Stars Move Still

By Brad Ramsay

> "It was wicked to let a young girl blindly decide her fate in that way, without any effort to save her."
> — George Eliot, Middlemarch

Chapter 1	3
Chapter 2	8
The Interview, St. Louis 1917	30
Chapter 3	38
Chapter 4	59
Fyodor's Grandmother, San Diego 1922	78
Chapter 5	84
Chapter 6	106
Clarissa and Dora, St. Louis 1891	128
Chapter 7	140
Chapter 8	160
Enoch's News, St. Louis, 1894	179
Chapter 9	185
Chapter 10	210
From Across the Pond, St. Louis 1915	242
Chapter 11	246
Chapter 12	274
Clarissa's Gambit, St. Louis 1923	304
Chapter 13	310
Chapter 14	329
Rosamond Vincy, St. Louis 1923	351
Chapter 15	355
Chapter 16	366
The Aftermath, Milligan 1924	380

Milligan, Indiana 1923

Chapter 1

A tear rolled down my cheek as I stared at the Seven Arches unable to decide what I would do. Would I leave on the train that would eventually take me to London, or would I stay home and become Mrs. Ruby Cleghorn?

If I wasn't sure that I had Harvey to come home to, I couldn't survive a year in London. Was gambling on the adventure of a lifetime worth risking everything I'd ever wanted?

The choice should have been simple, but I still felt divided. Should I marry Harvey or throw caution to the wind and spend the next year in London?

What might he say when he saw me off for St. Louis, leaving him behind once again? Things were a little different between us this time as I had made love to him, but I didn't do it to make him wait for me. I did it because I wanted him—needed him. It felt like goodbye, though I didn't want it to be.

I still wanted London. And I still wanted him. He had willingly given his blessing for me to return to work in St. Louis when I had asked him to wait for me before. This time was different. If I were to go, I couldn't ask him to wait again.

Nearly a dozen mushrooms found their way into my basket while I considered the future. They seemed to grow in abundance around the Seven Arches. I inhaled deeply trying to discern the scent of the fungi in the air as Ray had always taught me. The faint aroma hit my nose as I found my way toward the front of the first arch where I spotted three morels almost completely hidden by the overgrown grass.

Greedily, I picked them when I noticed one of the arch stones at the base was pulled away. Not even an arch stone, it was a rock fragment that wasn't even a quarter of an inch thick. It was difficult to get a grip on as it was lodged into the arch. There was enough space for me to wedge part of my pinky in the crack.

I winced as I felt a small prick, and I pulled out my pinky to see blood pooling on my finger tip. There must've been a jagged edge inside that crack that caught my flesh. Sticking my pinky in my mouth, I hit the stone with my other hand in retaliation. Much to my surprise, it gave just a bit and fell flush with the other stones in the arch. The small fragment puzzled me for a moment because it didn't seem to resemble the Indiana limestone which made up the rest of the arch.

Picking my basket back up, I strolled through the first arch and flowed right into the second. I had made this walk a hundred times before, but this already felt different somehow. An energy was flowing through me, or perhaps, it was the adrenaline from the prick on my finger.

As I passed through the third arch, I heard a low rumble—like distant thunder. I paused for a moment but the rumbling continued. I paused, expecting a storm—but the sky was clear, with only a few wispy clouds breaking up the blue.

The fourth arch amplified the sound as if someone had cranked the radio up to full volume. Confusion surged, followed by a strange curiosity. Still, I pressed on—through the fifth, then the sixth arch. By then, the noise was unbearable. My hands flew to my ears, but the cacophony felt like it would split my skull.

Something was wrong. It felt as if the world itself were imploding. Panic surged. I turned to run home—but instead, I sprinted forward, from the sixth arch into the seventh.

The moment I stepped through the seventh arch, everything went black.

I don't know how long I lay there on the ground, but when I came to, there were two baskets of mushrooms next to me instead of one.

"Hello?" I called out, still disoriented, but wondering if someone had come upon me while I was passed out.

Nothing seemed to be out of the ordinary as I examined the baskets. My mouth dropped open when I discovered that they were identical down to the fraying handles. The blue gingham towels were the same too. I took them both out and held them up in front of me. The blackberry juice stains were absolutely indistinguishable from one another.

The only difference between the two baskets was the three mushrooms that I had picked before I saw the gap in the stones. They were missing from the new basket.

Instinctively, I ran around to the first arch to see if something was awry, and there they were, the three mushrooms in the exact same spot where I picked them. A deep inhalation confirmed the subtle aroma of morels lingering in the air.

My eyes once again traveled from the mushrooms to the bottom of the arch where I first spotted the gap in the stones. I nearly gasped when I saw the gap had also reappeared. My finger brushed the gap again, but I knew better than to go poking inside it again.

"How is this possible?" I said out loud, completely vexed by the situation. It was as if I was reliving the exact same moment over again.

"Are you from hell?" a familiar voice called out to me from a small distance.

"I hope not," I replied, trying to place the familiar voice.

From behind a tree, a figure emerged.

The basket fell from my hand. My breath caught in my throat. She was me.

I mean, she wasn't me, but she was me.

She cautiously stepped toward me. I locked eyes with myself, but I was unsure if I was looking at another person because I could have just as easily been looking in a mirror.

We inadvertently mimicked each other for several minutes, making each of us realize that our instincts were identical. We laughed, reminisced without knowing why, and gradually grew suspicious of each other's motives.

She decided that I was an imposter, but it seemed ludicrous to me that I didn't belong. It eventually dawned on me that, perhaps, we were brought together because one of us could do something the other couldn't.

A burst of excitement coursed through our veins when we realized that one of us could stay in Milligan, Indiana and marry Harvey, while the other could embark on the adventure of a lifetime with Mrs. Byerly.

The arches had given us a gift—or a curse. We couldn't both have everything. So we split the life we'd once shared.

Oddly, there was little argument about who would stay and who would go. She volunteered to stay as if her heart had already been laid at the feet of our beau. I was so elated that I would be able to go to Europe without breaking Harvey's heart that I never considered the magnitude of what I would be losing.

Therefore it was decided that my duplicate, Ruby, would stay in Milligan and marry Harvey Cleghorn, while I, forever now Hazel, would chase our dreams in London. But first, I would say goodbye to our mother and Ray.

Chapter 2

As I opened the gate to Mother's house, I saw my Ray on the front porch leisurely sitting in the rocking chair and sipping on a cup of coffee. He'd been great three weeks ago when I'd arrived home from St. Louis, but a day or so later, the look on his face was strained.

Today was the first time I'd seen him out of bed all week. Activity was difficult after he came out of a long melancholy because stiffness and soreness settled into his muscles. I'm fairly certain he hadn't eaten in a few days either. As I glided up the sidewalk, he gently rocked in his chair with Jupiter lazing beside him.

Ray had our mother's deep blue eyes—eyes I'd always envied. He inherited our father's height with him topping out over six feet tall. If he ever ate enough to fill out his frame, he would be a formidable looking man with a strong jaw that made him look commanding and a deep voice that was also soft.

Anyone that didn't know him would think he was intimidating when in fact, he was the gentlest creature on the planet. His tall frame made things harder—he looked healthy, so no one understood how he could be bedridden for days.

I gave Jupiter a good scratching behind the ears before I took the rocking chair next to Ray. It creaked as I made myself comfortable. The old boards of Mother's front porch groaned a bit when our chairs were rocking in rhythm to one another, but neither of us had spoken. Still, we enjoyed one another's company.

With his eyes on the field across the road, Ray sipped his coffee, looking at nothing in particular as far as I could tell, but I knew he often fretted about being a burden to Mother.

Generally quiet in nature, it wasn't the easiest thing in the world to have a conversation with my oldest brother especially when it was right before or right after a melancholy. I was never sure if it was a natural quietness like Harvey, or if he lived in perpetual fear of saying something foolish. Words, it seemed at times, were meted out from Ray so sparingly that I wondered if he only had so many words he could speak in a single day. He never said "yes" or "no" if a nod of the head would suffice.

Aunt Nettie had gifted him Jupiter a few weeks after he and mother had moved into this house. Jupiter had been Uncle Ralph's dog. She had given him the pup on what turned out to be his last birthday. When Uncle Ralph died, Aunt Nettie couldn't look at the dog without crying, but she couldn't bear to get rid of it either. Ray always seemed to bond better with animals than people. Even that mangy old cat, Buster, never attacked Ray.

Ray was seven years older than me, and he had lived with Mother practically every day of his life. It was sad to know that the odds were slim that he'd ever be totally independent. Mother had been asked many, many times over the years what was wrong with Ray as people noticed he didn't have a job, and he was regularly absent from church on Sundays.

I noticed the dark circles under his eyes and a sallowness that came from shutting the light out. He looked closer to forty than thirty, and I always wished there was something that I could do for him. He admitted to me once that he had a girl he was sweet on, but she lived too far away. When I pressed him for details, he shrugged and realized he had already said too much. We both knew there wasn't much of a point for him to be in love. He couldn't support himself let alone a wife when he was struck with the melancholy.

My brother was a smart man, probably the smartest out of the three of us, but it did him little good on days when he would lay in his bedroom staring out, glassy-eyed, into the dark with Jupiter as his only companion laying on his bed beside him.

I rocked a few more times, and my mind wandered—I was twelve years old the first time he tried to kill himself, or at least, the first time I realized that he tried to kill himself. After spending three days in bed, he had disappeared from our lodging while mother, me and Roscoe were at church. She was frantic to find him, and she sent Roscoe and I out into the woods to call out his name until we were blue in the face.

We searched nearly an hour before we found him. He had obviously heard us but didn't answer as he was sitting at the base of a huge oak tree, trying his mightiest to make a hangman's noose.

I cried out when I realized what he was attempting, but he didn't look up. He kept working at the knot with his fingers and was obviously getting frustrated.

"Goddammit!" he said with anger and force in his voice before tossing the rope to the ground.

Meeting our wide-eyed gazes with the look of a puppy that had just been swatted, he flashed us his mournful eyes, vacant and red from crying, and my heart broke for him. Roscoe picked up the rope, and I led the way back to the house with my two brothers behind me.

Once we found Mother, Roscoe had the unfortunate task of telling her how we found him. She burst into sobs, and Roscoe did his best to comfort her while I sat by Ray's bedside reading to him from an old copy of Harper's Bazaar, more for me than for him.

Roscoe left home a few months later. They were in need of coal miners down in Arkansas, and he thought he was old enough to try his luck there. Mother was supportive as if she knew he had to go, but Ray was a wreck. I could still hear him begging Roscoe to stay, promising that he'd be better. Roscoe knew that Ray would never be better, and he couldn't handle it.

Mother struggled to deal with him when he was younger, and she was usually at odds with my father who seemed to understand something about Ray that she didn't. My father was always pulling Ray out of his comfort zone, but he was gone before it got worse.

I often wondered if my father walking out on the family was what initially caused Ray's melancholy, but Mother said that she always knew he had it. My father's mother suffered from it as well so he easily recognized the signs in Ray at a young age.

Always coddling him, my mother worked tirelessly to protect Ray and shield him from bad news or anything that could upset him. It never helped, and it caused everyone in the family to go crazy.

After Roscoe left, money was tighter than ever, and it was so bad to see Mother plastering on a fake smile when we were eating scraps. She never knew how loudly she cried in her bedroom at night because Ray and I would both hear her, and there was little that either of us could do to make it better.

My father taught him chess sometime before I was born, and they would play night after night, sometimes three or four games. Ray loved chess, and we all loved watching him play my father. There was a certain calmness in the house during those chess matches.

My father would come and go so often back in those days working odd jobs around O'Fallon that those chess games were the only time we felt like a cohesive family. Occasionally, Ray would set up the chess board in Mother's front porch and play both sides of the board. He realized many years ago that neither Mother nor I had a mind for the game.

Despite his delicate nature, Ray was my father's favorite. I'd like to think that Ray saw all my father's flaws, but I'm not sure. He never spoke up if Roscoe and I were speaking ill of him, as we often did after he left us for good, but Ray never said a cross word about John Wesley Sutton. Then again,

I'm not sure that Ray ever said a cross word about anyone ever.

Ray was the last one of us to see my father. A letter arrived at our house in O'Fallon saying that our grandfather had passed away and left my father a small inheritance. Ray traveled back to Milligan, Indiana with him to collect the money, but only Ray came back. Mother took the seventy-five dollars that dad had collected with the message that he'd be along shortly. Fifteen years have passed since then so we figured he must be long gone or dead.

"You weren't waiting on me to speak first, were you?" I asked Ray, breaking the silence that existed between the groans of the rocking chairs on the porch.

"A whole year, huh?" he said in between sips of coffee.

"Six months to a year," I corrected, and the conversation seemed to be over. It was easy to judge how well Ray felt based on the number of words he used. When he felt free of the depression, he could have a conversation, but when he was still grappling with it, words were difficult. I rocked a few more times when the memory of the first time Roscoe blew through town hit me.

Two years had passed, and he'd written us maybe twenty letters in total. Mining never suited him so he headed to Texas to become a cattleman on a ranch, and after a few months of that, he was all the way out in California picking peaches.

There was always a new job and a new adventure with each letter. He was always having the best time, and he was always driving the women crazy. Meanwhile, I was home trying to keep house and tend to Ray while Mother worked herself sick to keep a roof over our head.

Mother was always stubborn about me taking over responsibilities around the house because she knew that one day I wouldn't be there to lean on. I always countered that it was more of the reason for me to shoulder the burden with her while I was.

I hated Roscoe for abruptly abandoning us when life got difficult, and I didn't care if I ever saw him again. That hate multiplied when he came back for that first visit. He had brought me ribbons for my hair. They were pink and lacey—exactly the sort of thing a girl outgrew. I accepted them with grace, but all I wanted was to throw them back in his face and shout, 'We can't eat hair ribbons, asshole!

Time didn't stop for us just because he wasn't there. He had no idea how hard those years were. We didn't always eat or have light some nights, but Mother never said a word to Roscoe about it. Refusing to speak to him unless he spoke to me first, I treated him with cold civility.

To make matters worse, Mother decided to have a potluck to celebrate the return of her prodigal son, and when she ran into town to buy some food and liquor for the party, Roscoe cornered me in the house.

"Ruby, why are you looking at me like you want to carve up my liver?"

I eyed him for a moment before choosing to ignore him, and I hoped that he would get the message. Roscoe was not, however, adept at taking hints. He pushed me and pushed me until I answered him.

"Life has just been full of peaches and cream since you decided you were John Wesley Sutton and walked out on your family. We've been living like royalty. Sometimes, we each got our own lima bean for dinner instead of having to carve one into three portions."

His face went bright red. I could tell he wanted to shout back at me, but he turned around and walked out with his tail between his legs.

I wanted nothing to do with Roscoe's party so I avoided the whole affair, choosing instead to tend to our vegetable patch. Listening to the raucous laughter from the house, I tried not to enjoy the delightful smells from Mother's chicken and dumplings as they wafted out to me.

Even though I was hungry, I didn't want to be a part of anything celebrating my brother. Roscoe had a million stories to tell, and he had a flair for entertaining everyone. He was like the pied piper enthralling all the guests with his stories.

Blotting out all the happy sounds and smells of food was impossible, but it didn't stop me from trying. My attention turned to aggressively attacking the poke weeds that were wreaking havoc on our garden.

Ray appeared at the garden fence while I was on my hands and knees trying not to rip out any of our cucumber vines with my angry gardening. The shadow he cast let me know it was him without even looking up.

"Mad?" he said.

I kept on pulling at those weeds, giving all my wrath to those broadleaf pests. There was no point in replying to such an obvious question.

"You're not angry at Roscoe for coming home. You're angry at him for not taking you when he left."

The weed I was pulling gave way, and I stood up to meet Ray's gaze with it still in my hand. The urge to chuck the weed at him was overwhelming.

"Tell me I'm wrong."

Shaking my head angrily at him, my eyes suddenly filled with tears. Roscoe and I had been best friends as children, and the fact that he could leave me behind without caring what happened to me broke my heart. Ray climbed over the fence and held me. The stress of the last few years was falling out of my body riding the tears away from my psyche. He was right, and I felt so damn guilty that he was right.

"I need to be better, Ruby. I will be better," he said as he walked me into the house where I finally hugged Roscoe and joined the party.

"Mother and I sure will miss you." Ray said, snapping me back to the present. I nodded and squeezed his hand before getting up to go inside.

A few exchanges of words was the best you could usually hope for with Ray. As the screen door squeaked open, he said, "I'll be better. Don't worry about Mother."

"I know," I said as I stepped inside. He said those words every time I left to go back to St. Louis. I knew that he always tried his best, but whatever was broken inside him could only stay fixed for so long before he shattered again. It was hard to be mad at him because it was like being angry at a snake for shedding its skin.

When I stepped into the parlor, I was struck by the vision of a gorgeous golden, yellow dress, laid flat on the table. It was cut in the latest fashion so I knew that Mother must've copied the pattern from a magazine. Feeling the material between my fingers, it was a sheer, rich fabric, most likely chiffon.

The sleeves were short and they draped just over the shoulders. Dress styles in St. Louis were vastly different to Milligan, Indiana where most women wore threadbare housedresses every day but Sunday. Mother's skill with scissors and a needle perpetually impressed me, and I was touched by the gesture.

"What do you think?" Mother said walking in the backdoor and noticing my gaze at her wonderful creation.

I threw my arms around her and planted a kiss on her cheek. It was so thoughtful, and it must've taken her weeks of saving to pay for the fabric and hours of sewing after spending the day with people's laundry.

Hugging her tightly, I said, "I love it, but you knew I would. I should be buying you dresses, old lady!"

She put her hand on my cheek with an expression of tenderness and then her eyes narrowed letting me know that she didn't appreciate being called an old lady.

"What are you waiting for? Put it on! I want the last time I see my baby girl for a year to be in this yellow dress that her old lady made for her."

I grinned and greedily went to my room with the dress to change. My room looked so bare as it always did when my belongings were packed up. When I wasn't home, the room was basically shut up. It must've been originally conceived as a baby's room because it was so tiny. There was barely enough room for a single bed and a vanity, but it was adequate to my needs when I was home from St. Louis.

Even though I had to clean out the cobwebs whenever I returned to it, the room was my little corner of the world in Milligan, Indiana so I loved it. Growing up, I'd never had a bedroom to myself. Our house in O'Fallon only had two bedrooms so after my father left us, I moved into Mother's bedroom.

Most of my possessions were already packed up in my trunk, but I had a few knick-knacks that I had left in the drawers of my vanity. Inside was my worn copy of Middlemarch by George Eliot. I couldn't count how many times that I had read it, at least a dozen. Opening to the middle of the book, I found a small bouquet of pressed violets that Harvey had given me before he'd left for the Great War.

Originally, I hadn't any intention of taking them with me because of their sentimental value, but there was no reason for me to leave them behind for Ruby. She got the man so I was taking the violets. There was a second book in the drawer called The Glorious Misadventures of Horatio

Huffington, and it was comically bad. The author's name was S. Pierson, but I had never run across anything else he had written, and I was not tempted to take it along.

There was a drawer on the bottom of the vanity that had not closed correctly in more than a year, but I never had the inclination to try to fix it. I shoved it a few times, but it definitely stuck out about half an inch. Finally feeling that it was time to remedy the overhang, I removed the entire drawer, and when I looked into the back of the vanity, I spotted a tiny little shimmer. My hand reached in and pulled out a pair of my mother's beads.

More than a year ago the beads had gone missing, but they must've only fallen behind the drawer. I had missed them. They were cheap, but they were a present from my mother. Clutching them to my bosom, I felt relieved to have found them at this particular moment in time.

The ability to take this small token of my mother with me on my travels was so important, especially since it would be the only heirloom that I would ever be able to pass down to my own children.

I stepped out of my old dress and into the new one. It hugged my body perfectly. The look was completed when I added the beads around my neck. They were two gifts from my mother, and I would cherish them forever. After all, I wouldn't be getting any surprise gifts from my mother for at least a year.

My face furrowed as I looked in the mirror adjusting the beads. "No, not a year. Forever." Only now did it begin to sink in: I was saying goodbye to my mother forever. How had I let myself forget that?

Down at the arches, I understood it, but the implications of it all hadn't hit me. The only solace I could take was that Mother wasn't saying goodbye to me forever. She would always have Ruby just down the road at the Cleghorn Farm.

Positivity was impossible. A wave of regret crashed over me. I hadn't only given up Harvey but my entire family. Never again would I see Mother, Ray, or Roscoe after today. Ruby was their relation. After London, I would be nothing more than a stranger to them. Somehow, I agreed to all of it without truly considering the magnitude of my sacrifice.

A sense of utter remorse coursed through my veins. I had agreed to essentially erase my entire existence up until now. My past wasn't mine anymore. It belonged to Ruby now, and I had given it to her without even realizing what it meant.

All I had left was Mrs. Byerly and London.

"Ruby?" my mother knocked on my door, hearing my muffled crying, "Is everything all right?"

I stepped out the door and fell into her arms. She held me tightly and soothed me as best she could. This embrace could very well be the last time my mother ever comforted me. It made me sob harder. How could I leave her forever? How could I give up my own mother?

She maneuvered me down onto my bed, and I continued to weep for my lost family. Holding my hand, she patted my back while I tried to get a hold of myself. The smell of my mother—my childhood hugged me as I bathed in the grief.

"What's this?" she said as she grabbed my pinky finger. It looks like you got poked by a thorn here.

The cut on my finger from the jagged rock had scabbed over. It was not even a quarter of an inch long, but it was definitely noticeable when she held my hands.

"It's nothing," I said, pulling my hand away and attempting to change the subject, "I'm just going to miss you so much."

"Ruby, a year is no time at all, you've been in St. Louis upwards of six months at a time before. You won't be just a train ride away, but we'll manage. We will exchange weekly letters if that is what it takes to make you feel comfortable. The year will be over before you know it."

I couldn't argue with her. For her, our parting would only be an hour, maybe two, but for me it would be forever. Knowing that Ruby would be here full time to look after her and Ray took the sting out of it a bit. Ruby would also be able to write to me about them. Even if I wouldn't be physically with them, I would always know how they were doing, and I would have to take solace in that.

One deep breath and I was ready to be done with feeling sorry for myself. The stray tears were wiped out of my eyes, and I was ready to look forward. My future was wide open to me, and while I was losing my family, I was also losing the responsibilities that went along with them. They belonged to Ruby, and I knew that she would take excellent care of them.

Briefly imagining a couple of towheaded children sharing this little room while spending the night with their Granny and Uncle Ray made me smile. Granny would always make sure they had gingersnaps, and Uncle Ray would show them all the tricks he taught Jupiter. It was both beautiful and painful to imagine Harvey and Ruby's children.

Ruby!

This dress. She couldn't come home from the train stop wearing this dress if I was already wearing it. Unlike the dress I passed through the Seven Arches in, there was only one yellow chiffon dress, and I was wearing it.

"I'm going to change back into my other dress. This is too nice to debut on a train ride to St. Louis."

Mother nodded at me, "Make sure you take care of that finger. The last thing you want is an infection while you're crossing the ocean."

I cringed but nodded.

When I came back out into the parlor in my old dress, I saw Harvey out on the front porch leaning against a railing fiddling with the straw hat in his hands. I opened up my trunk to pack away the dress, the beads, and my copy of Middlemarch before going outside to meet him.

I almost cried out when locking eyes with him. The events of the last two hours were more emotionally draining than I had ever experienced in my entire life, and now it was time to say goodbye to the future I'd always imagined for myself.

When I walked out onto the porch, I fell into Harvey's arms, and he embraced me tightly. We were cheek to cheek and I could feel the golden stubble on his cheek rub against me. He was usually clean-shaven, but I knew when he slept poorly, shaving was the first thing he skipped.

My news from last night had taken its toll on him. I wanted to kiss away all his pain and reassure him that everything was going to be alright, but I didn't get to do that. That would be Ruby's job. Saying goodbye to him was my job, and I was dreading it.

We pulled our heads away so we could look into each other's eyes. There was still love in his eyes, but it was hiding behind a mountain of pain. I could only imagine what his own mother said to him when he told her that I was leaving again, for possibly for a whole year. She had never particularly liked me, and I think she liked me less and less each time I broke Harvey's heart by going back to St. Louis. Oftentimes, he told me that she paraded a series of single girls in front of him to tempt his heart, but my man was never tempted.

And he was my man. My mind particularly emphasized the past tense. Harvey once told me that he believed that he dreamed me into life because his future wife always looked exactly the way that I did. It was one of the most romantic things he'd ever said to me, and it clawed at my heart like an eagle's talon.

Never would I find another Harvey. This strong, quiet man adored me with his whole heart upon the first moment we met a decade ago. My big, strong farmer was irreplaceable, and I would always carry a piece of Harvey in my heart. He was my first love, and although it gutted me to think about, he might be my only love.

I had worried from time to time that Mrs. Cleghorn would hate me even more when I married her son, but Harvey always assured me that she would welcome me into the family with open arms once we were husband and wife. For Ruby's sake, I hoped that was true.

"Listen Ruby," he said, taking a deep breath.

I froze. He never called me Ruby. A cold chill ran down my spine, and I was suddenly afraid of what he might say.

"No Harvey, I want to speak first," I said, noticing that we didn't have any privacy on the front porch with the screen door open. Leading him by the hand, I took him down to the chicken coop which was out of earshot of the house and tucked away behind a beautiful cedar tree that Mother had transplanted to her yard because she always loved the smell of cedar.

"Every time I leave for St. Louis," I said softly, "I make you promise to wait for me. And I know, it's selfish. I swore I wouldn't put you in that position again.

Loving you has always been the easiest thing I've ever done, Harvey. You're the first thought in my mind every morning, and the last dream I have before sleep pulls me under.

I do want you to wait for me.

God, I do.

But I won't make you promise."

His eyes filled with tears, but they stubbornly wouldn't fall. He wiped them away with his sleeve. "Thank you," he said, "I came over here hoping that I'd have enough strength not to promise to wait for you. I 'spect I will, Gem, but I don't want to promise you that."

"I know," I said, taking my turn to let the tears well up in my eyes.

He pulled me to him. Our cheeks touched once again.

"I love you," he said.

"I love you too," I returned.

Our cheeks burned together this time. The bristle of his facial hair felt coarse, but I liked it. Feeling the heat from the man that I loved pressed against me, I turned my cheek just a bit, eager to meet his lips, and he turned with me.

Before I knew it, we were kissing again with the same passion we had at his fishing hole the night before. This was the last time that I would ever kiss Harvey and I wanted to savor every ounce of it.

Overwhelmed with the pain of it all, I found myself looking for the same comfort that he offered me on the previous night. Needing to feel his bare skin against mine, I pulled at his pants. He looked deep into my eyes again as if he were asking permission to continue. God, I loved this man.

Nodding violently, my head leaned into his hungry lips harder than before. Then he pulled away and kissed all the way down my neck as he lowered me to the ground. The satisfaction of our bodies together even though we were still fully clothed made me moan out softly in his ear. I pulled at his belt, urging him onward, and he fumbled while trying to pull up my dress.

"Ahem," said a voice that startled us both from behind the cedar tree, "Hack's here."

"Okay," I said, my face coloring bright red, hoping that Ray had only heard us and not seen us.

Harvey kissed me again one more time while we were spread out on the ground before helping me up. He pulled a few stray blades of grass out of my hair and gently brushed away the dust from the back of my dress.

"Goodbye, my Gem," he said, taking out his hanky and blowing his nose.

"Goodbye, my love," I said, taking one last look at him before I walked away. The memory of my pale-skinned muscle man with his light blue shirt waving goodbye to me would stay with me forever. Harvey was a man that always loved me more than I deserved.

My trunk was already loaded in the hack by the time we made it back up to the house. Giving Ray an innocent smile, I knew he wouldn't tell a soul, but I suppose it didn't matter if he did as Harvey and Ruby would be together in a matter of hours.

After nearly making love to Harvey yet again, the thought that Ruby would warm his bed every night stung as much as it comforted me.

The last long embrace with my mother was difficult to get through without crying. When it ended, she handed me a parasol. There was no way I would accept another gift from her, but she insisted. I feigned hesitation because I knew she'd have it back in her hands soon.

The three faces seeing me off filled my heart with both joy and regret as I felt like the luckiest and dumbest girl in the world. They loved me, and they would be thrilled to see Ruby come back into their lives to stay forever. Each of them thought they were losing me for a year, but they were gaining Ruby forever.

I gave one final, tear-filled wave—and just like that, I was off to start my new life.

The Interview, St. Louis 1917

The interview was set for mid-morning, and Clarissa Byerly began dreading it the moment she walked into her office at the Women's Charity Organization. She knew beyond a shadow of a doubt that she wouldn't be hiring the girl as the interview was granted only as a favor to her phlegmatic brother-in-law.

The girl was supposedly connected to a blacksmith once in Enoch's employ, and both Felix and Tabitha had insisted she grant the interview. Clarissa had previously made it her business to be nothing but hateful to Enoch Byerly, but she needed to stay in good graces with her son and daughter-in-law as there was to be a baby soon.

She hoped it would be a girl, but the due date was still several months away. Girls mattered more than boys these days—especially if you hoped to save them. Women were expected to always be reactionary to men. They had no power unless they came from money and remained a spinster.

Many women had come through the doors of the WCO woefully unprepared for life when they had been abandoned or discarded by men. Clarissa had teetered on destitution more than once in her life because of men, and it made her angry that young women weren't better prepared for the cruelty of the world.

Recently, she had started formulating plans to open up WCO offices across the country. She had the vision of a branch of the WCO in all forty-eight states. The organization would be a beacon for women of all ages to be protected, educated, and given the proper tools to survive in life.

The proposal for a Department of Outreach was still in its infancy, but she would never pull it off without additional staff to help her with the sundry details. Her current, lone secretary, Miss Lowery, was duller than a butter knife on a ribeye steak and twice as useless.

She wondered what sort of idiocy could be expected at this upcoming interview. The girls she had seen pass through the halls of the WCO were wide-ranging over the last few years. Some were driven and had enough brains to go far in life, while others were merely empty-headed chatterboxes.

All the good ones, it seemed, all had one thing in common. They hoped to marry or, in the case of some young widows, remarry some day. Clarissa had tried in vain to talk many girls out of marriage. Lectures of her own short-lived happiness in marriage were given to every girl with potential. She spoke in earnest about how Sam Byerly had managed to absolutely sweep her off her feet, but their bliss fizzled shortly thereafter. Marriage, in her opinion, rarely made women happy, but it did keep them subservient. These horror stories rarely swayed the girls, and she watched one after another throw away their careers for marriage.

The cacophonous racket of Miss Lowery arriving for the day broke Clarissa from her thoughts of marriage and the interview. Her morning was packed: a board report to write, the fiscal budget to reassess, and—eventually—dealing with the hopeless applicant.

She had little time for introspection. A harried meeting with Mrs. Schiff took twice as long as she expected and ended in raised voices and pointed sarcasm. An urgent message requiring her to address a discrepancy in the kitchen budget led to the discovery of a girl who was pilfering from the pantry and resulted in an uncomfortable amount of crying and pleading in her office. When she finally sat down to write her report to the board, she was interrupted by Miss Lowery, who clattered into her office to announce that Miss Sutton had arrived.

A glance at the clock told her the girl was more than thirty minutes early. She would have admired her promptness if it wasn't so inconvenient at the moment. If Clarissa was even remotely considering this Miss Sutton for a position, she wouldn't have minded making her wait for hours, but it seemed cruel to make the girl wait when she had no intention of hiring her.

"Send her in, Miss Lowery. Let's see what jewel my brother-in-law has sent us from the rural wilderness from which he dwells."

Miss Lowery stared at her for several moments without moving.

"SEND HER IN, MISS LOWERY."

The old woman finally got the message and soon the fresh-faced Ruby Sutton was sitting in front of her desk, smiling widely and obviously eager to impress.

Clarissa studied the girl for several seconds after greeting her. She was most definitely young, probably not quite 18 years old, but her youth would make her more malleable. Comparing her to the ancient Miss Lowery made Clarissa pause in her original intent to immediately dismiss her.

The overall first impression she got of Miss Sutton was positive. The girl's dress had been expertly pressed, and her hat had a small brim that she decorated with a bit of white ribbon. She looked quite put together, and the slight tremble in her hand told Clarissa that she was placing the utmost importance on this interview.

"I'm sure Miss Lowery told you that I am Mrs. Byerly. I run the finance department here at the Women's Charity Organization, and you are interviewing as a secretary and errand girl. You'll likely be asked to do the most menial tasks. We help women who have endured all kinds of abuse here. I'm afraid it isn't a glamorous job, Miss Sutton."

"Yes, ma'am."

Clarissa expected more of a reaction, but the girl was completely unfazed.

"Where do you come from? Indiana?" she asked, trying not to sneer with disdain at the state her son and his wife now called home.

"No, I've lived practically my whole life in O'Fallon, Missouri, but my mother's family comes from Indiana. I often visited over the years."

"And your father's family?"

"Oh, I don't rightly know. If you'll pardon me, I do not think highly of my father. He was a disaster of a human being, and I am ashamed that I am biologically connected to him."

Clarissa was taken aback by the pluck the girl displayed, but she liked her immediately. A girl raised by a strong woman was the exact kind of employee she was looking for. Without even censoring herself, Clarissa began a conversation with Miss Sutton on her own low opinion of most men citing her own husband and father as perfect examples of terrible influences.

Miss Sutton spoke with quiet fury about the father who had abandoned her family a decade ago, and one of her brothers who left them just a few years later. The two ladies got so engrossed in their conversation that they both completely lost track of time.

"It's lunch time, Mrs. Byerly. Would you like me to fetch you a sandwich?" Miss Lowery said, poking her head into the office.

"Capital idea, Miss Lowery. I'll take a chicken salad from Kopperman's. Miss Sutton, can we get you anything?"

"Oh dear, I have to be at the train station in less than an hour. Many apologies, Mrs. Byerly. I had no idea that the interview would last this long."

"We better finish up then. What are your qualifications?"

Miss Sutton carefully went over the secretarial correspondence course she had taken, and how she had practiced taking dictation with her mother and brother. She was still refining her shorthand, but she felt with a few weeks of practice, she would be more than proficient.

Clarissa considered how much easier it would be to dictate her board report to a secretary rather than writing it out longhand, and she knew Miss Sutton would be a great asset to her team in the finance office.

With every word the girl spoke, Clarissa liked her more and more. The grace and ease with which she could slide from a conversation expelling the villainy of men and the virtues of women into her education and tenacity for the position was inspiring.

This was the girl she needed by her side to eventually set up the Office of Outreach, but there was the ticklish question that could ruin it all.

"Why do you want to work, Miss Sutton? Most young girls your age are more interested in marriage than careers."

"I'm not most women, Mrs. Byerly. My mother has supported my brothers and I since I was a little girl. I know poverty, and I don't like it. I do believe that I want to get married and have a family some day, but right now it is important for me to know that I can support myself and my family if I need to."

"I promise you, Ruby, that I will do everything in my power to talk you out of shackling yourself to a man for the rest of your life."

She smiled, and Clarissa was charmed. It was quite a feat to charm the formidable Mrs. Byerly, and no one knew that better than the woman herself. Where this girl came from didn't matter. Clarissa had found her assistant.

"I also must admit that I loathe the name Ruby with all my heart. I knew a Ruby once and didn't care for her. What's your middle name pray tell?"

"Hazel."

The name Hazel had earth in it, strength, sense. A name to survive on. Clarissa could groom a protege named Hazel, but one named Ruby—not a chance. After all, Hazels endure, and rubies shatter.

"Perfect. Yes. That name will do. Hazel, when would you like to start?"

A smile escaped her lips when she saw how excited Miss Hazel Sutton was to be in her employ. They were going to change the world together, and Clarissa had already forgotten that unfortunate link Hazel had with her brother-in-law.

Chapter 3

"Goodbye, Hazel" was still ringing in my ears as my train bound for Terre Haute came whistling down the track. She had thought I said "Goodbye, Ruby" to her at our final parting, but I hadn't. I said it to myself. Ruby Sutton had a loving mother, two brothers, a sweetheart, and a tiny little room in Milligan, Indiana. Hazel had none of those things. A job with the WCO and a trunk full of clothes were her only possessions in the world.

I thought I would feel some sort of emotion at seeing Ruby for the last time, but I only felt emptiness. The elation followed by the depths of despair in such a short time period was taxing on my emotions. A hundred lifetimes' worth of tears had been shed—and it wasn't even noon.

At first, I thought I was gambling one year of my life. I hadn't realized I was gambling *the rest of it*. I was sad, scared, and utterly unprepared to face life without anyone who cared about me. My racing heart began to calm as I took several deep breaths and realized that I wouldn't be alone. Mrs. Byerly would be there to guide me every step of the way.

Mother had insisted on waiting for me to arrive the first couple of times I rode the train into town, but it lost its appeal after a while. It was much simpler to send a hack if she couldn't find anyone else to transport my trunk. I stared out across the landscape of Greene Township and the small community of Milligan for one last look from the small platform.

The train stop was so small that most days the train blew by never picking anyone up or dropping them off. There was one state senator that lived a few miles down the road from my mother's house, and he used it regularly on trips to Indianapolis. Most of the time when I was visiting home, I was the only one arriving or departing.

There was another woman waiting at the stop, sour-faced and silent, a boy beside her who must have been her son—they shared the same disapproving mouth.

The old lady looked at me for a moment and looked away. Not recognizing her in the least bit, I had to assume she was one of my mother's neighbors. I considered saying hello, but I changed my mind at the last moment. Her harsh countenance didn't invite small talk.

Milligan residents by and large were mostly unknown to me as I had never lived here full time. I'd been to church with Grandpa Nick and Bernice as well as my mother and Aunt Nettie a couple of times, but my visits were never regular. Harvey was the only person I talked to outside of Mother, Ray, and a smattering of relatives.

The train was already roaring down the tracks as it was. I tried to focus on the limitless possibilities of my new life as it arrived. Trying not to dwell on everything that I had given up, I focused on the freedom at my fingertips.

Ruby would be happy with the stability that Milligan provided, but Hazel could be as cosmopolitan as Lady Elizabeth Bowes-Lyon whose upcoming marriage to Prince George, I had read all about in preparation for my time in England.

The train halted and let off who must've been the old lady's granddaughter. The poor girl appeared a little pale, and she had a muffled cough. The lady wrapped the girl in a shawl and led her off the platform while the conductor loaded my trunk for me.

I was comfortably seated by a window where I caught one last glimpse of Ruby hidden away in the trees. We nodded to one another, but the old lady was in my sight line. She scowled, as if I'd nodded to her and she wanted me to know she took no pleasure in it. However, she was quickly occupied by loading her granddaughter into the buggy, and I convinced myself that I had imagined it.

The whistle blew and the train started chugging on down the line. As the train was pulling away, I took one last look and found that the old lady was back staring at me with a look so cold it made me shiver. My last feeling in the town of Milligan was unsettling.

Bound for Terre Haute, the train was usually more crowded than I found it to be. It was curious that there were only a handful of people in this car. More often than not, the trains didn't have more than a few empty seats, and my fellow travelers generally smelled like a mixture of pungent perfume, bathtub gin, or body odor. Hygiene, I noticed, was not a priority for many passengers when I started traveling.

Depending on the stops, it wouldn't take much longer than an hour for us to arrive in Terre Haute. Mother told me once that our family had lived in that city for a few years. I was too young to have many memories of living there, but I recalled Roscoe's first day of school very clearly. He did not want to go, and Ray had to drag him out the door toward the schoolhouse.

I would switch trains at the Terre Haute station before the longer leg of my journey to St. Louis. With only three days in town, I had to finish packing up the necessaries from the office and running last minute errands for Mrs. Byerly before boarding another train for New York. From there, we'd set sail on the *Leucothea* for England. The first portion of this journey I'd made what felt like a thousand times. So for the first moment since I was introduced to Ruby, I felt normal.

The further I got away from Milligan the safer I began to feel. Ruby's insistence that I had entered her world made me feel like an imposter who would get found out at any moment. The way that old woman stared at me gave me the creeps like she knew that I didn't belong there. I was glad that I'd never see her again.

While traveling between Milligan and St. Louis, I'd always felt safe. There had only been one singular time when I felt discomfited, and I was a few years younger. Two brothers were traveling from St. Louis to Indianapolis, and they noticed that I was traveling alone the moment I walked on the train. It was clear to me that they had boarded the train intoxicated on some dangerous liquor that they no doubt bought on the black market.

My Aunt Nettie, being a member of the local Temperance League in Parke County, had scolded us many times about the dangers of whiskey and drunkards so I was no stranger to the behavior. They were seated to my left, and I noticed that the pair would look at me and giggle. The older brother looked as if he were attempting to whisper in his brother's ear, but he was speaking at full volume.

He asked his brother if he thought I had a cherry, and I didn't blush, only blinked at the mention of fruit, unaware of the filth behind it. It was my mother who later clued me in that they were discussing whether or not I had known a man carnally. The lascivious glances they made toward me quickly disabused me of the notion that their attentions were innocent. I wasn't a prude as my brother Roscoe with his filthy mouth had immunized me to shocking behavior and language. Because they were being rude and making me uncomfortable, I planned to ignore them, but I didn't see them as a danger.

They eventually got loud enough that someone complained to the conductor, and they were moved to another car before getting booted off the train at the next stop. Even though I was the object of their lewd conversation, I had been able to disregard them. After they were gone, a young gentleman apologized to me for not stepping in sooner. He said that I had handled myself exquisitely, and those louts should be forever ashamed of themselves.

I had no idea how rude they had been at the time, and the whole ordeal made me more aware of my surroundings when traveling. Sitting near women, married couples, or just friendly faces in a pinch became one of my rules when it came to trains. Most people in the passenger cars had manners, and while I may have occasionally felt nervous over the years, I never felt fear.

The small crowd on my car to Terre Haute didn't make me feel nervous at all. There was a young couple with a small child, two ladies traveling together, an elderly gentleman, and a man with a newspaper.

The mother of the small child was doing her best to keep him quiet for the other passengers. Her husband, who barely looked old enough to be married, eyed his family with annoyance. I felt a twinge of pity for that woman as if she would never be able to make either her husband or her child happy.

Most likely sisters, the two ladies traveling together were both in their late forties or fifties. They were discussing some picture show they had seen together. I liked them, and they seemed like kind people who genuinely enjoyed each other's company.

Half asleep, the elderly man had a halo of sadness—neither smiling nor frowning, just steeped in some quiet grief. There was loss in his face, and I wanted to comfort him.

The man with the newspaper, I had yet to see his face, was somewhat of a mystery. I only saw a few flashes of him as he turned the pages. It almost became a game to catch a glimpse of his face, but to no avail. He seemed agitated, like a man on his way to deliver bad news.

It was a long time before he folded his paper up, and I actually saw him. Taken aback by how handsome he looked, I tried not to blush just looking at him. He had thick chestnut hair perfectly combed, and a little raffish mustache that made him look almost dangerous. His eyes, however, were too kind for you to even cater the idea.

He wore a black pinstriped suit complete with a wide red-striped tie. A black derby hat on top of his head made him look rather debonair. Despite my best efforts, I flushed, a traitorous wave of color giving me away.

I'd noticed that men other than Harvey were handsome before, but seeing this stranger and feeling my heart skip a few beats made me feel incredibly guilty. It was absurd because Harvey wasn't even mine anymore. Still, it felt too soon for me to even appreciate the looks of another man.

His eyes looked up and met mine, and I quickly averted my gaze. I willed myself not to flush because I knew that it would incriminate me further. He seemed not to notice me, and after his brief respite, he picked his paper back up and continued to read.

The newspaper made me quite envious as I had completely forgotten to bring myself something to read. Middlemarch was packed away in my trunk, and I cursed myself for not keeping it close. The emotional goodbyes left me too agitated for forethought. The quiet desperation of Dorothea

Brooke as she yearned to be taught by that old, bitter husband of hers would definitely pass the time, or the malevolent ingenuity of Nicholas Bulstrode would certainly keep my attention during the long train ride.

Perhaps, I would retrieve my copy of Middlemarch and buy a magazine as well when we reached Terre Haute. The newspaper stand would be easily accessible, and I would have a bit of time to buy something before my train to St. Louis departed. The rest of the journey was much too long to daydream about London for the entire ride.

There was no way I'd be able to pass the time staring at my chewed thumbnails or picking the scab that grew over my pinky so I started learning the little eccentricities of the people who shared my train car. The woman that I pitied often rolled her eyes at her husband every time he barked at her and looked away. Her look was downright hostile at times. It made me feel as if she could give just as good as she got. She calmed her child with quiet efficiency. Clearly, she was more in control than I'd given her credit for.

Those two ladies who I assumed were sisters were anything but. There was a tenderness between them that transcended sisterhood. They gave each other looks that I'd give Harvey but never Ray. There was a deep love between them that was hard to deny if you watched them for any length of time. Most people noticing the two women's love for one another would be shocked, but I'd encountered more than my fair share of "sisters" through my work at the

WCO. Some of the sweetest women I met were old maids that lived together. Perhaps, it was saying goodbye to Harvey less than an hour ago, but I envied the love between these two women. Somehow, I could tell that they'd never part from one another.

The elderly man kept turning to the window, as if about to point something out—then faltered. His face dropped every time. I suspected he'd recently lost a wife. This was most likely the first train ride he had taken alone in many years.

Mr. Newspaper was left-handed, I noticed, as he kept folding up the newspaper and placing it at his right side before pulling it back out again a few moments later. There was an article in the newspaper that he kept reading over and over, and judging by the distance he held the newspaper from his face, he was somewhat near-sighted. He also carried some sort of hard candy in his breast pocket that looked to be lemon drops.

When the train stopped, I mentally said goodbye to the people I'd been watching. They would continue on without me, but I was stepping onto a new path. Middlemarch waited in my trunk, and I had just enough time to grab something light to read before my train to St. Louis departed.

With Middlemarch clutched tightly in my arms, I made my way to the stand where I considered my options. I'd already read this month's edition of *Harper's Bazaar*. There was no point in reading *Good Housekeeping*. That would only lead to wistful thoughts of Harvey. I decided that *Cosmopolitan* was my best option as a man stepped in line behind me.

The hair on the back of my neck immediately rose as I could feel him standing much too close to me. Hot breath hit the nape of my neck as I tried to maintain my composure. I took a small step forward, careful to keep an acceptable distance from the gentleman in front of me, but much to my dismay, the man edged closer.

A squat man only a few inches taller than me, he was dressed in a threadbare suit and a fedora he'd likely fished out of the garbage. His shoes were cap toe lace up boots, and they made a little click when he moved his feet. There was too much hair oil in his dark, slicked back hair, and his eyebrows met just over the bridge of his crooked nose. He exhaled a cloud of moonshine breath that clung to me like damp wool, and he had a gold tooth that he licked with his tongue when I turned around and offered to let him ahead of me in line.

"I couldn't take your place, not a pretty young thing like you," he said, leering at me.

Ignoring his comment, I turned my back to him once again with an offended huff.

"I don't see many pretty ladies traveling alone," he said, whispering in my ear. His breath tickling my earlobe was hot and felt dirty. I wanted to take a bath immediately, but mostly I wanted to bolt for my train. Resisting the urge to run away, I hoped he was inwardly a coward as most bullies were.

I turned and glared at him, attempting to find the words to make him stop talking to me, but none of them were decent enough to utter in public. Mother had warned me that lecherous men often said shocking things to women hoping only to provoke a reaction. If they didn't get the attention they wanted, they would simply give up so I remained quiet.

"Hey, I'm talkin' to you. Don't you hear me?" he whispered in my ear again. Little droplets of spittle were released from his mouth as he spoke, and my heart began to race as shivers fell down my spine.

That was enough. No magazine was worth this man's harassment so I stepped out of line and dashed to my train. Then came the click of his shoes on the concrete. He was following me.

Click, click. Click, click.

His shoes weren't moving as fast as I was, but I felt like he was gaining on me. Beads of sweat popped out of my forehead as my pulse quickened. I *knew* I was in danger.

"Good. I'm going to enjoy your company all the way to St Louie," he said as I boarded the train with trepidation.

Scanning the car, I looked for a group of ladies that I could feign traveling with, but the one group of three ladies had no seats near them. There was an empty seat next to my Mr. Newspaper, and I felt a bit of relief wash over me as if he were a friend and not a complete stranger. Attempting to doze before the train departed, he was sitting next to the window with his eyes closed. I sat down next to him hoping to deter my stalker, but the click-click of his shoes followed me wherever I went.

"I don't bite," he said, taking out his flask and taking a heavy drink. "Would you like a little nip, it might loosen you up a bit."

He grinned, prominently displaying his gold tooth. I scowled at him while scanning for the conductor who was still taking tickets so I couldn't appeal to him for help until the train took off.

"I don't take kindly to being ignored," he said, grabbing my arm, "and you've done nothing but ignore me."

"Please let go of me," I said, quietly even though I was screaming inside my head. His grip tightened, intending to hurt. My last option was to scream and pretend to faint. I could feel the blood rushing to my head and briefly worried that I would actually faint.

"Sir, I'll ask you to unhand my wife," Mr. Newspaper said, eyes narrowed, fixing the scoundrel with a look that could make a grizzly bear turn tail and run.

I looked at my rescuer wide-eyed, and the cad loosened his grip immediately at the behest of Mr. Newspaper.

"If she's your wife then I'm your brother," the man sneered, "I saw her get off the train alone."

"What business is it of yours what errands I send my wife on," he said, his voice edged with threat.

The gold toothed man let his jacket open and showed that he was carrying a revolver. "I made it my business." He once again passed his tongue over that sinister tooth.

"Don't make me laugh," the handsome man said, suppressing a chuckle, "What exactly are you going to do? Shoot me and drag my wife kicking and screaming off the train? You're an ass, and I'll ask you to move to another car."

The man's sneer fell and his face went white. Expecting Mr. Newspaper to fold at the sight of his gun, he was genuinely surprised when he hadn't. He opened his mouth, but nothing came. Angrily, he bolted up out of the seat, closed his jacket, and disappeared into the next car.

Only then did I realize I'd been holding my breath.

"You're welcome," the handsome man said before opening his newspaper again.

I had wanted to thank him, but why had he been so brusque about it? Was he annoyed that I had brought that nuisance of a man near him? And why did he have to call me his wife? It was ridiculous. Gratitude flared into irritation. Smugness was never attractive

"I didn't ask for your help," I said a little indignantly.

He smirked at me. "I suppose you were going to wrestle the gun away from him?"

"For your information, I have been traveling and dealing with those people for several years. I'm not some damsel in distress, and I'll thank you not to sneer at me. It reminds me of the heel you just intimidated away. And another thing, your wife? You didn't have to insult my honor to get him to stop harassing me."

"Your honor?" he said with his voice rising slightly, "Pardon me, you should have just told him that I was a liar and you didn't know me from Adam. I apologize for not minding my own business, miss."

He noisily opened his newspaper once again, obscuring his face, reminding me of how long it had taken me to see him on the train ride here.

I had overreacted. The man had a gun, and I did need help. It was just that his "You're welcome" was so smug that it caught me the wrong way. He deserved a thank you from me, not an insult.

"I was flustered, and I do apologize. You did me a service, sir. Thank you." I said.

The newspaper fell, and he quickly smiled at me. "Think nothing of it. I was married to a woman with a quick temper. That man was a rough character, and I'm sorry you had to endure him as long as you did."

"Are you no longer married?"

He cocked an odd glance at me, "You talk about honor, and now you want to know if I'm married?"

He let off a little laugh when he saw that I colored. The laugh made me angry all over again.

"I'm a widower," he said with his smile dropping.

"I'm so sorry."

"She passed away a while ago, no need to dredge up bad memories."

"My apologies, I haven't properly introduced myself. I'm R..." and I was already trying to introduce myself as Ruby Sutton. It was a stupid mistake. I dropped my eyes and saw the copy of Middlemarch on my lap.

A smile slipped out before I could stop it.

"Pardon me," I said as I faked clearing my throat, "Rosamond Vincy."

He looked down at the copy of Middlemarch on my lap, and he raised an eyebrow at me. "Nice to meet you, Miss Vincy. I'm Tertius Lydgate."

Caught in the lie, I wanted to disappear. What kind of idiot uses a name from the very book in her lap? In Middlemarch, Rosamond Vincy married a handsome, young doctor named Tertius Lydgate. I should have said Ruby and given him a fake last name. I'd made a fool of myself in front of this man, and I wished that I could crawl into a hole and disappear.

He was obviously pleased with himself, and he was waiting for me to fess up, but I had too much pride.

"Do you travel quite often, Mr., I'm sorry, Dr. Lydgate."

Erupting in laughter, he appreciated the joke. It was a deep pleasant laugh which was quite disarming. My mortification began draining away, and I joined him in laughter. Assuring me that he would not require any other name from me, we settled our introductions. After that louse threatened to assault us both, a little anonymity would be comforting, but even though I couldn't put my finger on it, there was something so familiar about Tertius Lydgate.

In St. Louis, he was joining his mother to begin an extended trip. She had gotten some disappointing health news and insisted that he accompany her at least for a few months. He loved his mother, but the idea of going on one last holiday in anticipation of her dying was morbid to him. Grief seemed to follow him around these last few years, but God was obviously insisting that he have more.

I shared a bit of his grief when I told him that I had recently lost my mother as well. It was technically true. Mother was as dead to me as if she were buried in the cemetery. Although I did have the comfort of knowing she was alive, I would never sit down with her and discuss politics or hear her bawdy jokes.

"Goodness, you're competitive," he said with a smile, "My mother is dying, and yours is already dead. I'm also a widower. I suppose you've already buried a couple of husbands."

He had a dark sense of humor that reminded me of my own mother's. "Well, the man I intended to marry has decided to marry another woman," I replied, giving him a playful smile.

He laughed again. I laughed too. All the pain and loss I'd experienced was tragic—but teetering on the edge of absurdity.

We talked a little about Middlemarch. His favorite character was Fred Vincy as he could relate to him a little bit. When he was in school, he was a little reckless, and his uncle told him he needed to rein himself in, otherwise, there would be consequences. Once he was married shortly after graduation from college, he cleaned up his act. When Prohibition came around, he had no problem cutting out his occasional snifter of brandy.

"Oh, and I do have a dead father too," he said, eyeing me carefully.

I looked at him suppressing a smile and said, "My father is dead too. I think, but I don't know exactly as he abandoned the family many years ago."

"I give up. You win."

We shared another laugh, and as we conversed, I had found him to be more and more handsome. I hated the scoundrel who had accosted me at the newspaper stand, but if he hadn't, I never would have shared a lovely conversation with Tertius Lydgate. In a way I was thankful for him.

Our conversation had its lulls, and I turned to my book, and he to his paper. The article he kept turning to on the other train was an announcement of a printing factory being built in Crawfordsville. He had convinced his uncle to invest in it, and he was nervous that it wouldn't be a success. The prospect sounded interesting, but I knew very little about the printing business.

"This is going to sound forward, but I noticed you when you first boarded the other train. I wanted to talk to you then, but obviously, I have better manners than to force an unattended lady into a conversation. I'll be gone for a very long time, but may I look you up when I come back that way toward Milligan?"

My heart fluttered for a moment. Harvey had been the one and only man that I'd ever had romantic feelings for, and here I was wondering what it would be like to be married to this stranger. I didn't even know his real name, but he'd made me laugh and feel joy in the midst of everything that I'd gone through today.

But, if he asked about me in Milligan, he would be describing Ruby, who would no doubt be a married woman by then with no memory of him. I was off to London where I may never come back. No, there was no way for me to imagine a future with this handsome stranger.

"I'm afraid not. I've left my home for good—there's nothing left for me there. If you asked about me, it would most likely cause trouble. I'm sorry, Dr. Lydgate. You are the most chivalrous and charming man, but let's just stay Rosamond and Tertius."

He smiled and offered me his hand. "It was enchanting to meet you, Miss Vincy. I sincerely wish you the best."

I read Middlemarch and dozed the rest of the way to St. Louis. The conversation between us died out, but it was comforting to have his presence next to me.

Damn Ruby. She had my family and Harvey, and she robbed me of the chance to get to know Tertius Lydgate better. I comforted myself with the knowledge that in about a week's time I would be in England and thousands of miles away from her. The remainder of the train ride was uneventful. Thankfully that cad never resurfaced, and I was undisturbed.

It felt like I would never see that handsome stranger again, but I was indebted to him. He gave me hope that someone—somewhere—was waiting. Not Ruby's someone. Mine. Maybe I would buy a copy of *Good Housekeeping* for my train ride to New York in a couple of days.

As the train arrived at the station in St. Louis, Dr. Lydgate kissed my hand, and color crept up my neck. We bid each other farewell. I let out a gasp when I saw a figure outside my window.

"Is it that scoundrel? I won't let him near you!" Dr. Lydgate said rather heatedly.

"No," I said, trying to retain my composure, "It's my brother."

Chapter 4

Shit. What was Roscoe doing here? If he saw me when Mother knew damn good and well that Ruby was with her in Milligan, the jig would be up. My meathead brother would blow the whole thing just so Ruby could politely hold onto our slice of cake while I stuffed fistfuls into my mouth.

The logical plan was to ditch the trunk and give him the slip. It was the least messy option, and if I succeeded, the ruse that Ruby stayed behind wouldn't be compromised. Ruby would not want me to talk to him as it would complicate things for her and Roscoe too, since everyone would be convinced he was a loon.

I wasn't Ruby anymore. Even if we'd been the same person this morning, everything that happened today had made Ruby more herself—and me, someone entirely different.

The man's spittle on my ear was not something that Ruby would ever experience. She would not see how that rogue had folded so easily when Dr. Lydgate didn't even flinch at his little pistol. I had experienced all that, and it was odd to realize that Ruby would never know that feeling.

However, there was a man skulking around the St. Louis train station with a pistol who might be a little miffed at me for ignoring him and embarrassed that he'd turned tail and ran away. I'd let Dr. Lydgate go on about his business so my only male protection was Roscoe if that worm wanted to cause me more trouble.

I had said goodbye to Lydgate for Ruby, but maybe God, or whoever brought me through the Seven Arches was giving me the gift of seeing my brother one last time.

With an air of determination and a thought of self-preservation, I stepped off the train and made my way toward my brother, the wanderer. Roscoe hadn't aged much since the last time I saw him. He had our father's dark hair and black eyes. I thought my father would still be taller than him, but I couldn't be sure since he had left us before Roscoe reached manhood. His coloring was all Sutton, but his face was unmistakably Mottern. My grandfather had a daguerreotype of himself when he was a youth, and Roscoe was practically the spitting image of a young Nick Mottern.

He was better dressed than I expected. Roscoe had spent the last decade as a ne'er-do-well, drifting from job to job whenever the spirit moved him. I hadn't seen him in respectable clothes since he was still going to church with us.

The suit he wore was obviously new. The cut of the fabric and the way it shaped his frame told me it hadn't been cheap. Money burning a hole in your pocket was something of a Sutton family trait so I assumed that he'd decked himself out and was left with nary a dollar to his name.

"Hey wise guy, you lose something?" I said, sidling up before he noticed me.

He was startled, nearly falling backward at my sudden appearance. I had caught him so off guard that I knew instantly he'd heard word that I wasn't supposed to be on the train. At first he looked like he had seen a ghost, but that slowly melted away into a mischievous smile and a halting laugh. Once he'd recovered himself sufficiently, he held his arms out and pulled me in for a long squeeze.

"Dear sister, let me get a look at you," he said, backing up and giving me the once over.

"No one looks the tops after spending the day traveling on the train, I would expect you to know that since you've been practically everywhere," I said, nervously brushing a stray lock off my forehead and tucking it into my hat.

"You'd be fine arm candy for any gentleman worthy of you, I reckon," he said, giving me a wink.

It was obvious he was the same fun-loving Roscoe that he'd always been, and while I loved him, sometimes the eternal showman in him, always living to impress people with his jokes and quick wit, got tired fast.

"Enough Vaudeville. Can I just talk to Roscoe?" I said, hoping that he'd cool it for a little bit.

"Still the little spitfire, I see," he grinning as he pulled a piece of paper out of his pocket. It was a telegram that had arrived at his digs not more than a few hours ago. I didn't have to read it to know what it said.

Ruby stayed home STOP
Collect trunk from station STOP

Exhaling heavily after reading the telegram over and over again, I handed it back to him. There wasn't much I could do to explain it. It was the truth. Ruby did stay home. I had no story that I could tell him that would make a lick of sense to him, and as understanding as Roscoe was about philosophy and all that nonsense, I didn't want our last conversation to leave him thinking that I belonged in a padded room with a straitjacket.

"Do you know why Mother thinks you stayed home?" he said, as an explanation for the telegram churned over and over in my mind.

"Because I did. I'll be marrying Harvey soon. Mother will want you at the wedding," I said, walking to claim my trunk as it was unloaded off the train.

"Am I talking to a ghost? Because I ain't Icabod Crane, and you've still got your head," Roscoe said, thinking that I was playing some sort of game with him.

"No," I said tersely, arriving at my trunk where I opened it and took out the yellow dress and the beads. "You need to take the trunk back home like Mother has asked."

"Why can't you do it?"

"Mother asked you to do it, didn't she?"

He met my gaze, and the folksy smile that he wore on his face faded. We were at an impasse. He could unravel everything. One word, one poorly timed letter, and Ruby's whole world would burn down before it even began.

Roscoe wanted an explanation, but I needed time to think. An alibi? For what? Ruby was my alibi. She was probably sitting down to dinner with Harvey somewhere contemplating her future. No one would believe Roscoe had seen me in St. Louis.

"You're acting all suspicious," he said, grabbing me by the arm, "Are you in trouble? Is someone after you?"

He was the problem now, demanding explanations I couldn't give. I assured him that I was in absolutely no danger.

"If you ain't talking, maybe I'll just ring up Aunt Nettie. She'll explain why Mother's telegram said you weren't on the train, but you're standing right in front of me."

"I wouldn't be standing right in front of you. I'd be long gone. Aunt Nettie would think you'd hit the booze too hard, and she'd give you a lecture on drinking until you finally hung up on her," I said, calling his bluff. He looked at me like I was the one who'd been hitting the booze too hard, and he arranged for the trunk to be sent to his boarding house.

He could tell I was cooking up a little scheme, and if there was something that Roscoe Sutton loved it was schemes. I knew he'd want to be in on it. Ever since we were kids, Roscoe could never stand being left out of the joke. Pressing me for a nugget of information, I wouldn't budge because I hadn't figured out what I would tell him yet.

My stomach growled, and I told him that there was no way I could go into particulars on an empty stomach. Old Sally's wasn't far, and with any luck, Mrs. Byerly had left word that wouldn't send my stomach into a tailspin.

As we left the train station, I promised to take him to dinner at a little Italian place that I knew. He agreed but insisted that he'd be the one to pay. Intimating that he was some sort of big shot here in St. Louis, he said that he had a dozen other expensive suits back at his digs. Apparently, he made more dough in a week than he had in his whole dang life.

"I suppose that you've sent some money home since you know all about how your family struggles," I said, giving him the side eye as we walked down the street.

He coughed a couple times. I could tell that he hadn't even considered it, and he was embarrassed the thought had never occurred to him. Roscoe was known for living in the moment, and he never saw what Mother and Ray endured, so he didn't know they were struggling.

"Ray ever find work?"

"He does odd jobs when he can. He runs errands for Bernice and Aunt Nettie. Uncle Tice employs him now and then, but he can't get regular farm work from anyone else because he has a reputation for not being reliable. It all makes him feel worse about himself and so he spends more time hidden away when he thinks about it too much."

Roscoe nodded. It wasn't what he wanted to hear, but it was what he had expected.
We took a couple of detours as I filled him in on Mother and Ray. The walk from the train station to the boarding house normally took me fifteen minutes, but it ended up taking us over an hour.

When we walked into Old Sally's boarding house, I was reminded of the work that lay ahead of me. Mrs. Byerly didn't trust the post so she wouldn't hear of me sending the boxes, files, and other contents of her office to London by mail. She wanted me to personally escort them to New York, and she wanted them on the boat with us as we crossed the Atlantic. Estimating that it would take me only a day to get everything into crates and ready to ship, I'd made hypothetical plans to say goodbyes to some of the gals I knew around town.

Now, thanks to Mother's telegram, I'd have to spend that extra day putting together a trunk—otherwise, I'd arrive in England either naked or in the tatters of my only two dresses. I barely had enough money to buy myself the trunk let alone fill it with a decent supply of clothes and hats, but I had to deal with one problem at a time. What was I going to say to my brother about why I was here?

Old Sally greeted us warmly at the boarding house. She'd been like family since I moved to St. Louis, a retired madam turned boarding house owner whose heart had always been bigger than her scandalous stories. Introductions between her and Roscoe were made, and she handed me a letter from Mrs. Byerly, which had been delivered only moments ago.

Alterations had been made to our original plans as she'd made arrangements to do a bit of sightseeing in New York City so she was leaving as soon as possible. She had every confidence that I would get her boxes and files crated up and safely escorted to the *Leucothea*. Our boat, she said, rivaled the Titanic in luxury and hopefully would avoid the icebergs. I laughed not because Mrs. Byerly's joke was funny, but how painful her attempts at humor often were.

The thought that we wouldn't be traveling together to New York unnerved me a bit as it would be the first time that I'd traveled on an overnight train by myself. I shivered a little bit thinking of that louse with the gold tooth, but I was sure that he was long gone by now.

On the other hand, without Mrs. Byerly's looming presence, I could get everything packed up twice as fast and still have time to put together an adequate trunk. I dropped Middlemarch, my yellow dress, and Mother's old beads along with Mrs. Byerly's message in my room and led Roscoe off to the restaurant.

Flavio's was the Italian place that my girlfriends from the WCO dined at on occasion. The spaghetti with basil pesto sauce was my absolute favorite, but I never tasted a dish at Flavio's that wasn't absolutely divine.

We were seated near the kitchen in a dark corner, and I wasted no time in relieving the basket on the table of a slice of garlic bread. I was about to apologize to Roscoe for my poor manners, but his cheeks were already puffed out from the garlic bread that he'd inhaled. We looked at each other and laughed. Growing up poor and even poorer after our father left us, we were never shy when there was a bounty of food on the table.

The atmosphere wasn't much to speak of. There were candles burning on the table in old wine bottles, a red and white checkered tablecloth covering a slightly wobbly eating surface, and a man sitting in the corner playing an accordion. It was barely clean enough, but the smells from the kitchen distracted patrons from the occasional cockroach that scurried across the floor.

Flavio's could best be described as a hole in the wall, and it was almost exclusively locals who ate there. There weren't many tourists or rich folks who frequented this part of St. Louis, but the clientele added to the charm. I liked that it was always busy but never crowded.

Roscoe seemed pleased enough with the joint. He ordered my pesto and himself a plate of spaghetti bolognese in nearly flawless Italian. I was floored to hear how cultured he sounded as he spoke. He attempted to order us a couple glasses of wine, but the waiter assured him such a thing was illegal to sell. Waving his hand that Prohibition laws were meant to be ignored, he ordered us a couple bottles of coca cola.

Seeing how impressed I was by his Italian, Roscoe sheepishly admitted to shacking up with an Italian widow for nearly a year back when he was too young to know any better. They were mad about each other, but he knew that he could only play house for so long before it was time to move on. He was man enough to say goodbye to her, and he got a couple of black eyes in the bargain. In the end he had helped her with the rent for a while, and she gave him a second language and an appreciation for Italian food. I shook my head. It was amazing how much life Roscoe had squeezed into a little more than 25 years as he'd been on his own for nearly a decade.

He asked if I'd scarfed down enough garlic bread to tell him what was going on with me because he smelled a rat in my story from a mile away. Eyeing me sternly, he couldn't be put off for much longer, and I was suddenly indignant that he would demand anything from me.

"I'm not your puppet, Roscoe. You've got some nerve expecting anything from me. You left us to starve. Did you know we slept outside sometimes, after you ran off?"

He stared back at me in disbelief as if he hadn't known how bad things had gotten after he and dad both left us. We actually only slept outside a few times when the house had gotten so hot in the summer that the outside was cooler at night. However, I wanted to hurt him just a bit so I left out that detail so he'd think we'd been homeless.

Looking ashamed, he shook his head, and I was glad of it. He never knew what we went through because he was never around. After I got my job at the WCO and Mother and Ray settled in Milligan, we finally found our feet, but it didn't mean that Roscoe hadn't left us out to dry by running away. No doubt, he remembered the sparse food we had in the months after Dad disappeared. Mother was determined to stay in the house we rented in O'Fallon as it was the only place Dad would know to come back to. Her meager laundry business barely paid that rent. We scavenged for food. Ray took us mushroom hunting. We weren't above begging.

I never realized how much I'd needed to say that to him. Mother and Ray had never once given him any grief for leaving. Maybe they couldn't because they felt they should be able to manage, but Roscoe and I had been close. He shouldn't have left me, and I still hated him a little bit for it.

"Gee, Ruby. I didn't abandon you. Honest. I had to go. Seeing Ray with that noose again and crying because he couldn't get the knot right, it broke me."

Again? What did he mean by again? We only saw him try to kill himself that one time.

"Did you catch him trying to hang himself more than once?" I asked, tenderly.

He looked at me with wide eyes and a confused expression.

"Did you forget the first time—after he came back from Milligan with Dad's seventy-five bucks?"

Ray had returned from that trip happier and fuller of confidence than I'd ever seen him. He didn't try to kill himself. If anything, that trip helped him cope when we were resigned that dad wasn't coming home. Maybe in Ruby's world, it happened that way—but not in mine.

"I guess, I blocked it out," I said, "There were a lot of bad things that happened when we were kids that we shouldn't dwell on."

Roscoe nodded as if he understood all too well the memories of hunger and moving in the middle of the night to avoid eviction.

"If I didn't get out on my own, I was going to retreat inward just like him. I've always thought I had the melancholy like Ray. I just learned to hide it, and I knew that I wouldn't be able to hide it much longer. When it starts to creep in on me, I run. I know, I don't have it as bad as he does, but what if it gets worse?"

I was floored to hear what he was saying. Roscoe was like Ray? He was a little stronger than Ray as he could hold down a job for a while, but the blues would eventually take hold of him. His Italian lady helped him find at least three different jobs before he knew that she'd be better off without him. Playing like life is all fun and games was how he coped because if he didn't, he'd blow his own brains out.

We ate our meals while he apologized over and over for his shortcomings, and I could suddenly see a lot of Ray in him. I told him that I spent years angry at him because I never knew, and if he would have trusted me, I would have helped him just like I helped Ray.

He shook his head and brushed me off. Ray could live like that—he couldn't. He had to get out or die.

Our meal was completed in uncomfortable silence, and Roscoe asked me if I'd like to go somewhere with a more lively atmosphere. I was tired, but it was my last time to make a memory with my brother so I let him lead the way. Before we were out the door, he gave the waiter a business card with a wink and said, "If your boss has a supply problem, I'd be happy to talk it over with him."

We took a streetcar toward the heart of the city where we ended up in a dark alley with Roscoe looking over his shoulder, several times as if he was concerned we were being followed.

"Should I be worried about where you're taking me?" I asked.

He assured me that there was no danger, but he didn't want any tails. A fellow had to cover his bases when he was headed to the type of establishment where we were going. He rapped on the door at the end of the alley, and a slot slid open revealing a pair of eyes giving us the once over.

"Yeah?"

"We're here for the poetry," Roscoe said to the peepers.

"Who're you?"

"Charles Dickens."

The eyes disappeared and the lock of the door popped open. We were let inside, and the door immediately closed behind me.

It was a speakeasy, and it was hopping. My relatively chaste life in St. Louis hadn't acquainted me with much carousing. I'd always had Harvey back home in Milligan so I only went out with my girlfriends to the occasional lunch. Otherwise, I was curled up in my room at Old Sally's with George Eliot, Jane Austen, or ironically, Charles Dickens.

Roscoe was obviously known in this joint, and he had a table waiting for him when we got inside. He asked me if I'd like a drink or if Aunt Nettie's sermonizing had turned me pious. He informed me they were out of gin, but they had enough vodka and whiskey to take down a herd of elephants.

I left my drink order up to him, and I took in the atmosphere. It wasn't very big, but it was packed with people drinking up liquor and dancing like they'd never stop.

The name of the author changed every few days in case the feds get wise to the password. Roscoe had been in town working there for nearly four months, but he figured I was too respectable to make time for him so he hadn't bothered to look me up. By the time he'd gotten around to writing to mother, I was already gone so she cooked up the surprise at the train station.

The owner was a friend of a friend from Kansas City who said he needed a strong pair of hands who wasn't afraid of cops or making lots of dough. Roscoe followed him to St. Louis and they started running liquor from across the Canadian border.

After he had answered all of my questions, he said that it was only fair that I answer a few of his. I told him that he wasn't supposed to see me at the train station, and I was only staying one night in St. Louis before hightailing it back. The business was secret as it involved a meeting with a man tomorrow morning, and I couldn't go into any more details.

"Does it have to do with that yellow dress I saw you pull out of the trunk?"

"Yes, it does," I said, pouncing on his lead, "Look Roscoe, I'm no angel, but I'll make Harvey a good wife. Don't rat me out when you go home for the wedding, and I don't ever want to speak of it again. If you bring this up to me, I'll pretend I don't have any idea what you're talking about."

His jaw dropped for a beat before a smile spread across his face. He asked what Mother did to raise a couple of rabble rousers like the two of us? We drank a toast, and I felt the weight of the world lift off my shoulders. I had no idea that I was quite so good thinking on my feet, and while it wasn't ideal for my brother to think of me as some two bit floozy, it was better than him knowing that I'd walked through the Seven Arches, somehow created an exact double who was headed to London never to return.

He agreed to keep my secret as long as I promised him that I was in no danger. I told him that I was in more danger on the train from Terre Haute than I would be upon meeting my gentleman friend.

The whole story of the man who had harassed me on the train came out. He said that the Lydgate character sounded like a cool customer because he would have socked that loser in the jaw from here to kingdom come.

I told him he didn't have to worry because after this trip, if I did any traveling at all, it would be with Harvey. Roscoe had only visited Mother and Ray a handful of times since they moved from O'Fallon to Milligan, and my visits didn't always overlap. He'd been able to meet Harvey, but he thought he was too stiff for me. I, of course, told him to mind his own business.

"You really marrying this Cleghorn fellow?" he asked.

"I am."

What's this other fella's name?

"Listen, I'll tell you all about him if you tell me why Octavia Lanning's son born about nine months after the last time you were home looks almost nothing like his daddy?"

Roscoe almost choked on his drink at the mention of Octavia Lanning. That girl apparently followed Roscoe around like a puppy when he was home the last time, and after he left, she got hitched pretty quickly. Mother had figured it all out, but she doubted that anyone else had. She could always tell a Mottern baby, and Octavia's boy was most definitely a Mottern.

"I think the question and answer portion of the evening is at a close," he said as he caught his breath again.

Begging for just one more question, I asked if he'd ever run into our father in all his travels. Almost certain the man was dead for the longest time, I didn't know what prompted me to ask.

I was surprised to hear him answer that he had in fact seen our father. It had been more than two years ago when he was down in Texas working as a cattle wrangler. He had gone into a saloon for a drink after the sun went down, and he saw him sitting at the table playing poker.

"He had aged a couple years, but he still looked exactly the same. I sat down and had a drink trying to get up the courage to speak to him, but the next time I looked at the table he was gone.

"The bartender had never seen him before, but told me if I ever saw that man again, I should thank him because he bought my drink."

Two years ago my father was alive in Texas? I couldn't believe it. I had hoped for Mother's sake that he'd died in a ditch an hour after he sent Ray back to us with that seventy-five dollars. Roscoe thought about telling Mother that he'd seen him, but he figured it would only cause her more heartache so he kept it to himself.

We reminisced for a few more hours, only having a couple of drinks each. He escorted me back to Old Sally's where I reminded him that he never saw me in St. Louis. He peeled off a couple of greenbacks and laid them in my palm. I thanked him for his kindness and hugged him tightly.

"As long as you don't go on having any chat with Octavia Lanning's husband, your secret is safe with me," he bowed and walked on down the street.

Roscoe disappeared into the night—my last connection to Ruby's world fading with him.

Fyodor's Grandmother, San Diego 1922

Clarissa Byerly was finally beginning to feel like her old self again. Thanks to a letter from her son, she was bubbling over with rage and indignation—enough to overcome her lingering physical weakness.

"The impertinence!" she shouted, hurling his letter across the room of the boarding house where she'd been staying to finalize the budget while Hazel oversaw the delivery of office furniture to their newly leased space.

It had been a long few weeks. She'd barely recovered from the flu that nearly killed her before boarding a train to San Diego with Hazel.

From the moment she boarded the locomotive and felt her constitutional weakness, she realized that she had acted rashly. It was hard for her to believe that she wasn't invincible, and her son had acted so arrogantly that part of the reason she left so abruptly was to spite him. Felix demanded she convalesce in Indiana so he could tend to her—but she refused to let her own son tell her how to live.

Privately, she knew that she'd have to be lobotomized in order to endure any time in the house of Enoch Byerly, but her son was as stubborn as she was so she lied. He'd left to prepare her room in Indiana, and she immediately directed Hazel to arrange their travel accommodations to San Diego.

Felix was unreasonable and uncompromising regarding her health. He believed that he could control her life, even though he had made it abundantly clear to her that she didn't have any sway over his life.

Clarissa wasn't about to alter her future plans for any man, even her own son. She wasn't going to die in Waveland, Indiana. That, to her, was fundamentally certain. Dying in San Diego opening up a second satellite office for the WCO was much more dignified.

There was a chance that an enraged Felix would hop on the next train to San Diego to fetch her, but she had felt it was unlikely. If he did, their battle of wills would likely be bloodier than Gettysburg, and her son would be forced to retreat because she wouldn't compromise.

Felix occupied much of her thoughts on the journey, but the illness had made her more introspective about her own legacy. Before the damned flu, Clarissa was confident that she could open up a dozen WCO offices before slowing down. Hazel's ridiculous intention to marry that farmboy had certainly thrown a wrench into her plans, but she'd managed to keep Hazel from resigning—at least for now.

The New York office plans were scrapped because of her illness, but the opening of the San Diego office was to be followed by the opening of an Atlanta office. After those two went smoothly, she could make plans for five more offices in the next year.

All the work that lay ahead of her seemed exhausting, and she barely had the energy to make it from the train to the boarding house. Hazel was constantly by her side or managing the affairs needed to open the office. The girl knew that her employer had a bad bout of the flu a few weeks ago, but she didn't know the woman had been at death's door.

Hazel did most of the heavy lifting in those first few weeks. The first office space they were offered was completely insufficient and the rent expected was highway robbery. The girl had been an ideal student in the Clarissa Byerly School of Persuasion. She'd secured a better office in a better location for a lower rent, and, as a bonus, didn't pry about Mrs. Byerly's persistent lethargy.

They were staying in the shabbiest of places run by a very domineering Russian lady named Mrs. Petrova. The woman was charming at first, and Clarissa didn't like to judge women too harshly especially business owners as there were so few of them. She lived with her grandson, who was only a few years older than Hazel—a boy duller than ditchwater.

With Hazel out and about so much, Clarissa spent a fair amount of time at the boarding house answering letters, writing reports, and conserving her own meager energy.

The Russian kept the living spaces clean enough, but there was no real privacy to get work done with her coming through with a broom, a feather duster, or an irritating announcement.

Clarissa attempted to convey the importance of her work, and the solitude and quiet she needed for concentration, but it fell on deaf ears. The Russian lady and her grandson didn't seem to understand the concept.

Her irritation with her innkeeper coupled with the letter she'd just received from Felix, who'd called her a 'rancid, short-sighted idiot too stupid to listen to medical advice.', made her especially volatile that afternoon when she heard Mrs. Petrova clomping up the stairs.

"Fyodor likes your daughter. They marry, yes?" The Russian woman said after barging into Clarissa's bedroom under the pretense to fluff the pillows.

"Madam, it is exhausting to correct you this much. Miss Sutton is not my daughter. Now, please my pillows are much too fluffy as they are," she said without removing her reading glasses.

"Girls travel with mothers. You let her marry Fyodor, and they be happy. Yes?"

A moment ago, her wrath had been aimed at her son and his letter, but Mrs. Petrova had moved Clarissa's target with her incredulous demand for Hazel to be married to her grandson. Felix had blown the battle horn, but it was this woman who would feel her wrath.

Heated words were exchanged, and Clarissa, who usually shied away from unladylike profanities, unsheathed the sharp edge of her tongue. The shouts were loud enough to bring most of the terrified renters out of their rooms to witness the fracas. Fyodor's grandmother had as hot a temper as Mrs. Byerly, but the language barrier caused most of the insults to miss the target. They knew they were fighting—but had no idea just how caustic the other was being.

After the fight was over, Clarissa and Hazel were standing on the sidewalk outside of the boarding house with their bags in hand.

"Mrs. Byerly, you're finally returning to your old self. I was wondering if my employer had transitioned into a shrinking violet."

"Hazel dear, I admit that the flu had caused considerable weakness that I'm starting to shake, but I will not tolerate any more insinuation that I'm some sort of pushover. I've got a good mind to lecture you on the proper way to address your superior," she said acidly, but quickly softened with a smile.

Her relationship with Hazel was very reminiscent of a mother/daughter, but she still didn't share much of her personal life with anyone at the WCO. When they lost Tabitha and her grandson a few years ago, it was devastating. She couldn't bear to talk about it so she kept all personal talk to a minimum.

She also preferred Hazel kept talk of her fiancé—the farmboy—to a minimum. The girl had foolishly promised to marry him before he went off to war. He came back two years ago, and Hazel kept dropping hints that she couldn't delay the wedding for much longer.

Perhaps Clarissa was supposed to retire. It had been nearly 30 years since she'd seen her cousin Dora. They had made plans over the years to visit one another, but the distance between Chaffinch Fields and St. Louis was always difficult to overcome. It would be so much easier if Dora lived in the States as Clarissa could open up a new WCO office almost anywhere in the country.

Why couldn't she open up a WCO office in England? She could bring the mission of the Women's Charity Organization to Europe! It would be the crowning achievement of her entire career.

When they arrived at their new boarding house, Clarissa immediately set to work drafting a proposal for the first international WCO office—in London.

Chapter 5

The rhythmic pull of the train roaring toward New York City became a familiar friend to me on the overnight ride from St. Louis, and the excitement in my bones grew larger as the distance grew shorter.

I took out my first class passenger ticket for the *Leucothea* again to look it over. By the end of the day, the *Leucothea* would be departing from the Port Authority on Pier 88 and arriving at the Port of London in just seven days' time.

It was all happening, and my new life was beginning! Spending so much time since Milligan mourning what I'd lost, I hadn't appreciated everything I'd gained. Daydreaming about crossing the ocean on a luxury cruiser was definitely something to be excited about.

When I arrived at St. Louis a few days ago, life seemed so fraught with peril. The uncomfortable encounter with the gold-toothed man and Roscoe demanding an explanation that I could never give had unnerved me.

My only saving grace was Tertius Lydgate, a man who I was certain I would never meet again. He gave me hope that in my new life I could forge new connections. This gift from God I had been given started to suddenly feel real, and I felt like he was finally smiling down on me.

The ability to live this dream without an ounce of guilt for what I was leaving behind was magical. People would not be worse for the wear because I was gone as Ruby would be there to take care of all my loved ones.

After my triumphant meeting with Roscoe, everything seemed to fall into place. The three days that were allotted for me to finish up closing Mrs. Byerly's WCO office were more than sufficient.

I had the necessary books and files packed and crated by the end of the first day with only sundry details to work out the next. Mrs. Byerly leaving early to sightsee in New York was a blessing in disguise as she would have needed to go over every last document in her possession. She would have talked my ear off about each file and how helpful or not it would be once we got to London.

Opening up a new office of the Women's Charity Organization in London was not going to be difficult work for us. Last year, we opened new offices in Nashville, San Diego, and Atlanta.

We had learned so much from the experiences that Mrs. Byerly and I both felt we had a good grasp on any problems we might encounter. We were concerned only slightly that there were cultural differences that we might not anticipate.

Knowing that she wouldn't be able to hold onto me forever, she assured me that this year in London would be 55%

work and 45% play. Try as she might, she wasn't able to talk me out of the idea that I wanted a family someday soon.

Most of her arguments for me becoming a career girl didn't hold water because even as much as she loathed being married, she was the proud mother of a son. She couldn't ask me to give up being a mother, and unless I was a widow, there was no way that I could work and raise a family.

The world was unfair to women as she often lectured me. She had a nanny growing up, but even if her mother wanted to work outside the home, she couldn't because society frowned upon it. Mrs. Byerly got me into a dialogue once on why society disliked married women working.

I thought, perhaps, society placed an importance on a mother's love in a child's upbringing, but she countered that not all mothers were good mothers as we had seen a lot in our work.

Many stepmothers had raised children that were not their own, and those children turned out perfectly fine. Too much emphasis was placed on mothers because it takes a village to raise a child, and while I agreed, she took it a step further.

Society rules concerning women weren't about child welfare, but they were about controlling half the population.

Even though she made good points, she couldn't dissuade me from wanting a family with Harvey one day.

With my WCO work completed a day and a half early, I had only to go shopping for a new trunk and clothes with the money that Roscoe had given me. I hadn't looked at the three bills he'd placed in my hand until I got back up to my room at Old Sally's that night, but I was astonished to see the face of George Washington staring up at me on three twenty dollar bills.

I took the streetcar to Washington Avenue that afternoon to the garment district, and as I was a Sutton with money burning a hole in my pocket, I first went to Rice Stix where their dresses were top quality and top dollar.

Many dresses were featured in famous magazines, and I recalled some from recent issues of Vogue. Filling out my wardrobe with these would mean paying more than what I'd pay Old Sally in a year, and despite being enthralled at the prospect of looking like a model, I knew better than to look at them for long. I couldn't even imagine what kind of life one would lead where a girl could wear dresses like those every day.

There was one particularly beautiful ball gown that caught my attention. It was a cream-colored satin. The satin was covered with an overdress made of tulle embroidered with sequins and stylized with hinted floral patterns. Overdresses of this type were mostly Parisian if my magazines could be trusted.

I pined for this dress, and I almost bought it. The cash Roscoe gave me would more than cover the costs, but my sense of frugality from growing up poor prevailed. Twenty-five dollars was nearly half the money that I had, and I hadn't even purchased a trunk yet.

If I was going to splurge, I would splurge on a new hat. Walking down the street to the Levis-Zukowski Mercantile Company, which prided itself on being one of the largest hat manufacturers in the world.

I tried on a variety of hats but fell in love with this gorgeous wool cloche hat ornamented with a silk rose. The cost for the beautiful hat was merely five dollars. When it was boxed up, I was proud of choosing something so sensible and versatile. It could be worn while sightseeing in Europe and later for my job, not to mention that it was much less expensive than the dress at Rice Stix.

My last stop was the Famous-Barr department store. I had been there many times as it was much more in my price range than the other shops, but it had its perks. A nice trunk could be purchased and filled with everything I needed for about fifteen dollars if I was frugal. The remaining money gifted to me by Roscoe could be saved and spent overseas, even though I was still dreaming of that dress from Rice Stix.

The sales girl in Famous-Barr spent a few hours introducing me to some of the newer fashions that were emerging that summer. She used the term flapper when describing a lot of the dresses with the shorter hemline. I wasn't exactly a prude, but I still wasn't sure how much leg it was decent to show—even if Europeans were known for being more relaxed and less uptight about such things.

It was time to change up my colors a bit. I'd always worn natural colors like browns, yellows, and greens. They were usually the cheapest fabric, and Mother still made some of my clothes even when I lived in St. Louis. Her dresses were nice, but every once in a while I felt like a dowdy country girl in some of the house dresses she made for me.

The housewife in threadbare muslin was more of who Ruby was becoming. Hazel would be a bit more daring so I chose a knockout red dress with a hemline that was just below the knee. It wasn't scandalous for St. Louis or New York even, but it would have been the talk of Milligan.

The sales girl talked me into a matching red lipstick, and I prayed that Mrs. Byerly wouldn't jokingly refer to me as the Whore of Babylon as sometimes her humor was biting sarcasm.

Arrangements were made for the trunk to be delivered to Old Sally's, and I still felt a little change burning a hole in my pocket. The necessity of a few books for the train to New

York and the voyage of the *Leucothea* entered my mind. There was a bookstore that I knew quite well two blocks outside of the garment district so I decided to head that way.

The first novel I bought was called *This Side of Paradise* written by a man named F. Scott Fitzgerald. It was released a few years ago, and there was quite a bit of excitement about it at the time. I was floored when I read that Mr. Fitzgerald was younger than I was.

At twenty-three, I thought I'd accomplished a lot, but he was a man. Wondering what my life would look like if I'd been a man, I quickly realized between Ray and Roscoe that the men in my family were troubled to say the least.

Since I would be spending most of my time in London, I naturally gravitated toward British authors. I came across Dickens, always a favorite of mine, but realized I had never read *David Copperfield*. I chose it as my second book, deciding it was time to remedy that. Between the two, I figured they would be enough to carry me through to New York and then on to London.

As I left the bookstore, I had the sweet realization that I had an entire day tomorrow to myself with no one expecting me to do anything, and I couldn't even begin to recall the last time that happened.

Even when I was staying with Mother and Ray, they usually expected help with dinner, a walk with Jupiter, or an errand of some sort. Tomorrow, there was nothing, and I would relish it. I considered making lunch plans with a couple of the girls from the office when suddenly I was struck with a horrifying and familiar sound.

Click click.

Could it actually be him? I paused only for a moment because I could feel the sound getting closer and closer whenever I delayed.

Click click.

It had to be him. I had inadvertently memorized the cadence of his shoes when he chased me onto the train in Terre Haute. A lump began to rise in my throat as I clutched the books to my chest and picked up the pace.

Click click.

The street car that would take me back to Old Sally's was still four blocks away, and while the streets weren't empty, they weren't exactly crowded. He would get in my street car and follow me home, perhaps to my door, and he had a gun. I shuddered thinking about it, feeling my pulse quicken.

Click click.

The horrid thought that no one would miss me if I was kidnapped struck me like a ton of bricks. Mrs. Byerly would inquire to my mother who would tell her I had left my job to be married. I'd be discovered in a shallow grave and be just another hapless, nameless victim who was violated and murdered at the hands of an unknown killer.

Click click.

My pulse raced as I crossed another street and stood on the curb. My feet were suddenly frozen to the ground as I knew that I couldn't let him follow me further. He was going to have to drag me off in full view of the public as I wouldn't give him the satisfaction of stalking me to Old Sally's.

Click click.

I turned around and saw the glimmer of the gold tooth catching the light of the afternoon sun. He wore the same clothes he'd had on two days ago. They looked somehow shabbier, and I doubted they'd been cleaned. Sneering at me from across the street, he knew that "my husband" was nowhere to be found.

We sized each other up, and I wondered if I could hit him in the crotch hard enough with my knee to incapacitate him. It could be my only shot to run away and catch the streetcar before he caught his breath.

"I'm not ignoring you now," I said as a bead of sweat dripped from my brow and hit the tip of my nose. I was terrified, but I was going to hold my ground. He was a coward at a confrontation, and I was gambling a lot on it.

Licking his lips and not breaking his gaze from me, he must've thought that I'd lost my mind. He was expecting me to run or scream, but I did not break his gaze for one single moment.

My heart was in my throat, but I steeled my resolve. I wouldn't be dragged away without a fight. Someone had once knocked out that man's tooth, I could at least take off an ear if I thought my life depended on it.

As he took one step off the curb, that was it. A Rolls-Royce plowed right through him as if he were made of cardboard. The THUNK his body made as it hit the road was even more memorable than the Click Click of his boots.

There were screams of horror as I watched passersby step toward him to confirm what everyone already knew. The blood was slowly leeching onto the street from the back of his head. The force had knocked him out of his horrible shoes.

This man and I had no connection—except that he died harassing me. So focused on stalking me, he stepped out in front of a car. And now he was dead.

I was glad he was dead, but I was struck by the fact that this man was dead because of me. There was no sense of guilt lingering as he made the decision to pursue me, and he had paid the ultimate price. He was a vile creature who I hoped was burning in hell already, but here among the living there was nothing left of him but meatloaf.

Getting ready to walk away, I paused upon seeing a glimmer in the distance. It was a shiny gold tooth sitting in the middle of the street. I picked it up with one hand, placed it in my handbag, and walked nonchalantly to my streetcar.

The next day, I found a jeweler that paid me five dollars for the tooth. It felt like a sign so I took that money along with a twenty from Roscoe and returned to Rice Stix to buy that cream-colored satin gown.

The suffering that man caused me made me feel as if I deserved it. Part of me knew that if he had lived, I'd always be looking out for him at every corner wondering when he was coming for me next. He was gone forever, and it felt like God was looking out for me.

Everything had gone like clockwork for my train ride to New York City. The crates were loaded. My trunk was with me and my gorgeous new gown was inside it. I remembered my books, and in just an hour I would be arriving in the city where I would embark on my great adventure in London.

Mrs. Byerly had cabled me the night before I left that she and her son would be waiting for me at Grand Central Station. He had made her aware that sometimes ruffians traveled on trains and targeted women traveling alone. As I was only traveling by myself because she left a few days early, it was only right for her and Felix to pick me up at the station.

Leaving the train, I located my trunk and the office crates. Then, I stood wide-eyed searching for Mrs. Byerly. The woman was rarely on time without my assistance so it was no surprise that she hadn't arrived yet. She'd make it eventually, but it could be an hour of waiting at Grand Central Station. On the train, I had started David Copperfield and supposed that I would open it back up when I saw a figure from across the station that made me gasp.

Dr. Lydgate!

He was in New York!

What was he doing in New York? He'd never said where he was traveling with his mother. Everything was suddenly awkward as I didn't know what to do. I was excited to see him, of course, but I'd rejected his attempts to inquire about me.

We locked eyes, and I could see the visible surprise on his face followed by a noticeable redness rising in his cheeks. He stopped moving, and we stared at each other across the crowded station at a safe distance.

The question of whether or not he would approach me flew through my head. Did he even want to? I had this inexplicable urge to kiss him on the mouth then turn and run the other direction away from him forever. It was so much easier laughing with him on the train to St. Louis, thinking we'd never see each other again.

It felt like minutes were passing as we were locked in that gaze, both afraid to take a step toward one another when I caught sight of a small hat bobbing through the crowd. It was a hat I recognized as belonging to Mrs. Byerly. To my absolute horror, Dr. Lydgate appeared to be following or more appropriately, dragged behind her.

Then it hit me like an explosion of dynamite.

It was him. Of course it was—the man from the train, the one I'd been calling Tertius in my mind for days. But here, standing in the afternoon light of New York with his mother at his side and his real name on his lips, he seemed different. More handsome. More real.

Felix Byerly.

My head was spinning at the realization. Behind the mustache and cocksure grin, he strongly resembled his mother, my boss. That was the familiarity that I bonded with when we met on the train.

"Hazel, darling!" Mrs. Byerly said, kissing my cheek upon meeting me. "I'll make introductions later. Felix, please arrange for Miss Sutton's trunk and the crates to be taken to the Port Authority to be loaded on the ship. This station is so filthy. You can meet us at that charming little tea room we passed on the way here."

Felix nodded to his mother, and he gave me a sideways grin with a finger to his lips when she wasn't looking. He obviously didn't want me to tell her that we'd previously met on the train, but I wasn't sure why.

She took me by the arm and led me down the street. "Isn't New York City just fabulous?!" she said, "Do you know that I haven't been here in over thirty years. It was a vacation with Felix's father, and it left a bad taste in my mouth. My goodness! Did you know the Statue of Liberty is green now? I'd never have believed it. It was a deep brown the last time I saw it. The color is not an improvement in my opinion. Oh, where are my manners? How was the train ride, my dear?"

Mrs. Byerly was always overly loquacious, and it did take some getting used to after spending the last few weeks with Ray and Harvey who combined barely spoke the amount of words in a week as Mrs. Byerly had in the last five minutes. My own tendency to prattle on was always significantly diminished when I was around my boss.

I assured her the train ride was splendid and mentioned that I'd packed all her office necessities from St. Louis. I'd even found a memorandum from the Alliance of Nashville Suffragettes that she had misplaced and given up for lost. She forced a smile and seemed wholly uninterested in talking about work.

"My dear, this trip is my gift to you before I release you back into the wilds of that charming little hamlet your mother lives in. I'm retiring after we open the London office. Mrs. Schiff is most likely entertaining applicants to replace my position as we speak."

"You're retiring?!" I was taken aback, Mrs. Byerly lived for her work. She wasn't even sixty years old, and she had always been so lively. At times I forgot that she wasn't my contemporary, but I had noticed in the last few years she had slowed down.

She had threatened to quit before I'd agreed to help her open the London office, but I assumed it was only a ploy. I had no idea she had been serious. So much was swirling through my mind that I didn't know which question to ask first.

"Yes, my dear. It's time for me to enjoy the fruits of my labor and become a languid, old dowager. I couldn't bear to train another secretary to manage my work affairs as well as you, and I know that marriage and family isn't something that I can tempt you away from. It's quite a shame too as you're such a talented young lady. As long as Mrs. Schiff could spare the funds, I would have sent you all over the country opening up new offices of the Women's Charity Organization."

Mrs. Byerly noticed my terrified expression. I hadn't anticipated losing my job at the end of the year. It was devastating to hear, but if Mrs. Byerly wasn't employed with the WCO they certainly wouldn't keep paying her secretary.

"Whatever is wrong, my dear?" she asked, suddenly startled.

I told Mrs. Byerly that I'd left Harvey behind for good when I came on this trip. I no longer had a future husband waiting for me, and I was more than available to assist her for the next few years. She scoffed at first, insisting we'd merely had an argument. But when I mentioned that, last I heard, he was planning to marry another woman, she began to believe me.

Admitting it hurt more than I expected. It made it all feel so real and so final. Harvey was no longer my anchor back to Milligan. I had thought of him, at times, as an anchor in a negative sense where he was holding me back, but now I thought about him as an anchor tying me to a life that I'd wanted as long as I could remember.

I wiped a few stray tears from my eyes as Mrs. Byerly looked at me in utter confusion.

"Did he give you an ultimatum? Did that pig tell you that you had to choose between my trip and him? Oh my, you are so much better off without him. My God, Hazel. He would have only gotten worse in his controlling behavior. That is not that type of man you want to tie yourself to. Didn't you tell me he was attached to his rancid mother? Why! He'd suffocate you. Not literally, I hope, but you'd waste away as some sort of forlorn housewife most likely scrubbing his britches on a washboard and dreaming about what your life could have been."

I thanked her for the kind words and told her that I wanted to look into opportunities in the London office that we open up. Assuring her that my brother Roscoe had come into a bit of money, I no longer had to worry about taking care of my mother and eldest brother.

She was delighted and couldn't imagine a better applicant to run the first international office of the WCO, but our work was months away. The office they had leased wouldn't be available until late June, and until then, she didn't want to hear anymore talk about our work.

Glancing around to make sure her son wasn't nearby, she confided that she wanted my help. Once we arrived in England, we'd be spending about ten days at her cousin's estate, Chaffinch Fields, before heading to the continent for a few months. Her cousin had only one daughter and heir, and Mrs. Byerly had already conspired with the Duchess to arrange a match between Felix and Olive Powlett.

Mrs. Byerly and her cousin had many written letters over the years hoping to make a match between Felix and Olive, and their hopes were dashed when Felix ran off and married another woman. She had died, and Felix had sufficient time to grieve for her so it was the perfect time.

"Can you imagine? My Felix running an English estate! Why he'd leave his uncle's house in a moment, and I could retire there. It all sounds so lovely to hear Dora talk about it. It's far enough outside of London to give clean air and quiet, but close enough to travel there to find amusement. Chaffinch Fields! Isn't that a divine name? Now, not a word to Felix. If he believes that I am trying to set him up with dear Olive then he'd detest her on sight just to spite me. You will help me, my dear? I knew you would. You're such a wonderful, young lady. Shh, here he comes."

Felix kissed his mother, and I extended my hand for him to greet me as well.

"Felix, this is my secretary Miss Hazel Sutton. You're no doubt familiar with the name as I do go on about her so much. She's been such a diligent worker for me. Why I quite doubt I would have been so successful without her. I say, where is our tea?"

"Wonderful to finally meet you, Miss Sutton," he said, winking at me to keep up the ruse.

I nodded, trying not to show how fast my heart was beating.

"Mrs. Byerly tells me that you are touring Europe with us. Are you planning to return home soon after?" I asked.

"My uncle has granted me three months before he requires my company again," he said.

"That uncle of yours. I detest him more than your father. My goodness, why does he demand or require anything of you? You're my son after all. This is ridiculous. I have half a mind to write him a letter containing a good scolding."

"That's plenty, Mother." Felix said.

Felix explained that he was the sole heir to his uncle's fortune on his father's side and that he was quite fond of him. He had taken on much of his uncle's investment work, which kept him away from his mother more often than she liked to admit.

"A month at Christmas is all he gives me anymore. I know that I've been working a lot, but I have only one son. I don't think that it is right that I should have to share him with some insolent uncle with a big purse that he dangles over him."

Felix let Mrs. Byerly go on a bit longer this time, and I could tell it was a complaint that she made frequently.

It was almost comical that mere moments after meeting Mrs. Byerly and Felix that I was keeping two secrets. First, there was Mrs. Byerly's hope of making a match between Felix and his cousin and secondly, Felix's desire to stay quiet about us having met before.

Why he didn't want her to know we had met on the train was puzzling, and furthermore, I didn't know when I was going to get the chance to discuss it with him. Somewhat disappointed that Mrs. Byerly had asked me to help make a match between Felix and Miss Powlett, I was conflicted as seeing him again made my heart flutter.

I spent the next few hours listening to them recall their adventures in New York. While they were constantly sarcastic and cutting with one another, it was easy to tell the byplay masked an esteemed affection. It made me a little homesick for my own mother.

We sipped our tea, and Mrs. Byerly also described Chaffinch Fields the best she could from the descriptions she had received from her cousin. The estate probably was so grand that we'd all fall in love with it upon sight. She mentioned that Dora was concerned about the future of the place as one day Olive's future husband would be the steward.

She remarked that she had extended an invitation for Dora and Olive to accompany us on our trip across Europe, but they might need a little arm-twisting to go.

"Is that right, Mother?" Felix said, suppressing a smile.

Mrs. Byerly's secret was not, in fact, much of a secret from Felix. It was painfully obvious as evidenced by his expression. I watched them playfully argue, and Felix always said the name "Miss Powlett" with sarcastic emphasis. His mother pretended not to notice, but I could tell that it vexed her.

It was still hard to believe that the handsome gentleman from the train to St. Louis was actually Felix Byerly. I had no idea how to act around him and knew that if I were overly friendly, Mrs. Byerly would take it as undermining her. But I didn't want to be cold either. He was so charming—and worse, he knew it.

Reuniting with him so quickly after a regretful parting felt so surreal. There were so many questions to be answered like how we ended up on the same train to St. Louis.

When we finished our tea, we headed toward the Port Authority to board the ship. Once settled into our various cabins, I was able to leaf through a few more chapters of *David Copperfield* before napping a bit.

Later that evening, I met Mrs. Byerly and Felix on the deck to wave goodbye to America with our white handkerchiefs in the air. The three of us had dinner together where Mrs. Byerly dropped more hints at how lucky the future husband of Olive Powlett would be, and I played my part by wholeheartedly agreeing with her.

Aboard the *Leucothea,* it was hard to believe that it was all happening. This luxury liner had so many leisure activities available on the journey, but if the food on that first night was any indication, all my senses would be dazzled as we crossed the ocean.

They served lobster thermidor for dinner, and I had never tasted anything so divine. It came with roasted asparagus and chestnut sauce that melted in my mouth, and for dessert, Baked Alaska, which was so decadent that I hadn't the words to describe it.

Shortly after dinner, Mrs. Byerly retired for the evening, and Felix and I managed to exchange a few words. He hoped I wasn't inconvenienced by withholding the information that we'd met before from his mother.

It was impossible to let her in on the secret. He'd gone on and on about how hopelessly besotted he was with Miss Rosamond Vincy, and she still clung to the harebrained notion that he'd fall for Olive Powlett. If she knew I *was* Rosamond, she'd never leave us alone long enough to let anything real unfold—and that was all he seemed to want on this trip.

"Besotted?" I asked.

He gave a wink. "I know what I said. Good night, Miss Vincy."

Then he vanished into the dark, leaving me breathless and smiling like a fool.

Chapter 6

The shock of learning that Tertius Lydgate was Felix Byerly left me reeling, and the word "besotted" rang out in my ears over and over again. We'd had such a wonderful train ride as strangers, and we'd said so much that we wouldn't have normally shared if we had known each other's identities.

I laid down on my bed to think about how serendipitous it was that Felix Byerly had been on my train when I left Milligan. Mrs. Byerly only said that his uncle lived somewhere dreadful, but I had no idea it was a place so close to where my mother and Ray lived. She always only concerned herself with the big picture. Sundry details, she always said, were my department.

It was quite odd that we'd never met, but then again, he wouldn't visit his mother when we were tied up with work. He would always visit St. Louis when I was leaving the city for Milligan. Replaying our conversation on the train over and over in my head, I laughed at the absurdity of it all.

The realization that Tertius Lydgate's mother was dying caused me to sit up in bed immediately. At the time, I didn't put any thought into it, but then again, I hadn't expected to know his mother. Panic surged through me. Was she truly dying? She was the only person I had from my old life. Ruby got everyone else, and now, Mrs. Byerly was dying! I couldn't believe that she hadn't told me she was dying.

Was that the reason for this beautiful trip she was taking me on with her son? Was it a goodbye? Mrs. Byerly and I were close, but she was still my employer. I couldn't ask her a personal question about her health, and if I did, she'd ignore it, no doubt.

I tried to calm myself. She was well enough to travel across the ocean to a new country, and she was known to scheme a bit to get what she wanted. It was well within the realm of possibilities that she embellished her health issues to make her son come with us on the trip. If I could get a few moments alone with Felix tomorrow, I felt sure he could ease my mind about her. Occasionally, Mrs. Byerly was known to tell little fibs to get what she wanted as women needed to use every tool they had as we were living in a man's world.

The following morning the three of us breakfasted together, and Felix could tell that I was preoccupied. He obnoxiously tried to wink at me a few times, but I ignored him. Mrs. Byerly occupied my time for most of the day. She dictated a letter for me to post when we arrived on land, I listened to the String Quartet with her, and we had tea before she retired to her cabin to rest her eyes for a few hours.

She normally rested in the afternoons, but I hadn't known of her health issues then. My mind jumped to panic. I imagined her in astounding pain and swallowing obnoxious amounts of laudanum before passing out onto her bed as the excruciating pain in her chest dulled slightly.

Left to my own devices, I frantically began to search the boat for Felix, but I didn't have to look far. He practically materialized out of thin air at almost the instant his mother had disappeared into her room.

"Are you quite angry with me?" he said, sidling up and holding out his arm for me to take.

"You mean your juvenile gestures to me over breakfast? I pretended not to see them because my mind was occupied with your mother's health. I had nearly forgotten that Tertius Lydgate's mother was quite ill."

He opened his mouth as if recalling the conversation we had aboard the train. It hadn't all been longing looks and quips about misery. Nodding quietly, he told me that it was almost as serious as I had feared it might be. She had contracted the flu last year, and it was a particularly bad case.

I confirmed that I had known this because her illness and inability to work sent me home early for my winter vacation in Milligan, and it canceled the opening of the New York office. I recalled panicking until a letter arrived from her at Mother's house that said her illness was not serious, and she had an overly cautious physician.

Explaining how his mother hated to appear weak in front of anyone, she willfully misled nearly all her acquaintances about the severity of her condition. She had written more than a handful of letters to various friends and family members stating that she had indeed contracted the flu, but it was not so serious.

Felix traveled from Waveland to St. Louis to nurse her, and he'd hired a physician and nurse to make sure all her needs were met. He read her books every night through the worst of it and worried that each labored breath would be her last. The flu developed into pneumonia, and the pneumonia had left her at the point of death.

Praying over her, he was prepared for her to pass away at any moment, but her fever finally broke. She suddenly began to get a little bit better every day. Convalescing for several weeks, she began to build her strength. The doctor was dumbfounded that she survived. The whole ordeal had weakened her heart and lungs, and while she seemed to be in decent health, another illness could be fatal.

Tears welled up in my eyes when I thought about poor Mrs. Byerly. She had been so kind to me, and the job was such a blessing for me and my family. It seemed unbelievable that she hid from me how close she was to dying. It hurt that she shielded people that loved her from such news, but I knew her to be a proud woman.

I wanted to believe we were more than employee and employer. Maybe I was wrong. Thinking back over the past year, she had indeed slowed down, but I hadn't wanted to see it. All the times she'd rested or put herself in precarious positions visiting hospitals with sick women and children were silly risks that I would have prevented had I known her condition.

Felix comforted me and made every assurance that she was as healthy as she had been for this last year. Her heart issues were nothing new, and she had indeed used her weakened heart as a tool to lure him to England. They had spent the last few days sightseeing in New York, and he was convinced now that she wasn't at all concerned about her fragility. She may have been his loving mother, but he also knew her to be a plotting conniver. He gave me a rakish wink, and to satisfy his vanity, I tossed him a smile.

"She'll probably outlive both you and me if she takes it in her mind to do so."

I giggled and was somewhat soothed. If Mrs. Byerly could claw her way back from the brink of death once, I was confident she could do it again.

Felix made me promise to meet him that evening after his mother went to bed. He claimed he was desperate to get to know me better. I was a tad anxious, but even more excited to get better acquainted with him as well.

I couldn't figure out how to make sense of these new feelings. The last several years I was devoted to Harvey Cleghorn so much that I rarely ever thought about another man in a romantic way. No one ever compared to my Harvey—until Felix. He was new, exciting, and impossible to ignore. He made me want to blush and flirt, but also at times, I wanted to bend him over my knee and spank him for his lascivious looks and jokes.

That night I met him at the Grand Piano on the main deck. He looked so handsome decked out in his gray suit, wide green tie, and bowler hat. The little red dress I had chosen was slit above the knee, and I wore my wool cloche hat. The red lipstick looked quite striking with my outfit. It felt a little naughty to dress this way as it was in
 stark contrast to the sensibilities of the future Mrs. Ruby Cleghorn.

"Stunning," he said standing up when I approached the table he had reserved for us. I blushed, but then he grinned and said, "You look good too."

It took a lot of effort not to smack him across the face, but I controlled myself. His raffish smile gave me butterflies in all the right ways.

As the pianist played *Clair de Lune,* Felix and I first started getting to know one another. He painfully recounted the rejection I'd bestowed upon him after our train ride. I colored and emphasized that I didn't want to say goodbye forever, but I knew that I'd never be returning to Milligan ever again.

He pried only a little, and I knew that I had to choose my words carefully. Felix lived in Waveland of all places with his uncle. I didn't know what the future held, but I couldn't exactly have him going back to inquire about me. I didn't want him comparing notes with Mrs. Byerly either.

"I've left everything and everyone that I've ever known behind with the exception of your mother. Honestly, I'm still trying to understand it all myself."

He looked solemn for a moment and answered, "Life throws up curveballs. Sometimes painful ones. It sounds to me like we've both known our fair share."

Reaching in his pocket as he spoke, he pulled out one of the hard candy that I'd seen him fiddling with on the train to Terre Haute. He offered me a butterscotch, and I politely declined.

"I thought those were lemondrops."

"Heavens no, what am I eight and taking castor oil?" he said almost indignantly.

Lemondrops are a superior candy to butterscotch, Mr. Byerly." I answered smugly.

"Likes disgusting hard candy. Strike one." he said with a wink as if he were making a list of my flaws.

"Makes condescending lists to himself, strike one." I said just to amuse him.

His guffaw was melodious. I loved the sound of his laugh.

We discussed the oddity that we knew so little about one another. Mrs. Byerly was apparently as good at not discussing her work life with Felix as she was at not discussing her private life with me. Felix was amazed to learn that I had been Mrs. Byerly's companion on all those trips she had taken across the country to open up new offices of the WCO. He'd pictured her taking an entire staff of people with her, not just one secretary.

I told him a few stories about the cast of characters we'd met over the last few years. When Mrs. Byerly dragged me to the Ryman Auditorium in Nashville to listen to an opera singer. It was a beautiful performance, but Mrs. Byerly had eyed a donor that she was dying to talk to halfway through the performance, and the rest of the evening was plotting how to corner the man into donating.

Felix cackled as I told him how his mother tripped me right in front of the man to get his attention. Needless to say, I got the next few days off, and the WCO got a hefty donation

He told me a little about how he lived with his uncle in Waveland, and now managed many of his affairs. Uncle Enoch was in his mid sixties now, and he was ready to live a life of leisure and travel. The town of Waveland housed most of the Byerly fortune. They owned everything from the telephone company to blacksmith to the barbershop.

I watched as Felix animatedly told me about his love of giving back to the community. In a town like Waveland, it was much easier to be benevolent because everyone knew everyone. It was easier for him to fall in love with Waveland than his hometown of St. Louis. St. Louis was too big and impersonal. He enjoyed his status of walking down the streets of Waveland and being greeted by everyone he met. His uncle had maintained a certain level of wealth, but they never grew it at the expense of members of the community.

He started to mention his wife, but he quickly caught himself. Then, his expression flickered.

I gathered that they had lived together in Waveland. An odd thought struck me as I wondered if Harvey knew Felix or vice versa, but it was such an awkward curiosity that I couldn't bear to ask it.

We sidestepped any mentions of our past paramours. I certainly didn't want to talk about Harvey, and I got the feeling that Felix wasn't ready to share about the wife whom he'd lost at some point in the past.

At the end of the night, stars were dancing in my eyes when I thought of Felix. It felt much too soon to be smitten, but I had fallen in love with Harvey so gradually that I didn't even realize I loved him until I couldn't imagine life without him. Felix was so different. I almost felt like I'd waited all these years to meet him.

The next several days and nights aboard the *Leucothea* were split between tending to Mrs. Byerly and getting to know her son. Prone to seasickness in the evenings, she retired to bed when the winds would rise on the water and the motion of the boat made her stomach turn. Consequently, she left us after dinner every night while we were crossing the Atlantic.

In the mornings, however, she called on me constantly to spend time with her as she generally gave Felix leave to entertain himself either enjoying a cigar in the smoking room or swimming laps in the pool. While he was pampering himself and enjoying his holiday, I became well versed on the music of Brahms, a favorite of the quartet; playing bridge, which I never quite played to Mrs. Byerly's satisfaction; and if she was feeling especially active, shuffleboard.

Felix usually took his meals with us, and when the dessert course was finished, he bid his mother good night, nodded to me stiffly, and headed off to the smoking room. Mrs. Byerly went to bed assuming that I retired as well with the stack of books that I had brought on board. She didn't realize that this was just a ruse. About twenty minutes after she was secured in her cabin, I met Felix on the promenade, and we started our evening together.

I learned a lot about Felix in those nights we spent together on the *Leucothea*. For starters, he was more shy than I'd previously figured. He had no problems trying to vex me with double entendres, but if I struck up a conversation with another young lady we ran across on the ship, he was usually too timid to speak. Once, I absolutely exasperated him when I asked an attractive young lady passing by us what she thought of the dimple on his left cheek.

"For Christ's sake, Miss Sutton, what are you trying to do to me?" he asked quite flustered after that encounter.

"I could ask you what you are trying to accomplish with lascivious questions about mermaid procreation?"

He smiled wickedly, "Touché."

It was almost a mark of how well he got along with someone, his shyness. If he liked a person, it melted away almost immediately, but if he didn't, he was practically a deaf mute. His shyness was mostly apparent around women. Other men didn't seem to intimidate him at all. I assumed this was due to the teachings of his mother, or possibly, an inherited trait.

The wickedly dark humor he possessed was the perfect antidote for the empty feeling in the pit of my stomach at leaving behind my family. His forwardness and open admiration for me notwithstanding, I felt comfortable with Felix, and even though I consciously tried not to, I found myself constantly comparing him to Harvey.

Harvey wasn't shy, but he always chose his words carefully, while Felix was shy, but once his tongue was unsheathed, he could rival me in prattling. Harvey was fair and boyishly handsome while Felix was dark and debonair. Harvey was a voracious learner when it came to farming, but he had little time for entertainment. While Felix was well-read and appreciated the arts, he found actual physical labor rather tedious. It took me by surprise when I realized how little these two men had in common. From their upbringing to their interests, they had as much in common as a mule had with a peacock.

What made me feel even more guilty was that I hardly missed Harvey. When I was working in St. Louis, I missed him all the time. Daily, I had thought about him, wondering what he was doing at any given minute of the day. Ever since I boarded the *Leucothea*, I only thought of him in comparison to Felix. I didn't long for him or even envy Ruby who by this time must be on the brink of marrying him.

Knowing Ruby would make him happy let me stop worrying about him, at least, I told myself that, but part of me wondered if that was true.

Absence was supposed to make the heart grow fonder, but I also knew that continuing to love Harvey forever was just an exercise in disappointment. He had every part of me in Ruby, and perhaps, that was why I was able to let him go so easily without falling apart. All the attention I got from Felix didn't hurt either.

When Mrs. Byerly retired for the evening, those first few nights we listened to the pianist below deck while we got to know one another. As the waltzes of Chopin played, I watched him laugh—so alive, so present—and wondered if I'd ever truly left my old life behind, or if I was just floating above it—somewhere between two worlds.

As those nights progressed, I got more and more than a glimpse into the private life of my employer. Even though she always had wisdom to share with me, she rarely went into any detail about her life. I only knew that she was widowed "by the grace of God," had a son she adored, and was no stranger to high society or poverty.

The last detail she often said helped her schmooze the donors for the WCO as well as empathize with the downtrodden.

Felix explained that she was born into the Venable family which had been prominent in St. Louis for several generations. They had made their money in steam-powered riverboats years before the Civil War. The family fortune had been mismanaged by her grandfather and squandered by her father. By the time she was a debutante, she only had the Venable name and a faint memory of wealth to keep her in society. Her family was proud, but she was little more than a charity case.

After her mother passed away, she distanced herself completely from the Venable family. She'd had only one cousin who had been her bosom friend growing up who she kept up a regular correspondence with.

The life of Samuel Byerly was almost the opposite of his future wife. He was born into abject poverty. Both of his parents died young, and he and his brother were completely on their own. Enoch Byerly, who never had a formal education, had a good mind for business. He accidentally fell into the Indiana Gas Boom of 1880, transforming the two brothers from paupers into thriving investors.

Enoch cleared quite a lot of money from the wells, and nearly as much when he sold his stake in them. Sending his brother to Wabash College, he settled in the nearby town of Waveland. There was enough money for them both to live quite comfortably on, and he started investing in the community. Discovering he had quite a knack for investing, he continued to steadily increase his wealth over the years.

At Wabash College, Samuel Byerly was a bit of a carouser, and he wasn't suited very well for academics. A charming fellow, he made friends easily. One friend who hailed from St. Louis happened to be a family friend of a certain Miss Venable. Shortly after being introduced, declarations of love were exchanged between Mr. Byerly and Miss Venable, and their wedding took place a mere month later.

"They were happy for nearly 30 minutes," Felix said with a smirk as he finished his story.

After his father died his Uncle Enoch made a point to be a fixture in his life. He came to see him quite regularly in St. Louis. Mrs. Byerly couldn't object to him because Uncle Enoch paid all of her expenses, and he allowed her to live in St. Louis while supporting her aged mother.

"They eventually came to an understanding that I would live with Uncle Enoch when my schooling was finished. He wanted to teach me the art of investing, and I was the only family he had in the world. Of course, Mother has been plotting for me to make my own millions independent of Uncle Enoch so she doesn't feel beholden to him. Hence, this trip where she expects me to seduce Olive Powlett."

"Isn't your mother fond of your uncle after all he's done for the both of you?"

He let out a loud guffaw, "Of course not, she hates him with a passion. She'll never forgive him for insisting that I move to the middle of nowhere and leave her behind. That stubborn old woman knew she was welcome to come with me to Waveland, but she'd rather cut off her own nose than share a roof with her brother-in-law. Uncle Enoch, on the other hand, is quite fond of her. I think Mother would like him too if he didn't remind her of my father."

Felix's childhood in St. Louis was quite happy. His uncle kept them quite comfortable, and he never wanted for anything. While indulgent in some things, his mother believed in being a strict disciplinarian with her only son. Always adventurous, he had managed to get up on top of the roof of their house when he was seven years old.

"She thrashed me good, and I have been petrified of heights ever since," he said, smiling at the memory.

"I've seen your mother angry a time or two, and I cannot imagine the fire that would have blazed in her eyes about you."

"Oh, she's as mean as a snake. Wait until she sees me not take to Olive. It will not be pretty."

Next, I told him all about my family, remembering that both of my parents were already described as dead. My parent's marriage, I said, was unhappy because of my father's shortcomings as a provider. Since he couldn't hold down a job for more than a few years, they traveled all around the Midwest mostly before I was born. I was born in Indiana, but by the time I was four, we moved to Missouri which was where I spent nearly all of my formative years.

Eventually, my father left and Mother supported the three of us the best she could. When I was old enough, I traveled to St. Louis and interviewed for a job which his mother had most graciously given me, while the rest of the family moved to Milligan to be closer to my mother's family.

When he asked me about my brothers, I lied and told him that I had quarreled with my oldest brother before I left home, and my second brother, the one that I met with in St. Louis, was a lot like my father when it came to holding onto jobs. I purposely didn't give anyone in my family names in case he may have crossed paths with them in one way or another. The lies felt so painful, but I didn't have a choice.

"Didn't you mention a fiance?" he asked, finally addressing the ghosts we'd been dancing around all these nights on board the ship.

"I did," I said exhaling. "Didn't you mention a wife?"

"I did."

"Isn't it rather painful to recall?"

He nodded as if he understood, and we closed the subject. It still felt too fresh to talk about Harvey with him. Also, with the amount of family the Cleghorns had in Waveland, he could at the very least be familiar with the name. Even though I was dying of curiosity about his wife and what happened to her, I couldn't very well press him for information while not offering any on my part.

Those nights on the ship with Felix were the best part of crossing the ocean. After we had talked about our childhoods, we discussed literature, the arts, and considered the possibility of taking in an opera while we were in Paris. All his attention was very flattering, and I greedily lapped it up. It was a familiar feeling too because when Harvey and I were in love, he used to come over to Mother's house every evening just to listen to me talk.

Thinking about Felix occasionally when I was entertaining Mrs. Byerly, I was scolded a time or two for daydreaming. Whenever she made a sarcastic comment about another passenger, I'd remember it to tell him later that night. If Mrs. Byerly said something cryptic about his father, I'd wonder if he knew something more to the story. I began to notice that whenever I thought of Felix, I'd smile.

When someone you find attractive gives you all of their attention, it is quite possibly the most intoxicating feeling in the world, and Felix knew exactly how to make me feel like the only woman on the *Leucothea*. He made me blush with his earnest admiration, and I began to think that he came up with new flatteries for the sole purpose of raising the color in my cheeks. That smug face, that while handsome, could make me angry in a flash.

As I lapped up the attention, I did my best to discourage it. He was, in fact, pursuing a woman that was indebted to his mother, and his mother had already arranged a bride for him in the form of Olive Powlett. He scoffed at the thought as he had seen pictures of Miss Powlett, and she was no great beauty. Leaving his uncle behind to live the rest of his life in England was not something that appealed to him. The Venables may have been loyalists in the American Revolution, but Byerly's were patriots he said with a playful sneer.

His mother had formed the insane notion about him marrying Miss Powlett when he was just a child. Dora, Olive's mother, had been Mrs. Byerly's cousin. She had been a member of the branch of the Venable family that had managed to hold on to most of their money. The two girls had been playmates as children, and Dora's mother had been from a prominent English family so it wasn't much of a shock when Dora became engaged to the 5th Duke of Cleveland.

"When the Duchess of Cleveland was pregnant, I believe that Mother was already putting me in line for the British throne," he said with a snort of derision.

Marrying Tabitha had ruined all her plans, he said with a hint of color rising to his cheeks. However, enough time had passed for his mother to start up her machinations to put Olive and him together again.

All his attention had gone to my head, and I vowed that I would set him straight before we landed in England. I couldn't interfere with his mother's plans for him and Olive even if I had begun to have feelings for him. Mrs. Byerly had been a wonderful boss to me, and I refused to undermine the matrimonial plans she had for her son. She brought me along to be an ally, not for Felix to become smitten with me although I did feel a pang of embarrassment that she never entertained the thought that Felix and I would be well suited for one another.

It was our last night on the ship and hours after his mother had gone to bed. We strolled above deck, chilled just slightly by the air but enjoyed the sights and sounds of the ocean. We had been quite chaste in our actions even if his words were flattering and filled with trace amounts of roguery.

Out of loyalty to his mother I told him after we got off the *Leucothea*, I could no longer entertain all the attention he had lavished upon me. His mother had been too kind for me to do otherwise.

He stiffened at my words, and I eyed his jaw clenching. We had been strolling at a medium pace, and he suddenly stopped. There was anger in his face, and his eyes danced with fire that I had seen occasionally in his mother.

"I know next to nothing about Olive Powlett, but I do know a lot about you. The more I know about you the more I like you, so you'll forgive me if I'm not too optimistic that another woman will capture my heart."

"How could I possibly look your mother in the face? She would think that I schemed or plotted to get you to fall in love with me, knowing full well what her plans are for you."

"Hang my mother, if she wants to get in the way of my happiness!" he said, the heat rising in his cheeks.

"Felix," I said trying to remain calm, "We've known each other for less than a week. Yes, I am fond of you, but unlike you, I am planning to stay in England when we dock there. I've already talked to your mother about working in the office we're going to open. Going back to America isn't an option because there's nothing there for me anymore."

He looked at me with that smug face, the rising anger falling away, "I'm quite enamored of you, and I promise you that it doesn't happen all that often for me. I also understand that we've only known each other a short time. Let's enjoy this trip, and we'll continue to get to know one another under my mother's nose. When it is time for me to go home, I will. If I discover in a few short months that I am unable to live without you, I will come back to London and relentlessly pursue you until I wear you down. If absence doesn't make the heart grow fonder, then we'll always have our nights on this ship to look back on fondly."

My knees buckled at his eloquence. He put his arm around my waist to catch me, and I looked into his eyes. The look of mild concern faded into a lascivious smile, and he kissed me. I kissed him back, and we melted into one another's arms. It was electric. Unlike the thousands of stolen kisses from Harvey, Felix seemed to be communicating his earnestness and a depth of feeling that almost overwhelmed me. When we separated, I couldn't look him in the eyes for fear that he would see the longing that I felt pulsating throughout my body.

If he never returned, I'd still have that kiss. These nights on the ship would be mine forever. The envy I once held for Ruby vanished in the heat of his breath, touched with wine and sea salt.

"I see a second trip to London in my future," he said as we broke apart.

After that kiss, a part of me burned for him to be right. I inhaled deeply—his cologne still lingered, tangled with the salt in the air.

Clarissa and Dora, St. Louis 1891

Clarissa Venable was pensively brushing her hair at the vanity on the morning of her wedding. So many thoughts were swirling through her head. After today, the world would no longer see her as her mother's daughter—but as Samuel Byerly's wife.

Wife was certainly not a title that she had envisioned for herself a month ago. Her mother had paraded her all around St. Louis society in the last few years, hopeful that she would impress any bachelor with a modicum of means.

The last decade had been difficult. After her father died in a Kansas City brothel, squandering the last of the Venable fortune, Clarissa and her mother sold nearly everything. They scraped by on help from relatives and remained visible in society only through careful maneuvering.

Miss Venable was raised to be a strong, level-headed young woman. Her mother envisioned Clarissa to enter society as an independent woman of means, but due to embarrassing circumstances thrust upon them by her father, the only way to acquire means was through marriage.

The marriage market was something that Clarissa detested much to her mother's chagrin. The young debutante was made to feel like little more than a gold digger when her mother would point out the assets of each and every young man they encountered. Marriage was less a dream than a deadline, as their dwindling funds left few alternatives. They often returned home from a night out screaming at one another over Mrs. Venable's pushiness, or Clarissa's complete dismissal of an eligible suitor.

Time was still on their side, however, as Clarissa had only turned 20 years old earlier that year, and her mother calculated that they could afford to be somewhat choosy until her daughter turned 22. Then, she would have the unfortunate task of marrying the girl off to any fat, drunken gambler with a respectable income.

All contingency vanished when Samuel Colt Byerly waltzed into her life just weeks ago. Clarissa paused her hair brushing as she thought about how quickly she had fallen utterly and inescapably in love with him.

A sharp rap at her bedroom door startled her from her reverie. She quickly glanced at her clock, confounded that her mother would disturb her so early on her wedding morning. She'd hoped for a few quiet hours before the guests arrived—most of whom, she suspected, came only to gawk at her good fortune.

Clarissa dramatically got up from her vanity and thrust open her door, preparing to exchange verbal barbs with her mother. At first, she was dumbstruck upon seeing the figure behind the door. Her mouth stood agape as the woman strolled past her into the bedroom.

"I whole-heartedly object to the accursed union!" the woman snapped as she sat down at Clarissa's vanity and fixed a few loose strands of hair untucked from her hat.

The room went quiet for a moment until the woman stood back up to face Clarissa. They stared each other down until they both erupted in guffaws and embraced.

Dora Venable was Clarissa's favorite cousin and constant companion when they were children. Her arrival in time for the wedding was wholly unexpected as Dora's mother and father had planned to embark on a European tour with their daughter.

"How in the world did you manage to get back here for my wedding?" Clarissa asked.

Her cousin explained that they had been sidetracked in New York when some of her father's friends insisted they stay in the Hamptons with them for a few weeks. Although her mother was not too keen on delaying their trip to London, her father had wanted to see what the fuss was about. When the telegram arrived announcing Clarissa's engagement, Dora threw an absolute fit until her father relented and brought her back to St. Louis for the wedding.

"Mum was more than a bit peeved that Dad would have the audacity to delay the trip to London even longer so he let her go on."

Clarissa was more than happy to see her oldest friend in the world, but their stations in life were quite different. Dora was always flitting off to New York, London, or Glasgow for holidays with her parents, while Clarissa and her mother scrimped and saved to afford new dresses. When they were children, both their families had wealth, but as Clarissa's father frittered away his fortune, Dora's father had grown his, leaving Isadora Venable a very wealthy heiress.

The two girls quickly fell back into their old dynamic as Dora demanded to know every last detail of her whirlwind courtship with Samuel Byerly. They corresponded with one another regularly, and Dora was absolutely flabbergasted that she had not heard one mention of the prospective groom prior to the arrival of the telegram in the Hamptons.

"I've never met a man like him before, and I knew that if I said no, I'd never see him again. That thought shredded my delicate heart so I had no choice but to say yes."

The figure of Samuel Byerly that Clarissa cut for Dora intrigued her to no end as Dora had generally been the one to fall in love with every man she met while Clarissa turned up her nose at the first sign of flirting.

Since Clarissa had been out in St. Louis society, she'd been disappointed often. The Venable name got her introduced to many eligible men, but soon the whispers of her family's finances got to the ears of potential beaus, and they were soon much less intrigued by her. She realized quickly that fortune favored those with fortunes.

Dora was a bit scandalized to learn that Samuel Byerly didn't come from wealth or breeding, but the picture Clarissa painted titillated her nonetheless. His parents had passed away when he was young, and he had been raised by his only brother who was a small-time hustler on the streets of Muncie, Indiana.

When they hit the big time, Enoch, whom Sam affectionately called Notch, wanted his brother to become the respectable man he never could be. So Sam was enrolled at Wabash College, where he began making connections.

Introductions were made at a society luncheon. Sam had made fast friends with the son of Mrs. Harrison Frisbee at Wabash College. Clarissa's mother had purposely lost many bridge games and engaged in base flattery to maintain her placement in Mrs. Frisbee's inner circle.

"I swear, Clarissa, your poor mother is a saint for putting up with that harridan, Mrs. Frisbee. You know, that she cornered me last fall and talked to me for nearly an hour about one of her sons. I can't even remember his name, but it was the one with all the hair in his nose."

Clarissa giggled. Poor Allan Frisbee—his nostrils were the least of his problems. A shiver went down her spine as she recalled her mother attempting to sing the praises of poor, humorless Allan as he had once been a prospect for her.

Sam Byerly walked into the dining room with all the refinement of a laughing hyena in the library. All the young folks crowded around him eager to hear stories of his exploits on the streets of Muncie in his youth. He had a story for almost everything, and he kept nearly the entire luncheon in stitches except, of course, Mrs. Frisbee, who was bemused by his presence.

"You had some sort of benefactor who lifted you out of poverty and sent you to school?" Mrs. Frisbee asked when the laughter died down during the beef consommé.

"You misunderstand, Mrs. Frisbee. My brother has become a self-made man by investing in natural gas. He has sent me to Wabash College to study business so that I can help him manage our fortune. And yes, while my past is a bit checkered to say the least, it has given me a greater perspective on what I've gained. I apologize if you find me gauche, and I will modify my behavior accordingly if it is unbecoming to your table."

Dora gasped, "He didn't say that to her?! Why Mrs. Frisbee would have died!"

He had said those exact words, and Mrs. Frisbee offered an abrupt apology while the party ate the rest of the meal in abject silence.

When the meal was over, the groups scattered. Clarissa couldn't join the men for cigars and brandy, and she didn't have any friends amongst the ladies her own age so she decided to take a few turns in the garden, fake a headache, and excuse herself.

The air in the garden invigorated her, and while she pretended to admire Mrs. Frisbee's hydrangeas, her mind kept circling back to Sam Byerly and the way he instantly shut down their hostess when she attempted to embarrass him.

She couldn't help but smile when a tap on her shoulder nearly made her jump out of her skin. As if she were in some sort of dream, Sam Byerly stood next to her in the garden. She quickly averted her gaze when he broke out in a grin before addressing her.

"Baby, you are the hottest girl here, and I couldn't head back to Wabash College without introducing myself to you."

The expression on Dora's face at hearing the first words Sam said to Clarissa mirrored exactly what she had experienced in real time.

"I couldn't believe the impertinence, and I couldn't believe how flattered I felt to be singled out by him. He lacked refinement, yet exuded a strange kind of debonair charm. And I'm embarrassed to admit what happened next."

Dora leaned forward, eyes wide with curiosity. She had known Clarissa her entire life, yet she felt deliciously scandalized at what happened next.

"Clarissa! What did you do?" she said, hoping the answer was wicked.

The color red didn't quite do justice to the flushing of Clarissa's face. It was deep, and Dora was even more intrigued by it.

There was something about the look on Sam's face. It was confidence that was masking a terror that his eyes couldn't hide. Clarissa couldn't decide if it was all Sam, or partly her fear of being saddled with an Allan Frisbee, but she kissed him.

Clarissa Hyacinth Venable, raised on strict decorum, had never kissed a man before, but one look into Sam Byerly's amber eyes weakened her knees.

"You hussy!" Dora said with the broadest grin on her face while Clarissa was still unable to control the flush in her cheeks.

She didn't know how long they kissed, but it took Sam propositioning her to head to a more secluded spot in the garden to snap her back to reality. With her head cleared, she immediately pulled away.

"Baby, we were just warming up! I thought you liked me?"

"I'm sorry. You must think I'm some sort of…well, I'm not. I'm afraid I've made a terrible mistake."

She turned and fled the garden, ready to run all the way home, but he caught her by the sleeve and pulled her close again.

As they paused from another kiss, he whispered, "I don't even know your name."

"It's Clarissa," she said before kicking him in the knee and running home as fast as she could in her dress.

Sam returned to the luncheon where he introduced himself to Clarissa's mother. He charmed her socks off with tales of the fortune he and his brother Notch had managed to secure at the start of the Indiana Gas Boom several years ago.

He confided in Mrs. Venable that he was instantly smitten with her daughter, and while he'd only be in St. Louis for another week, he hoped he'd be allowed to call on her.

By the end of the week, Clarissa and Sam had kissed about twenty more times, and she'd kicked him in the shin another three times.

Then he was gone.

Over the next two weeks, she received three letters from him, discussing his undying love for her. He talked of introducing her to his brother who earnestly wished to meet her and her mother.

Clarissa's mother was dancing on the ceiling when she read the letters. Somehow, her daughter had attracted a handsome, wealthy, young man who would make all their monetary problems disappear. On the other hand, Clarissa almost wished that Sam was poor because she hated for him to think for an instant that she cared about his money.

She had to admit that her attraction to Sam Byerly was combustible, but she worried that it was not sustainable. They were two very different people, and she was uncertain if they could ever be happy. She had a shining example of marital unhappiness in her mother and father's union. Would she be tempting history to repeat itself?

Mrs. Venable made the case that Samuel Byerly was not Clarissa's father in the least bit. Did Clarissa already forget the way that Sam had managed to put Mrs. Frisbee in her place during that luncheon? Her father would have never had that kind of courage. No, Mrs. Venable was more than certain that Sam would make an excellent husband for her only child.

"It is rather romantic," Dora said, having been silent throughout much of Clarissa's story as she'd gotten caught up in it.

Sitting back down at her vanity, Clarissa continued her story while Dora fussed with her hair.

When she first set eyes on Sam's brother Enoch, Clarissa loathed the sight of him. He had none of the warmth that enveloped his brother. He rarely smiled, his jaw always clenched as if perpetually unimpressed. The man looked like he'd never been happy a day in his life.

He intimidated her, and it put her on edge. Mr. Byerly was little more than a judgmental snob which didn't make sense in any way to the portrait Sam had painted of him. Clarissa's mother tried to turn on the charm, but Enoch was rather dismissive of her.

He mentioned that he had recently started investing in a small town south of Wabash College, and he'd fallen in love with it. He had hopes that he and Sam together could turn it into a thriving community where poverty didn't exist. The farrier he employed was shoeing horses from as far away as Indianapolis.

All of Enoch's plans bored Clarissa to tears. He was so dry and so uninteresting she could hardly believe he was Sam's brother.

"While I respect your charity when it comes to small communities, Mr. Byerly, I can't imagine you're sending your brother to Wabash College to only do your bidding? I have yet to hear Sam's words on this town improvement experiment."

The two brothers looked at one another as if they had no idea how to answer the question. Enoch had obviously expected Sam to return to the town of Waveland when he finished his studies, but what were Sam's plans?

"Notch and I haven't ever really discussed my future after college. I graduate in a few weeks, and I reckon I was thinking of looking for a life in a bigger city like St. Louis at least for a little while."

Sam's statement brought the largest smile to Clarissa's face, and before she recovered, she saw Enoch looking deeply at her. He looked from her to Sam, and he nodded.

"It's been a privilege meeting you Mrs. Venable and Miss Venable, but I'm afraid that I need to catch the next train back to Indiana. My brother, I believe, has made arrangements to stay for another day or two."

Enoch and Sam rose from the table together, and Sam walked his brother out the door. When he returned, he got down on one knee and proposed.

"Oh my goodness, Clarissa. I'm practically swooning, and I wasn't even there. You and Sam are so lucky to have found each other."

As Dora hugged her from behind, the future Mrs. Samuel Byerly could see her wedding dress in the reflection of her vanity. It was so refreshing for Clarissa to look into the mirror and see her cousin actually envious of her for once.

And for the first time in her life, Clarissa was happy that she leapt with her heart instead of overthinking every sundry detail.

Chapter 7

The next day we arrived at Chaffinch Fields in a motorcar sent by the Duchess of Cleveland. It was quite luxurious, and even Felix, used to a degree of wealth, looked impressed. I doubted his uncle's fortune compared to the silver spoons that fed Olive Powlett as a child. Mrs. Byerly, of course, sang endless praises to how well her cousin had married, and I caught Felix rolling his eyes more than once.

The motorcar we arrived in was one thing, but the estate was quite another! The manor house stood in a clearing overlooking a gorgeous, natural lake nestled in rolling green hills. It looked like a stone palace! There were three floors of windows with Ionian columns that shaped the front, and a marble statue out front that appeared to depict a famous, ancient resident. The bricks glowed white in the sun, giving the house an almost ethereal quality—as if it had been carved from clouds. Never in all our travels had Mrs. Byerly and I stayed at such a grand place.

"My goodness gracious, Dora never did her estate justice in her letters. It's breathtaking, wouldn't you say, Felix?" Mrs. Byerly said, giving him a slight jab in the ribs to get his attention.

I looked over and saw that the magnificence of Chaffinch Fields was indeed not lost on him. As we drove up to the house, we must've spooked a flock of ducks on the lake, and they squawked wildly while taking to the air. It was almost as if someone had released doves for our arrival. Felix marveled at it, and he admitted to his mother that he didn't expect it to be quite so exquisite.

"Imagine what it would be like to manage such an estate," Mrs. Byerly said, barely able to contain the excitement she elicited from Felix's reaction.

"Not in my wildest dreams," Felix said, still taking it all in as we exited the motorcar.

The Duchess of Cleveland came out to greet us immediately, and she was a pretty woman, roughly the same age as Mrs. Byerly but with fewer white streaks in her hair. I could tell fairly quickly why the two cousins had been such good friends as they were quite alike. They carried themselves with an air of self-importance. The pair both paid careful attention to their appearance with neither of them having a hair out of place, and they had stern faces with kind eyes. The Duchess' accent was a bit muddled, and it was quite clear that her childhood in America had affected her mostly British elocution.

The two ladies stiffly bowed to one another before laughing and sharing a friendly hug. They exchanged letters several times a year, but they hadn't seen each other in three decades. They began to talk a mile a minute as if they had never been parted while Felix and I stood patiently waiting to be introduced but still taking in the grandeur of our surroundings.

"Felix, allow me to present your cousin—the Duchess of Cleveland," Mrs. Byerly said with stately formality.

"Pish, call me Dora. I've heard so much about you over the years, I feel like I know you already, dearie. And who might this be?" she said, turning to me with an inquisitive eye.

"This is Hazel Sutton. She's my secretary with the WCO. She's here to assist me with setting up the new office later this summer. She's been such a loyal young lady that I wanted to take her on this trip before I formally retire."

I colored at the emphasis she put on the word loyal as I thought of the long nights Felix and I had spent together on the *Leucothea*. Catching a glimpse of Felix, I saw him smirk when the color in my cheeks rose as if he could read my thoughts.

The Duchess directed our bags to be taken to our rooms which she had airing out, and she invited us into the house for some refreshment. We were nearly halfway inside when I caught a glimpse of a young man galloping up to the house at a furious pace on the most magnificent looking stallion.

Felix and I stood mesmerized at how expertly the young man rode. He jumped a stone fence, landed with aplomb, and slowed down to a canter as he approached the house. Upon closer inspection, it was not a man, but a woman in trousers with her hair cut quite short. I was astonished that a woman rode so expertly, and she wasn't even riding sidesaddle.

"Olive! What am I going to do with you?!" the Duchess snapped coming back out of the house, her cheeks blazing with fire. "You were told to not greet our guests wearing those...those things!"

It seemed unbelievable that this woman in front of us was the heiress to Chaffinch Fields. I assumed Olive Powlett to be a portrait of modesty. In my imagination she was a mousy little girl with her hair plaited and hiding her face behind a silk fan. Instead, she was this self-assured, jovial young woman wearing trousers, and not in the least bit bothered by her mother's chastising words. There was an air about her that seemed to be in contrast to the solemn manor house in which she lived and stood to inherit.

She was tall—evident from the way her legs rested in the stirrups, and she had the same kind eyes as her mother. Olive was well mannered as evinced by her perfect posture even mounted on the horse. Her face was quite fair, and the riding had put a blush in her cheeks. Smiling with such a wide grin that it seemed to overtake her entire face, she looked even more beautiful. It was impossible not to feel inferior to her as she carried herself with such confidence.

"Greetings, cousins!" she said dismounting and running fingers through her short hair, "You must be Felix! My mother has talked about you endlessly. Tell me, do you still defecate gold bars, or has my mother embellished?"

Felix was a little taken aback by her forwardness, and I saw the shyness that he exhibited on the ship start to rise up in his shoulders. Sensing this, Olive took his hand in hers giving him a shake.

"I suppose the wedding will be in a few hours," she whispered, grinning when he burst out in a fit of laughter. It was quite clear that no matter how artful their mothers thought they were in pushing them together, they clearly saw through it. I cringed a little in jealousy as I saw the spark of an instant connection between the two. The Duchess and Mrs. Byerly knew their children, perhaps, better than they knew themselves.

Miss Powlett was quite an attractive young lady. Her brunette hair was short, but still showed traces of auburn highlights. She had the rosy glow of someone who spends a lot of time outdoors. Her deep blue, almost gray eyes were quite friendly. I watched her and Felix interacting, and it was as if they'd known each other their whole lives. Felix's face glowed with no evidence of shyness in a matter of moments, much the same way it had when he was expounding *my virtues* aboard the *Leucothea*.

"The candle that burns twice as bright, burns half as long," I thought to myself wistfully.

Felix and Olive were engrossed in a conversation about her horse almost immediately. She mentioned all the horses that this stallion had sired, and she hoped that there would be a racing dynasty coming from Chaffinch Fields in a few short years. While he had never owned horses, Felix had been to the Kentucky Derby a few times with his mother. He was captivated by her knowledge and seemed to hang on Olive's every word. When she offered to take him down to the stables to look around, he readily agreed. Chaffinch Fields had been breeding polo horses for generations, but the Duke had recently taken an interest in racehorses.

The Duchess and Mrs. Byerly continued into the house reveling in the nostalgia of their childhood escapades of more than forty years ago. I was torn between two happy groups of conversation, and I didn't believe that I fit into either one. Feeling awkward, I stood on the front porch and took in the lovely view of the English countryside from the manor house. The bond between Felix and Olive was growing before my very eyes.

"I sometimes take for granted the loveliness of the fields." Olive said, introducing herself, "I'm Olive Powlett. It is so nice to meet you, Miss Sutton, is it?"

"Hazel, please." I said nervously, coloring slightly at her friendliness.

"Well then, Hazel. You'll have to forgive Mr. Byerly and me. While we haven't formally met, our mothers have described us as a Greek god and goddess to one another. They really are quite gauche in their transparency," she said, turning to Felix who was stifling a laugh.

"I better go check on the ladies inside. They are no doubt readying the minister and loading their shotguns for a ceremony the moment we walk into the house," Felix said, tipping his hat to the both of us, obviously pleased with his joke.

Olive laughed a hearty, deep laugh, and her amusement obviously tickled Felix to no end. Grinning, he made his way indoors. I exhaled, feeling as if I had vanished the moment Olive entered Felix's field of vision—and I wouldn't reappear any time soon.

"I didn't expect him to be so charming," Olive said half to herself and half to me, "Have you just met?"

"Yes and I can assure you that he has a wicked sense of humor," I said, remembering some of his bawdy jokes.

"Good, it can get positively dreary around this old graveyard! Tell me, Hazel, do you ride?" she said, stroking the nose of her magnificent steed.

I had ridden a horse now and then, but mostly as a little girl. She immediately insisted that I should ride with her every day that I was her guest. The tour of the stables would include me as well after I got settled. If I wanted to pick out my own horse, she would help me make my selection. Assuring her that it sounded quite lovely, we parted company. I wanted to hate her. Why did she have to be so nice?

She swung back onto her horse and galloped off, and I watched her go, fully aware that Mrs. Byerly hoped I would befriend Miss Powlett just enough to sing Felix's praises in her ear. I sighed, feeling the childish fantasy of Felix ever truly falling for me dissolve into the lingering echo of Olive Powlett's rich, mellifluous laugh that still rang in my ears.

After dinner the ladies were all assembled in the parlor of the house, while the Duke and Felix were off in the smoking room, enjoying brandy and cigars—an English tradition kept up at Chaffinch Fields for the past three hundred years.

There was a look of satisfaction on Mrs. Byerly's face that said all was going exactly according to her plan. She looked quite content as she chose a book to enjoy with her glass of wine.

Having finished with riding for the day, Olive was no longer wearing trousers. She looked effortlessly striking in a midnight-blue drop-waist dress I envied so intensely it almost stung. The beadwork on the midnight blue fabric shimmered giving the impression that she was wearing the stars.

I had put on the gorgeous yellow dress that my Mother had made, and she eyed it with similar envy. While examining Mother's perfect stitching, she told me the obscene price she'd be willing to pay for a similar dress. Understanding that we had fashion in common, she beckoned me to follow to her suite in the house so that we could look at her newest copy of British Vogue magazine.

"Mother told me that I should apologize for you seeing me in trousers," she said, motioning for me to make myself comfortable in her sitting room, "But I won't. Side-saddle riding is, frankly, damned uncomfortable, and I will wear trousers on my father's property if I please."

Assuring her that I was not in the least bit scandalized, I said that Mrs. Byerly was probably beside herself. Olive chuckled to me, and she did an impromptu impression of Mrs. Byerly with her nasal twang. It was quite good, and I couldn't help but laugh. I hated that I actually liked her. It was impossible not to like her, and the thought of her with Felix depressed me.

She offered to have a bottle of red wine opened, and we chatted like old friends for the rest of the night. We carefully avoided the subject of Felix. I didn't know if she was conscious of the fact that I was jealous of her beauty, wealth, and promising future with Felix, but she didn't show it. People often talk about good breeding, but I'd never understood it. One evening in Olive Powlett's company was all the education I needed.

The week we spent at Chaffinch Fields before embarking on our grand tour of France and Italy was blissful. I had never had any idea how wealthy people lived, and it was decadent. A flurry of servants were always at my beck and call for any ridiculous request I could make.

The Duchess showed me the room and the pull to summon a maid, but I was too shy to ever use it. A pang of sadness hit me, knowing that Mother would have positively glowed at all the amenities at Chaffinch Fields. After all the years she had worked so hard for her children, here I was, her own daughter, able to ring for breakfast from the comfort of a private suite.

The main house at the estate was one thing, but the grounds were quite another. The rolling hills where Olive took me to ride were straight out of a Thomas Hardy novel. I saw all manner of people in their day-to-day activities, and I could only imagine how many hundreds of years their family had worked the grounds at Chaffinch Fields.

The gardens were exquisite. The East and West Gardens each had different species of flora as Olive informed me that sometimes the Duchess preferred to stroll in a flower garden, and other times she liked the hedges and hostas. I could stroll in any of the gardens all day or out to the lake to watch the ducks.

The family cemetery was also a sight to behold. Ancestors from Olive's family tree dating back to the 1600s were buried there. It was unbelievable how much history the estate contained. I could hardly fathom what it must feel like to belong to a place for centuries. My family's roots were tangled in hardship—not stone markers and rose bushes.

Mrs. Byerly walked me through the cemetery on one of the few afternoons she didn't spend with the Duchess. She showed me the tombstone of the Duchess' mother, and she had many fond memories of her.

"I was so glad she spent her golden years here with her daughter. That woman was good to me as a child," she said with tears welling up.

She asked me how well Olive and Felix were getting along, and I mentioned that they certainly seemed to be enjoying each other's company. Remarking that it was a magical place, she hoped that it would be enhanced with the birth of a child someday soon.

I forced a smile as she was already imagining her grandchildren here.

The Duchess of Cleveland and her daughter had a never-ending array of amusing activities for us to partake in. The library was the largest I had ever seen, the grand piano in the music room was well tuned, and they had all manner of pencils, sketchbooks, paints, and canvas for art.

I barely had time to write my promised letter to Ruby about the splendor of it all before I was called down for the next activity. Mrs. Byerly and the Duchess taught me to play whist one afternoon when they sent Olive and Felix out in the carriage to call on some friends. Olive had invited me, but Mrs. Byerly said I was much too necessary to her for me to go.

Olive woke me early most mornings to have a quick bite before we headed down to the stables for an invigorating ride. She had me mounted with a sidesaddle, but she encouraged me to try on a pair of her trousers because it was much easier riding.

For the novelty, I would have taken her up on it, but I thought it might displease or embarrass Mrs. Byerly. I could see why Olive enjoyed riding her horses across the fields. It was a lovely form of recreation, and if I had been born the only child of the 5th Duke of Cleveland, I would probably take up the sport as well.

I loved all the horses, but the one I took to the most was named *Resurrection*. He had been deemed a substandard as he was born premature and in bad health. Olive had taken him on as a vanity project, and he had grown into a fine young steed. She named him *Resurrection* because he had a new life after a rocky start.

Finally on one of the rides, she brought up the subject of Felix, and she said that she had noticed a few glances exchanged between us. She wondered if perhaps some exchange of feelings had taken place before we arrived in England.

Inwardly cringing at her question, I tried to imagine what glances she could have witnessed. Whenever I was in the same room as Felix, I had tried to be careful not to betray my feelings, but it was hard not to look at him longingly at times after the connection we had forged on the *Leucothea* even if it was fading away.

I told her honestly that we had struck up a mere flirtation, but as we hadn't spent much time together since our nights on the *Leucothea*, I was relatively certain it had run its course. He was a wonderful man, but we, perhaps, wanted different things out of life.

"Good," she said with a note of finality, letting me know that I'd eased her fears.

Her tone worried me somewhat, and I thought maybe Felix had told her to be wary of my intentions. I had successfully separated my love for Olive from my jealousy, and I didn't want to jeopardize our budding friendship.

"I prefer your company anyway, Miss Powlett. It's easier when it's just us girls," I said.

"I couldn't agree more," she smiled, gave her horse a little kick, and we galloped on.

The Duchess and Mrs. Byerly contrived frequent garden walks for Olive and Felix, and it was hard to miss Olive's laugh echoing throughout the property. I busied myself with the amazing library they had on hand, trying to forget that Felix and Olive were falling in love.

Because we'd only known each other a relatively short time, I tried not to be angry at Felix, but the way he seemed to fawn over Olive made me want to attack him for his change of heart. It wasn't his fault, I knew, and if I were in his position, I'd no doubt succumb to her charms as well.

I finished *David Copperfield*, and I'd already started *This Side of Paradise*. After falling behind on my reading on the *Leucothea*, it was nice to return to the literary world. I spent a few hours looking through the books belonging to the

Duke, but none of them caught my fancy as he seemed to collect a lot of religious texts.

On another morning ride, I mentioned that my work with Mrs. Byerly in England would be permanent for me as I had no plans to return to America. I told Olive that I was grateful for her friendship and hospitality, and I hoped that when I had a holiday here or there that she wouldn't object to a visit from me.

"Darling Hazel, I would be delighted. Most of the dowdy hens that the Duchess wants me to be friends with are so stiff and formal. I feel comfortable with you, and I am gratified to keep your acquaintance," she said, giving me a long glance letting me know that she was very much in earnest.

She had such a wonderful British accent that it was hard not to smile whenever she talked. It was nice to know that I had a friend in England. I felt less alone than I had for the first time since I waved goodbye to Mother, Ray, and Harvey. And unlike my attraction to Felix, Olive carried with her no chance of a messy romantic entanglement.

I got confirmation of Felix's intentions with her one evening when I hated to bother the maid, but I was hungry for a late night snack. Scampering down toward the kitchen, I walked past the library and heard Mrs. Byerly and the Duchess chatting in hushed tones. Pausing, I knew it was wrong to eavesdrop, but I couldn't resist.

"Felix was asking the Duke how he managed the estate just the other day, and this morning the butler informed me that Felix asked if it was possible to fall in love with someone in a few days!"

"Dora! You're fibbing! Really?" said the unmistakable voice of Mrs. Byerly.

I ran back to my room, having completely lost my appetite.

Those days and nights at Chaffinch Fields made me feel so torn. I absolutely adored Olive, but I hated her for how she had won Felix in such a short time. Recalling Felix's words that he didn't fall in love so easily, I scoffed at the thought. He most likely romanced every eligible woman that he ever encountered using that line, and I felt so foolish for imagining that I was special to him.

Olive was a dream, and I understood why Felix was so enamored of her, but I couldn't help but hate him for it. Lying in bed every night, I repeated to myself that my future was the WCO, and the happy couple were none of my business. I tried to be happy for them, specifically for her, but it was an exercise in futility.

Felix and I had only one brief interaction the entire week at Chaffinch Fields. I had purposefully avoided him after I had overheard Mrs. Byerly and the Duchess as I had no right to interfere with a courtship that would bring my employer the pinnacle of happiness.

He sent me several notes over the course of the week asking if I would meet him for a chat. There was no need for him to tell me that he was falling for Olive, and frankly, I didn't want to hear it. Some things are better left unsaid. We'd had a cute flirtation, and formally breaking it off would make it seem like it meant more than it did. I did not want to embarrass myself by getting choked up as I wanted to preserve my dignity.

After our morning ride, Olive invited me on a stroll in the East Garden as she had noticed how lovely the azaleas were looking this morning from her window. She needed an hour to change out of her trousers, and I grabbed my copy of *This Side of Paradise* to read as I waited upon her in the garden.

I was blissfully reading my book in the sun when a shadow appeared over me in the shape of Felix Byerly.

"Why Hazel, aren't you a sight for sore eyes?" he said, taking a seat by me.

"What on earth are you talking about? We see each other every day, Mr. Byerly." I said edging away from him.

Being referred to as a sight for sore eyes was insulting to both me and Olive. It was just another line he used on women he intended to string along.

"Mr. Byerly, is it? Not even Dr. Lydgate? What's made you so cold to me?" he said with a look of mild concern.

"Cold? I don't believe that I've been cold to you, *Mr. Byerly*."

"Stop calling me that. Call me Felix!"

"Mr. Felix Byerly, I don't appreciate being accosted like this. If you would like this spot in the garden, I would be happy to move to accommodate you.

"Is that how it is going to be? Well, Miss Sutton, I just want to clarify what Olive and I have been discussing lately."

"No," I said sharply, springing to my feet, flushed with anger.

How could he be so cruel as to try to make me talk to him as if there had never been anything between us! He shot up behind me and grabbed me by the shoulders. He pulled me to him and looked in my eyes. The fire was back. My pulse raced, and my nose twitched with indignation. He searched my face for answers, but I would betray nothing.

"I need to talk to you! Why are you being so difficult?" he said quietly, but deeply in earnest.

"Olive, dear!" I said sweetly, seeing her emerge from the house in another beautiful dress. I extricated myself from Felix's grasp, shot him a dirty look, and strolled up to meet her.

"Hazel, darling!" Olive called, looking past me and seeing Felix. There was a look of alarm in her face as if she had been scandalized at seeing us together.

"I'm afraid that Mrs. Byerly needs me for a few hours this morning to help her pack up her trunk for our trip abroad. I'm sure Mr. Byerly would kindly escort you around to look over the azaleas," I lied, but I didn't want to be a third wheel in their stroll around the garden.

The color drained from Felix's cheeks, and he suddenly looked quite guilty. The look on his face confirmed that I knew exactly what he wanted to talk to me about. I didn't need a formal rejection.

"Oh pish posh, a fifteen minute delay will not bother her a whit. Come look at the azaleas for a moment. I'm just beside myself that this is our last day here at Chaffinch Fields, and you aren't even coming back here after our holiday!"

I shook my head. I had plans to travel directly to London to begin interviews and set up the new office while Mrs. Byerly enjoyed the week in Scotland with the others.

"Yes and I'll need to get back to my uncle after Scotland, I'm afraid, unless I have a reason for staying." Felix said, first looking at Olive and then at me with the color raised quite high in his cheeks. I was enraged inside that he would say such a thing in front of me. Did this man have no tact? He pursued me day and night on the *Leucothea*, and the moment that he caught sight of a rich heiress, I was dropped like an inconvenient piece of trash. He had fooled me into believing he was different—that he saw me. But I was only ever a passing fancy.

"Oh, you should, Felix. With Hazel leaving me for her job, this place will be downright funereal. Otherwise, the Duke and Duchess will drag me to London for the tail end of the social season."

"I would like to see London myself," Felix said as if he were considering her offer.

Soon the easy and free manner with which Felix and Olive communicated began, leaving nothing for me to say so I excused myself to tend to Mrs. Byerly who I doubted needed my help in anything.

I took one last look at them strolling arm in arm among the azaleas of the East Garden, laughing all the way, and they looked to be the perfect pair. Their romance would bloom across Europe. And me? I would begin again, quietly, with nothing but the ashes of what might have been.

Chapter 8

The scent of blooming primroses lingered in the air as our trunks were loaded into motorcars bound for the Port of Dover. The lovely aroma reminded me of my rides with Olive that week—memories now tainted by how wretched I felt watching Felix transform into a lothario before my very eyes.

The group of ladies and the lone "gentleman" said goodbye to Chaffinch Fields and the Duke soon after. He would join us upon arrival in Rome in about six weeks. Felix and I hadn't spoken since our altercation in the East Garden. I hoped that he didn't feel the need to pursue the matter further as I was quite certain by now that he was smitten with our Olive.

I tried to hate Felix with every fiber of my being. The evidence was damning: he seemed to crave the estate and fortune that came with Olive, yet still wanted to keep me dangling on a thread. If he ever dared suggest I become his mistress, I'd slap him across the face without hesitation.

On the other hand, the picture I was painting of him in my head was not the same man that I got to know on our voyage across the ocean. He was deliciously dark-humored, but there was a quiet, almost bashful charm about him that didn't align with the opportunistic lothario I'd painted in my mind.

Part of me wanted to know what he was thinking, but I also didn't want to speak to him either. Pretending there was never anything between us was much more comfortable than any other option.

Our ferry departed from Dover and was bound for Calais on the French coast. Crossing the Channel thrilled me—it was the same passage Charles Darnay and Lucie Manette had taken in *A Tale of Two Cities*. That alone was enough to make my heart stir, even if Felix's betrayal weighed heavy on my spirit. Damn him.

The Duchess read over our itinerary, and we were set to spend two or three weeks in Paris. She informed us that she often found Paris to be a total bore and preferred the coastal cities like Marseille or Nice, which suited her tastes much better. I could hardly imagine a holiday in Paris being dull, but I deferred to her judgment.

She rented a chateau for us from one of the Duke's relatives and assured everyone that we would all be quite comfortable. The Duchess made it obvious that she loved to play hostess, and if there was ever a single thing we wanted for, all we had to do was ask. It felt so decadent, and I wished that I could share it with Mother who deserved such attention. The thought gave me a small pang of self-pity, thinking of the family I had once had.

The Duchess and her daughter had a never-ending list of acquaintances they promised would keep us amused. Olive intimated that most of the Duchess' friends were snobs who would ignore me the moment they heard I didn't come from a prominent family. She promised to shield me from them, claiming it was their loss, "You're one of the most delightful creatures I've ever met," she said without a hint of irony.

The woman was too kind to me, and I told her so very often.

Her friendship was the saving grace of this trip. I'd never had a friend quite like her. She thought my modesty was so charming but thought nothing of disrobing in front of me to change her dress or undergarments. In situations that would normally make me blush, she had such a way of putting me at ease. In her, I felt a little bit like I found the sister I never had.

Mrs. Byerly, who I had only spoken to a handful of times while we were at Chaffinch Fields, begged me to sit with her aboard the ferry to cross the channel. I agreed to be at her complete disposal throughout the entire journey and hoped she wouldn't scold me for not checking in on her more often.

The woman was such a master of self-possession that it was entirely possible that she was seething with anger at me, and I wouldn't know until she told me. On the other hand, she could be thrilled with how well mannered I had behaved. She took my arm and pointed to an area of the deck that appeared to be well shaded as the sun would wreak havoc on her complexion.

"Hazel, dear. I want you to forgive me," she said while we were quite out of earshot of the rest of our party.

I certainly didn't expect to be begged for forgiveness, but at least I knew she wasn't angry or disappointed. Mrs. Byerly's disappointment was much worse than her anger.

"Mrs. Byerly, whatever for? This trip has been a dream so far!" I said, thoroughly confused.

She worried I might feel forgotten—that in rekindling her bond with her dear cousin, she had left me adrift. The two ladies spent so much time getting reacquainted that she had quite forgotten me, and as Felix and Olive seemed to hold each other in high regard, she hoped that I didn't feel too left out.

Assuring her that while Felix and Olive spent much of their time together, Miss Powlett had made a point to include me in many activities. There were a variety of amusements that kept me occupied at Chaffinch Field such as horseback riding, garden strolls, and fashion. She seemed pleased that I was so fond of Olive.

While looking across the ferry at Felix and Olive, Mrs. Byerly enjoyed watching them sharing a glass of wine, laughing, and talking like they had known each other their whole lives. I could see the pride she felt in making such an advantageous match for her son.

"They certainly are well suited for one another. I had no idea they'd become smitten so quickly. Oh you do think they are smitten, don't you, Hazel?"

I did not wish to continue the conversation where we discussed just how enamored Felix and Olive were with one another. Not being blessed with the same self-possession that Mrs. Byerly had, I felt that I would fly into a passion if she forced me to continue singing the praises of the match.

Particularly galling was the fact that Mrs. Byerly failed to even entertain the thought that Felix might have been attracted to me on the trip. She didn't worry one iota about going to bed early when we were aboard the *Leucothea*. A jealous, petty voice inside me screamed to tell her everything—how Felix had once whispered that I'd captured his heart, how he'd known me as Rosamond Vincy. But I bit my tongue so hard it ached.

My beauty wasn't particularly striking, but I was far from ugly. Olive even commented on how fetching I looked several times, and others thought that I possessed certain charms. I was able to keep Harvey's love for several years while living in St. Louis. Why had she assumed that Felix wouldn't take any notice of me?

"That reminds me, dear. Have you and Felix quarreled recently?"

Shocked by the supposition, it was a little unnerving that she could possibly read my mind. I suppose she could have seen our heated conversation in the East Garden, but her room had looked out into the West Garden so it seemed unlikely. The best course of action was to feign ignorance.

"Why ever do you ask, Mrs. Byerly?" I asked with a trace of indignance in my voice.

"I commented to Felix at how nice you looked in that yellow dress before we got on the ferry, and his jaw clenched as if he were about to launch into a tirade. He gruffly admitted that you did look nice, but my son cannot hide anything from me. Felix is a passionate young man, and he isn't always in control of himself when he is perturbed."

Flashing to the angry face he had aimed in my direction in the East Garden, I blushed. He saw me as insolent because I wanted to avoid an awkward conversation with him. Recovering quickly, I said that I had barely exchanged a handful of words with her son during our time at Chaffinch Fields. If we had quarreled, it was definitely news to me.

"I wonder if he is jealous that you and Olive have gotten along so smashingly. Perhaps, he is annoyed that you take up much of her time," she laughed, "It is good for him though. He'll appreciate their time together even more, don't you think?"

I unclenched my own jaw to smile and nod at her.

The wind on the English Channel swept over the deck which chilled me a bit. Pulling my shawl a bit tighter to shield the cold air, I was quite grateful that she appeared to change the subject when she spoke next.

"Wasn't Chaffinch Fields wonderful? I do believe the air there did my lungs good. It is so much cleaner than what we have in St. Louis with all the factories. I could see myself retiring to Chaffinch Fields. I do hope that Felix is being forward enough with Olive. She's had suitors, but the Duchess said they were all too timid for her daughter. Olive is a strong personality, and she needs a strong man to keep her in check. Doesn't that sound just like Felix?"

Exhaling heavily, I realized the whole ferry ride to Calais would undoubtedly be all about the storybook romance of Miss Olive Powlett and Mr. Felix Byerly. I let her babble about them for a while, only half listening as I dreamed of crossing the channel again in a few months to start our work. Bringing the Women's Charity Organization's mission to England would be a noble endeavor, and I wouldn't have to watch Felix and Olive making love to one another every day.

"Why yes, and it would be nice to have you at Chaffinch Fields while I'm working in the London office of the WCO. You would be an invaluable resource to me." I said, hoping to pivot away from her favorite topic for a moment.

Her face lit up, genuinely delighted by the idea. "I hadn't thought about that! How lovely—semi-retirement and a purpose. I'd adore being your sounding board," she said with a twinkle in her eye.

It was nice to see her happy, and I knew the only reason she planned to retire was worry about her own health. Even now, she looked a bit frail. I promised to keep her abreast of everything going on at the London office. She patted my hand, and we reminisced a bit about our work over the years.

When we first began traveling and opening up offices, there wasn't much of a budget for it. Mrs. Byerly and I often stayed in the shabbiest of boarding houses. She recalled the rather large Russian woman who tried to marry her grandson to me. The woman refused to believe that Mrs. Byerly couldn't force me to get married. Standing up to the woman who was more than twice her size, Mrs. Byerly got quite red in the face, but she wouldn't allow the woman to intimidate her in the least. The remembrance made us laugh until our sides hurt.

"I don't want to pry, Hazel, but are you still doing okay about the loss of your former beau? I do know how much you cared for him. Harvey, was it?"

It was touching that Mrs. Byerly remembered Harvey. I supposed she had picked up on my jealousy of Olive and Felix's love and assumed that I still missed Harvey. He and

Ruby were probably disgustingly happy by now and all moved into their new home. The new Mrs. Cleghorn had chosen the safer path—warm arms to fall asleep in, a quiet, predictable life. I envied her ease, her certainty. And yet, I had chosen this path. I would make it mean something.

"From time to time I think about him, but I suppose it was never meant to be," I said, with a little more emotion in my words than I expected.

"Oh dear! I hate to see you in pain. I never wanted to let you go for my own selfish reasons, and I was always against marriage for women, you know. I think it is the whole issue of power that is so unfair. A woman must fight for it so much in this life. Once married, her power vanishes. If she complains, he can strike her into silence. That's why I never encouraged it—for anyone. If Felix had been born a girl, I'd have steered her far from marriage. But this world doesn't reward that kind of wisdom, does it?"

Squeezing her hand when she finished, I was going to miss her little speeches when she retired. I really was.

Paris looked exactly as I had imagined—like a dream pulled from the pages of a novel. I felt that any moment I would see Monsieur Defarge roll a cask of wine out of his shop. The Duchess said that there was a bit of an economic boom in Paris, and it made the social scene rather exciting. The Duke, ever practical, kept up with Parisian affairs for business, but the Duchess waved off those details with a smile. However, there were new productions of plays, operas, and concerts. Paris was alive with vibrance and excitement.

"I thought Paris was going to be a bore, Duchess," Olive said with her voice dripping with sarcasm.

"That's enough cheek from you, my dear," she shot back at her daughter.

The first few days in Paris had the Duchess and Olive calling on friends and introducing their relatives Mrs. Byerly and Felix. I was invited to come along, but I declined, partially because of Olive's advice and partially because I had begun to feel a deep fatigue from our travels. And if I could avoid Felix—even for a moment—I leapt at the chance.

There was another reason I needed time to myself, and I didn't know it until we arrived in Paris. As we drove up to the chateau from the train station, I was struck by a window we passed. It had seven candles on pedestals shining into the street. There was a red one, a white one, and five more in various shades of pink. They were lit in a circle with the red and white one next to one another. The Seven Arches were definitely in a half circle, but the matches of color could not be denied. A sign in the window said, "Madame Leveau, Le Diseur de Bonne Aventure" which Olive informed me meant fortune teller.

It took me a few days to work up the nerve to inquire about the candles. I feared that Madame Leveau would tell me that I had indeed come from hell, and if I didn't go back through the Seven Arches, life would be agony for me and anyone I came in contact with. The occult and supernatural fascinated me on some level, but it also scared me out of my wits. Was there a connection between the colors of the candles and the Seven Arches, and if so, what was it? The curiosity of it all was killing me.

I stood on the sidewalk outside the l'atelier of Madame Leveau and prayed that she spoke English because the amount of French that I spoke wouldn't get me directions back to the house. Mesmerized by the candles on a small table in a perfect circle, I finally took a deep breath and walked inside.

A pungent wave of sage and something sharply astringent hit my nostrils—what I imagined magic might smell like. The entrance was red and gold wallpaper with Turkish rugs on the stone floor. There was a noticeable crucifix on the wall as well as a pentagram directly above it.

"Bienvenue!" said a voice the moment that I walked in. I assumed that it meant welcome, but it could've meant that she planned to slit my throat. Hoping for the best, I answered "Merci," one of the few French words I knew.

Madame Leveau was a tall, slender woman. Her skin was the color of rich coffee, and her hair was hidden beneath a jewel-pinned turban. Towering over me at least four inches, she smelled faintly of cinnamon. Her silky voice was perfectly suited to her craft as I trusted her but was slightly scared of her as well.

"Parlez vous anglais?" I asked, hopefully.

"But, of course, Mademoiselle!" she said jovially, "Are you here to have your fortune told? You must be an American!"

She had a way of making me blush without even knowing why. When Madame Leveau looked at me, I felt like she could almost see my soul and all the secrets that went along with it. Before what happened to me at the Seven Arches, I wasn't sure that I even believed in fortune tellers or soothsayers, but with my exact duplicate living life as a married woman in Milligan, Indiana, anything had to be possible.

"I'm curious about my future, yes, but it was the candles burning in the window of your shop that first caught my eye. Is there a significance to the colors?"

She eyed the candles and surveyed me a bit suspiciously. I was afraid for a moment that I shouldn't have asked about them. Grabbing my arm, we strolled over to the candles burning in the storefront.

Her voice lowered for a moment, and she said almost in a whisper that no one had ever asked about the colors. The hair on the back of my neck stood on end the same way it did with the gold-toothed man.

My sense of fight or flight kicked in, but Madame Leveau had my arm tightly in hers. She appeared to be meditating with her lips moving in a way that I knew she was repeating some verse or perhaps, even a spell to herself.

Her eyes snapped open, blazing fire for one terrifying instant. It nearly made me scream out loud, but in a moment, Madame Leveau's face relaxed into the calm serenity that first greeted me.

"My apologies, mademoiselle. The colors of these candles are not something that I speak about to people very often. Other fortune tellers use black or blue candles which symbolize the passing of a loved one or spirituality."

She released my arm as her grip was unnecessary, for I was no longer in any fear. Her intensity, though palpable, was not aimed at me or my query. Rather, it was tethered to the vivid recollection of those white, red, and pink hues burning in the form of the candles before us.

They signified what she called "le chemin de l'esprit terrestre" or "the path of the earthly spirit." The white color represented the divine or heaven, while the red was the blood or earthly body. Every soul must travel from the mortal body to heavenly body. The path was forged when

Cain killed his brother Abel as Abel was the first mortal to move along the path of the earthly spirit.

I was enthralled by the story, and a little flattered to think that what happened to Ruby and I had origins all the way back to Cain and Abel.

"Are the pink colors as important?"

"Oh quite important! The white and red are the end and the beginning, but the pink is everything in between. They are your transition into the divine, but they also represent an infinity of paths," she said with her thick French accent dissipating.

"Infinity of paths?"

The pink candles acted as a gradient from red to white. The deep pink candle across from the gap between the red and white candles was an equal marriage of the two colors. The other candles were redder or whiter as they approached the others.

While the white represented the divine and the red represented mortality, the pinks were everything in between. Each pink candle held a balance—part mortal, part divine. The gradient was infinite, just like the paths we walk.

Each pink candle had a little of the mortal and a little of the divine. The red and the white, while next to each other in the circle, operated independently of one another, but the pinks had some of the red and the white within them which meant that there were infinite ways to get from white to red or red to white.

My confusion must have been obvious because it all seemed to make sense when discussing colors, but I couldn't see how it translated to Cain and Abel or Hazel and Ruby for that matter.

She tried to explain that it represented life, and we all start as the blood of the mortal, but as we get closer and closer to death, we obtain more and more of the divine if we are lucky.

"So it is only representative of life and death?"

She shook her head. Life and death was the basis, but life is much more than birth. Our lives are not only existence, but the choices we make. Different choices make different paths, and endless possibilities of change in the same life.

My head was swimming with the choices that Ruby and I made that led us to one another, which in turn led me into Madame Leveau's shop.

"Mademoiselle, you came to see me today. Did you have any apprehensions about coming to have your fortune told?"

I nodded.

"Perhaps, that part of you, under the right circumstances may have conquered yourself and kept you away from here. That is the formation of a new path. The path of the earthly spirit explores that path as you work to get to heaven. The red and the white are the final destination, but the pinks are all the ways to get there. Seven candles—one for each path, for each choice. Seven: the sacred number found in Scripture and ancient rites alike."

"Is there a way to travel between the paths and see different choices you've made?"

"The worlds are much like the rings in a tree. They are all circles. There is no crossing between them." She pulled a small piece of firewood from a stack in the corner to illustrate her point. Wiping off the edge of the wood for us to examine the annual rings, she pointed to one of the rings in the center of the wood and traced it with her finger.

"Let's say this is our world. This one that is next to it must be almost identical to our world. The rings are roughly the same size, and the color of the wood is an exact match. The choices made in this world are so similar that it is likely indistinguishable from our world."

"Traveling as far as here," she said pointing to the last ring, "I cannot even fathom. Unlike this piece of wood, there are an infinity of worlds between here and here. These infinities are where we get *The Path of the Earthly Spirit,* and the path from the mortal to the divine."

I nodded, having gained a mild understanding. My ability to see those mushrooms and Ruby's inability to see them was the difference between our two worlds. Had I not seen them, or if she had seen them, we never would have met.

After she set the piece of firewood back down, she picked up her stack of tarot cards which she had wrapped in black silk. Carefully unfolding them, she asked me to hold the cards in my hands so they could gather some of my energy.

I'd never had my fortune told, and I was a little unnerved by the intensity of the experience. However, I felt that Madame Leveau was seasoned in her ways to continue attracting customers to her shop. I felt like part of what I was experiencing was an act, but I was still excited and apprehensive at the same time.

"What brings you here today? Do you have a specific question or need guidance?"

"I want to know if I made the right decision, leaving home and coming here," I said, feeling the heat in my hands transfer to the cards that I held.

She asked me to cut or shuffle the cards as many times as I was comfortable with, and then hand them to her.

Three cards were dealt face down.

"This is your past. This is your present, and this is your future or the final answer to your question."

I nodded suddenly, nervous as to what she was going to show me with each turn of the cards.

With a quick flip, she revealed the first card.

"This is The Fool reversed. Upright it is an excellent card. It symbolizes new beginnings and the innocence of the soul, but reversed it tells me that you have been reckless and inconsiderate of the rippling effects of your actions. Does this sound familiar?"

I swallowed hard and nodded.

Flipping over the second card, she said, "The Five of Cups, upright, which tells me that you are experiencing much loss in love now. Perhaps, you have lost more than one love recently, and you are feeling very sorry for yourself."

With terror-filled eyes, I fought the urge to shoot up out of the chair and run away from the table. My legs turned to water. A cold shiver crept up my spine.

The final card was flipped, and she immediately whispered, "Mon dieu! The Tower!"

"The Tower?"

"Yes, mademoiselle. The Tower is a sudden change. It can foretell disaster and upheaval, coupled with the reversed Fool and the upright Five of Cups, the Tower is predicting unexpected changes in your life."

"Is it good or bad?"

"The unexpected can be good or bad. It is not for me to say," she said, staring into my eyes as if she were looking straight through me.

Standing up abruptly from the table, I paid her fee and fled her l'atelier. I walked around the block a few times after I left Madame Leveau's to clear my head. The entire reading had left me unnerved.

I tried to form in my head what I expected, and the only aspect of my life that I was quite certain about was opening the London office of the WCO with Mrs. Byerly. If Madame Leveau was correct, that wasn't going to happen. Would Mrs. Byerly's health deteriorate while we were on this trip, or would I be fired? The whole ordeal left me frazzled.

Back at the chateau, I wept—though for what exactly, I couldn't say. Maybe for the Tower. Maybe for everything.

Enoch's News, St. Louis, 1894

On a damp autumn afternoon, Clarissa stood at the window, watching the street for Enoch Byerly's arrival. Her brother-in-law was due for one of his weeklong visits, like clockwork, and she braced herself.

Enoch took the train from his beloved town of Waveland to St. Louis every few months to check in on his sister-in-law and nephew. Whenever he invaded her home, Clarissa remained frosty but cordial.

She never knew the right words when it came to Enoch. Of course, she hated him to his very core, but he was the one providing for her and her son. With the exception of her increasingly infirm mother and Dora, an ocean away, the only family Clarissa and Felix had was Enoch Byerly.

From their icy meeting before her engagement to his frequent weekend trips to visit Sam, Clarissa and Enoch had never been able to find common ground with one another. Clarissa assumed that her brother-in-law hated her because she'd ruined all the plans he'd had for Sam, and she kept that chip on her shoulder for as long as they'd known one another.

Sam had abandoned his family about three months after Felix was born. He had the decency to tell her that it wasn't necessarily all her fault. They had spent the last year and a half bickering which was roughly the amount of time they had known one another, but Sam claimed that he still had amorous feelings toward her.

No, Clarissa's husband attempted to bow out gracefully by talking about how he'd never been able to live for himself. He knew deep down he'd never please his demanding brother, and he'd made a worse decision by marrying an even more demanding woman. He had decided that their marriage would only survive if they spent some time apart, and he was catching the last train out of St. Louis. And he did.

She'd spent most nights after Sam left burning everything that he'd left behind and cursing his name up and down the halls of the home that Enoch had purchased for them as a wedding gift.

Enoch showed up on her doorstep a few weeks later attempting to guilt her for the very first time to move to his house in Indiana with Felix, and he even invited her mother. He had taken a vested interest in his nephew, and he wanted the boy to grow up with a man's influence.

Clarissa still fumed at those words. What business did her brother-in-law have in the raising of her son? Sam barely looked at the boy, and he was out the door just a few months after he was born. Why should Enoch give a fig about how he was brought up? And there was the impertinence that he needed male guidance?

They argued, but Enoch quickly folded and tried to smooth things over with Clarissa before he casually mentioned that he was the one keeping her bank account flush.

She would have thrown all the money in his face and cut ties with every Byerly man forever if it hadn't been for her mother, who deserved to enjoy life after years of sacrifice while married to Clarissa's fool of a father.

And on some level she knew that Felix should know his uncle not only for his wealth, but because she knew him to be a good man despite how much he hated her. Enoch would have made a better father to Felix, but the man lacked any of his younger brother's charisma, vivaciousness, or magnetism.

Thus, the visits from Enoch came every few months after Sam disappeared. They never talked about him, but they had an unspoken agreement that if either of them heard of his whereabouts they'd let the other one know.

It was coming up on 2 years since he'd left, and they'd heard no words on his travels. Clarissa figured he went east toward New York City, but hell, what did she know? The amount of time she'd lived with him was less than the amount of time he'd been gone.

Still, Enoch's visits made her nervous. She knew she had a temper, and one wrong word could have her mother and her son sent to the slums to live. Clarissa relentlessly educated herself on a variety of subjects, but for what cause? She was a woman. Outside of working in service or laundering clothes (both which she regarded as only marginal better than prostituting herself), what choice did she have?

There was also a certain level of pride in Clarissa's bones. She knew all those shrews like Ruby Hollingsworth who gossiped behind her back when she was younger would be more than happy to renew their talk. She couldn't bear to have that witch see her doing manual labor for her bread. It would destroy her and her mother.

So she endured the visits from Enoch, but she was always plotting her and Felix's escape from his clutches one day. She had long considered crossing the ocean to raise her son at Chaffinch Fields in Dora's palatial estate, but Clarissa was certain that her mother wouldn't be able to survive such an arduous journey.

When Enoch's cab arrived at her front door, she watched him alight. He never was as handsome as Sam, but there was no doubt they were brothers from their identical gait and height to their coloring and strong jaws. Enoch was slower today than normal. Most of the time, she could tell how excited he was to see his nephew Felix from the hop in his step. The hop was noticeably absent, and his shoulders were decidedly slumped.

She almost immediately surmised that he'd heard word of Sam. She wasn't sure how she was certain at that moment, but she knew.

They had barely exchanged stiff pleasantries before Enoch blurted out the news.

"He got shot."

Clarissa gasped upon hearing, and then almost involuntarily tears began to roll down her cheeks. The tears, she couldn't even explain to herself because she hated Samuel Byerly. She hated him more than any other person on the planet, and on some level she was glad he was dead. While he was alive, he would never have been anything but a source of pain to her and Felix. Now that he was gone, she could at least pretend for Felix's sake that his father would have been in his life.

The telegram had arrived more than a week earlier, but Enoch had not taken the news well. His brother had always been his only family, and now Felix was the last hope for the Byerly legacy as his uncle would never marry. Anyone who met Enoch could tell at once that he had little interest in the fairer sex.

He did have a soft spot for Clarissa, but only because she had been his brother's wife. If she'd shown any interest he would have married her if only to add security to Felix's upbringing because he loved his nephew. He'd briefly considered selling all his property in Waveland and moving to St. Louis, but he couldn't do it. Waveland was supposed to be the Byerly legacy, and as much as he wanted to help raise his only nephew, he couldn't let go of his magnum opus.

Later that evening, Clarissa and Enoch sat down in the parlor to discuss their business. As always, he asked her and Felix to move to Waveland. She promptly refused and launched into a rant about how she would not raise her son in the wilderness when their lives were firmly rooted in St. Louis.

"Now that Sam is dead. I'm the boy's benefactor, and I want a say in how he is raised."

"I'm his mother, and I'll be cold in my grave before I allow you to have any say on how I raise my son."

"Don't be cross."

"I'd sooner drink strychnine than continue this discussion. If you want to cut us off, I'll take Felix to England to live. My cousin Dora is now the Duchess of Cleveland, and I can assure you we will be well taken care of."

"Fine. You have total control of his upbringing, but I want him to go to Wabash when he is ready for college."

"Absolutely not. He will attend college right here in St. Louis."

Enoch had to relent. She would do almost anything to spite him if he held his support over her head, and she would see to it that Felix grew up not knowing him. Yes, Clarissa must be placated until Felix was old enough to be reasoned with.

After he had handed over the money necessary to cover her expenses for the next few months, tensions began to cool. They drank a toast to Samuel Byerly because both had to admit that without Sam there would be no Felix.

Over the next few days of Enoch's visit, Clarissa witnessed how much her son bonded with his uncle, and she knew that despite hating him to the core, Enoch would always be in Felix's life.

Chapter 9

One afternoon after we'd been in Paris for several days, Olive tracked me down to look at some French fashion magazines. There was a particular style of dress she wanted, and she planned on dragging me out on a shopping trip. I protested that I had no extra money to buy a dress, but she perished the thought. It hadn't even occurred to her that I might pay for the dress. I kept objecting, but she stayed firm. She thought it would be a total gas if we had matching dresses for dancing.

"And this is exactly what I want," she said, passing me a picture of a fashionable young lady in a sleeveless red dress cut practically up to her hips! It was about three inches shorter than anything that I would ever consider wearing and had rows of fringe all the way down to the thigh.

"Olive, my goodness, what would the Duchess or Mrs. Byerly say! Or Felix for that matter?"

"Darling, they won't see it. They'll go out long before we do, and they'll be asleep long before we get home. Live a little. I'm afraid you're going to be absorbed into that bed before long. Besides, I've missed you with visiting all these stuffy, old biddies. Haven't you missed me?" she said with a feigned pout.

Examining the picture of the dress again, I couldn't imagine wearing something so scandalous, but no one I knew would see me. I supposed if we were caught, Olive would take the blame, and who was going to punish an heiress?

"Is Felix not a dancer?" I asked, perhaps with a hint of tartness in my voice.

"Felix and his mother have to spend some time together, love," she said with a wink.

That afternoon she took me to several boutiques, and I was gratified that nearly every shopkeeper recognized her. I felt a little like I was traveling with a celebrity. She kissed everyone she met on both cheeks before showing them the photo in the magazine. The first few stores didn't have what she was looking for, but she finally got lucky. The last shop we went to had one red dress and an exact copy in white.

We tried them on, and they both needed small alterations that could be done and delivered to the chateau by tomorrow. Matching black gloves and headbands adorned with black feathers completed our outfits. It felt a little bit naughty, but I was no angel, I thought to myself, recalling that lustful night at the fishing hole with Harvey.

The next morning, I felt a little more energetic than I had in the last several days. The social calls had been completed, and Mrs. Byerly was quite excited to see the Louvre. Everyone was pleased that I felt well enough to go to the museum, and I thanked them all for their concern. Privately, I wondered if my body was fighting off infection as I was still quite tired, but I rallied.

Mrs. Byerly had always considered herself a lover of the arts, but the art scene in St. Louis was perpetually a disappointment to her. She and Felix visited the Metropolitan Museum of Art in New York, and I knew she was eager to show off to the Duchess all she had learned.

We entered the Denon Wing of the museum, and I watched Felix offer his arm to Olive. A huge smile spread across her face, and she gratefully took it. Mrs. Byerly and the Duchess tittered at each other, and the thought of appreciating art vanished from their minds. They would spend the morning watching for evidence that their children were in love.

At first, I lagged back to let them all move ahead. The memory of Madame Leveau's Five of Cups lingered in my head. Self-pity. Loss in love. I tried my best to appreciate the French impressionist paintings, but it was harder to appreciate art alone. In the throes of self-pity, I began to see Felix and Olive's faces on all the paintings that depicted lovers.

I left the first floor believing that I had given Felix, Olive, and the two old busybodies tailing them sufficient time to be ahead of me, but when I got to the top of the stairs, I saw the Duchess and Mrs. Byerly eyeing something with great interest. Standing on my toes to see the painting they were pointing at, I colored immediately. They were pointing at Felix and Olive off in the distance, and I watched as Felix laid a tender kiss upon Olive's lips.

The ladies clutched each other in jubilation, and I, red-faced, kept climbing past the second story to the third, completely shaken by what I had seen. I found a seat and dabbed my eyes with my handkerchief, suddenly feeling unbelievably foolish. They clearly cared for each other, and I had seen how well they got along. Why their kiss had taken me by surprise, I could not say. Felix was never mine, and he had never made me any promises. In fact, I had gone out of my way to stop him from telling me how enchanted he was with Olive.

"You stupid fool!" I said to myself, taking a deep breath. Here I was in arguably the finest art museum in the world, and I was pouting because two attractive young people shared a kiss. Putting my handkerchief away, I smoothed my dress and continued to appreciate the art on the third floor.

I was staring at the *Death of the Virgin* with bemused interest as Olive sidled up to me twenty minutes later.

"I was wondering where you ran off to, darling! Come see the *Venus de Milo* with me," she said, taking my arm and leading the way.

The Venus de Milo was located in a whole other wing of the museum, and I protested that I was taking Olive away from Felix and her mother. She had willingly left them as she spent the last few days up to her elbows in Felix's stories and her mother's insinuations. There was fun to be had, and she indicated that I was the only fun person on the trip.

"Tired of Felix already?" I asked, recalling the kiss that was no doubt fresh on her lips.

"He's off tomorrow to explore the city with one of the old fuddy-duddies the Duchess threw at him. If I'd stayed, she would have insisted I go along to play chaperone, which sounded absolutely dreadful. So we gave them a little something to keep them entertained, just enough to buy ourselves a bit of space."

"What?"

"We pretended to sneak away, and when we knew they were looking, he planted a kiss on me. It was such a hoot. I'm sure the ladies just ate it up."

I was puzzled, but I didn't want to go into grave details about Felix's prowess with his lips. I knew how well he kissed, and I recalled being weak in the knees while the softness of his mustache tickled my upper lip.

Olive was in a wonderful mood practically humming with excitement as she led me through the museum to see the famous *Venus de Milo*.

"We can go dancing tonight too! Isn't that wonderful news? I've arranged it all with Felix. He's taking the two old battle axes to the opera tonight. After they head out, we can go over to my friend June's salon. It will be my first night of freedom on this trip, and I get to spend it with you."

She grinned. I smiled at the thought of a whole night out. I really hadn't done much more than brood in my room since we'd arrived in Paris aside from my experience with the fortune teller and shopping.

At the sculpture, I was struck by the long torso on her. She had a haunting beauty about her, and the missing arms reminded me of the conversation Mrs. Byerly and I had on the ferry ride about married women being powerless.

"I do love this sculpture," Olive said. "My pedantic art friends, you'll meet some of them tonight at June's, say that it is passé, but I say it is classic. Ugh, most of my friends are such prigs, but when you get a couple of drinks in them, they really let loose."

"It is so beautiful," I said as I walked up a bit closer to the sculpture, "She reminds me a bit of you."

A sly smile spread across Olive's face at my comment, "Do you really think so? I certainly think my tits are a bit bigger than hers."

We laughed and headed back to the Denon Wing arm in arm to join the others.

That evening The Duchess, Mrs. Byerly, and Felix bid us goodnight for their evening at the opera. The Duchess interrogated her daughter about our plans, but Olive smiled and said she was a big girl and so was I.

"Please keep my daughter reined in if you can," the Duchess said to me as they departed.

"I'll do my best," I smiled.

The scandalous dresses had been delivered while we were out at the Louvre, and they fit perfectly. We dressed in Olive's room, and she admired my figure in the white dress. She wore the red one and was the model of feminine beauty. After some initial apprehension, I agreed with Olive that the highness of the hemline was somewhat complementary to my shapely legs so I decided not to be self-conscious about it.

We took a car to the home of her friend, an American expatriate. Olive knew that I would just love her. Her name was June Barrett, and she had come to Paris a few years ago on assignment as a magazine writer. She stayed to write poetry and short stories. It seemed like such a glamorous life.

June had short cropped red hair and alabaster skin that almost resembled porcelain which was resonant of Harvey's paleness. She smoked her cigarettes with a long cigarette holder, but what surprised me the most about her was that she was wearing a man's suit. I wanted to ask about it, but I felt it would be gauche so I tried not to stare.

"Olive, where do you find these intriguing girls?" June said after we'd been introduced.

"Don't scare her away, Junie. I like this one, and she thinks I resemble the Venus de Milo." Olive said, giving me a squeeze before pouring a drink for each of us.

She handed me a snifter of brandy which went down quite smoothly, and I was immediately invited to refill my cup. The rest of the party would be arriving soon. Olive talked to June about her writing for a bit, and they began to read a draft of her most recent work, *The Honey Pot*.

"Darling, it is perfect. The language you use as you describe the woman's fingers with the golden sweetness is quite titillating."

While they talked, I walked around the salon and took in the artwork. June had quite the appreciation for the female body as most of the prints depicted women with their bare breasts.

Throughout the next hour or so, more and more women began to show up, and Olive introduced me dutifully to each one. Some of them were dressed in fancy cocktail dresses like the two of us, and some were dressed like June in men's suits. It struck me as odd that everyone was female.

I had at least three or perhaps four glasses of brandy waiting for the dancing to begin, and when the band arrived, we all shuffled into the next room with a small but adequate dance floor. The music was hopping in a moment, and I was a little shy about dancing so I watched Olive and her friends do the Charleston. It was such a riot to see how much fun everyone was having, and I understood why there were no men as it wouldn't have been so easy to cut loose. The alcohol was making me light-headed, but I didn't care as I was lost in the music and atmosphere. Nothing would compare to this experience.

After the dancing began, I switched to gin, which may have been a mistake. I had only been drunk a handful of times in my life, always careful about what I drank, but with Olive handing me glass after glass, I found myself laughing more and more as the night went on.

The music was incredible. It was much more exciting than what was playing in Roscoe's speakeasy in St. Louis. The alcohol took away almost all my inhibitions, and I danced with Olive all night, laughing and giggling while she twirled and dipped me.

I finally got to the point where I couldn't dance anymore, and we went outside to get some air. In the night, I hit on the memory of Felix and I aboard the *Leuchothea* when he told me that it was not so easy to capture his heart. It all seemed unfair how lucky Olive was to have her fortune, Felix, and friends who threw raucously delightful parties.

"How do you think Felix would enjoy this place," I said rather spitefully as the liquor had brought my resentment to the surface.

"My God, Hazel, are you jealous?" she asked rather taken aback.

At this point, I had no idea how I was standing, but I wasn't going to cower about my feelings anymore. "Yes, and I don't care who knows!"

"You are the absolute sweetest. I wasn't sure about you, but this jealousy certainly clears everything up. Darling, Felix isn't your competition."

Smiling, she rubbed my shoulder for a moment before planting a tender kiss on my lips. In my drunken haze, my eyes popped open widely, but she smiled back at me. She had kissed all her friends on the lips at some point. It was just a custom that I wasn't used to. My head spun with liquor, and I couldn't remember anything after she said, "I'm very French tonight."

I had the faint memory of her tongue inside my mouth when I woke up the next day so hungover and tired that I had no inclination toward ever getting out of bed.

I laughed when I realized how silly it was that I'd imagined Olive's tongue in my mouth. She was practically engaged to Felix, and I knew she wouldn't do any such thing to jeopardize that. Her group of friends were just more relaxed about affection than Americans.

Suddenly, I remembered admitting that I was jealous of her and Felix, and I felt completely embarrassed. Everything after that seemed a bit fuzzy, and I was sure that I passed out a little bit later as I wasn't even completely sure how we got back to the chateau.

My head was pounding, and I quickly got over my hesitation about using the bell since everything hurt. I had the maid bring me an aspirin, some breakfast, and a pitcher of water.

After taking the aspirin, I drank the water greedily. But when I lifted the cloche covering my breakfast, the smell of scrambled eggs hit me like a slap. I stumbled to the water closet and threw up everything I had just taken in. The scent of eggs made me violently ill.

As the day went on, more and more pieces of the evening began to fall into place. Things I had brushed off under the influence of liquor now struck me as strange. The honey pot poem seemed far less innocent in the light of day, and the fact that so many of the ladies were wearing suits stood out more than it had the night before. The art on June's walls had shown women in various states of undress, and I realized there hadn't been a single man at the dance aside from the musicians.

I suddenly remembered Olive reassuring me that I had nothing to worry about when it came to Felix, and just like that, the memory of her tongue in my mouth came rushing back with clarity. Olive hadn't thought I was jealous of her—she thought I was jealous of Felix!

The scent of Olive's perfume came flooding back to me as I flashed at the two of us kissing out in the night air. I felt flushed with embarrassment. Olive liked women, and I had made her believe that I did too! Oh God, I felt so awkward. There were so many things I said to hide my fondness for Felix that were obviously misconstrued.

My face felt hot not only from the shame of it all, but at the uncomfortable conversation that would need to take place. How would I tell her? She was Olive Powlett, and it was her kindness and friendship that had sustained me since arriving at Chaffinch Fields. I couldn't disappoint her, but I couldn't pretend to have romantic feelings for her either.

She wasn't the world's worst kisser, but no, I couldn't see her that way.

After lunch, my physical body began to recover from the liquor, but my embarrassment deepened. I had no idea how to address what had happened the previous evening. Since I first met her, Olive had been so kind to me. How I was to tell her that I was flattered by her attention, but I only loved her in a sisterly way. I didn't think she was spiteful, but she could run to Mrs. Byerly and demand that I be sent away.

That afternoon she looked in on me, and the look of happiness on her face made me feel like an utter beast. I did not relish telling her that I didn't normally go around kissing girls.

"How are you, darling?" she asked, knowing how much I'd had to drink last night.

"I'm a bit better, thank you." I said, looking at my hands rather than meeting her gaze. I didn't want to see the look in her eyes, and I feared that I would disappoint her.

"If you're up to it, I think I can finagle another night with my friends. They certainly thought highly of you."

After taking a deep breath, I told her that I was little more than a naive country girl. I did love her dearly but as one would love a friend or a sister. Meeting her eyes for the first time, I saw how confused she looked. We'd had great fun at June's salon so I was more than happy to go back, but I didn't feel romantic toward her.

"Had you never done anything like that before? I know it can be unnerving to give into those feelings."

"I don't really have those feelings."

"I don't understand, dear. You said that you were jealous of the time I was spending with Felix, and you called me the Venus de Milo."

"I was jealous of you, not Felix. Felix and I shared a few stolen moments on the *Leucothea*, and I felt like he tossed me aside for you. It hurt. You two looked so happy together that I didn't want you to think of me as a threat."

She laughed at the thought that she would ever in a million years marry Felix for love. If she were looking for a marriage of convenience, he was exactly the type of man she'd choose, but their entire romance was a show for their mothers. He had told her that he had a girl he was sweet on, but he never mentioned it was me.

I asked carefully, unsure whether she had told him about her friends—or if I even had the right to ask.

"Of course not, I couldn't risk him telling his mother, who would instantly tell my mother. In our circle, my love life's already gossip fodder, but I'm lucky. If my parents had another child, they might have me institutionalized or something."

"Do they know?"

"The Duke knows to a certain degree that I never want to get married. Mother, on the other hand, remains eternally hopeful that the right man will change everything for me," she sighed.

She explained that she and Felix had decided right away that there was nothing romantic between them, but they were fond of each other. No matter what they felt, their mothers would keep pushing them together as long as there was a glimmer of hope. They decided it would be hilarious at the Louvre if the old biddies saw them share a kiss.

"When did you plan on telling them? They will both be disappointed," I said.

"My mother is used to disappointment, but it serves them both right for trying to push us together as if we were puppets to manipulate."

I realized that Olive's life, while glamorous, wasn't even what she wanted. She couldn't be herself with most of the people in her social circle. It suddenly made sense why she didn't like making those calls with her mother. My heart went out to her, and I squeezed her hand.

"I hope we're still friends."

"It's such a shame, love. Even when you were blindingly drunk, you were one hell of a kisser." she chuckled, extending her arms for a hug.

Blushing, I betrayed myself by how flattered I was by her compliment.

Then her words took me back to Madame Leveau and the infinity of paths. Perhaps there was a version of me that would be more than titillated at Olive's attention. The kiss was tender—even lovely—but it didn't make my stomach flip the way Felix did. A couple of rings away there was doubtless a Hazel out there that would have gladly shared a life at Chaffinch Fields with Olive Powlett.

When she walked away, I realized I faced the daunting task of asking Felix to forgive me for how terribly I had treated him. Ever since arriving at Chaffinch Fields, I had gone out of my way to avoid him. We had shared such a wonderful time getting to know each other on the *Leucothea*, and I had allowed petty jealousy to steal any chance of more quiet, meaningful moments between us in Paris.

It was suddenly clear that he wanted to tell me out in the East Garden about the ruse he had with Olive, but my overly dramatic reaction to his attention kept him from it. I should have trusted him. Everything he had said to me had been true, capturing his heart wasn't easy, and I was ashamed of myself.

I didn't know where I stood with him, and quite frankly, I didn't know where he stood with me. Before arriving in England, I had been all ready to relinquish him. England and the WCO were supposed to be my future. Why had believing him to be in love with Olive deepened my own affection for him? Was I really that shallow? Did I only want him more because I couldn't have him?

That night, I barely slept. And when I did, my dreams betrayed me, I dreamed that I was in the East Garden back at Chaffinch Fields. There was an altar surrounded by my favorite flowers, white-petaled daffodils. A String Quartet was playing Chopin. I looked down at my attire and saw that I was wearing a wedding dress. My chest tightened, heart climbing into my throat.

Suddenly, my father appeared out of nowhere to walk me down the aisle. I couldn't understand why he was at my wedding—I hadn't wanted him there—but he was insistent. At the altar, I saw Felix waiting for me. He looked so handsome and dapper that it was hard to believe I was actually marrying him. The thought of being his wife thrilled me. I wanted to run to him, throw my arms around him, and promise myself to him forever.

But as I stepped closer, I saw that familiar, confident grin on his face, and to my horror, Harvey and Olive appeared behind him. All three of them looked as if they were waiting to marry me. My father's arm tightened around mine, and I kept pulling, trying desperately to break free from the strange procession of suitors that awaited me.

Soon the wedding march began to play, and against my will, I was marched down the aisle toward the three people who had romantic feelings for me. The three of them looked excited as if they had worked out how a four way marriage would operate. I continued to shake my head and pull against my father, but he had a tight grip.

As a last ditch effort, I threw myself on the ground, and it felt like I shattered into a million pieces. I laid there for a moment, but I could stand—uninjured. As I stood up, I saw two other Ruby Hazel Suttons standing up as well. We looked at each other and up at the three suitors at the altar.

We all screamed, and I awoke in a cold sweat.

The next few days I schemed to catch a moment alone with Felix, but he was invariably out by the time I conquered my extreme tiredness. I sat down to write him a letter, but I thought better of it as it could easily end up in the hands of his mother.

Finally, I woke early one morning, and I caught him in the library reading while enjoying his morning cup of coffee.

"Good morning, Mr. Byerly," I said, happy to see him but worried that he might be angry.

"Mr. Byerly is reading, Miss Sutton, if that is how it is going to be."

"Felix, I owe you an apology."

"Yes, you do."

We made plans to meet at a cafe down the street in a few hours. The walls in the house had ears, and if we still wanted to keep our connection a secret, we couldn't be seen alone together.

Arriving at the cafe before him, I ordered a slice of the pain au chocolat as it looked absolutely divine. I made a pig of myself, but since I wasn't able to keep down eggs and cheese, bread was just about the only Parisian fare I could rely on. French food was supposed to be a highlight of this trip, but it was actually a nightmare. All the dishes seemed to have cheese and the texture no longer agreed with me. It was a shame, but I knew we'd move onto Italy in a week or so. I'd heard wonderful things about macaroni and pasta. The thought of spaghetti with basil pesto sauce at Flavio's sounded heavenly.

"May I say that you're a sight for sore eyes now, or are you going to yell at me again?" he said with a smirk as he sat down at my table.

"Oh Felix, I'm so sorry. I've been sick and moody lately, and I'm such a horrible person. You've been so kind to me," I said, starting to cry.

What was wrong with me? I'd never cried so easily in my life, and the tears were flooding my eyes.

"What's all this? I couldn't be angry at you for long. Are you sure you're feeling alright? I've heard you've not been well."

I took a few deep breaths and managed to get a hold of myself. That outburst was so unlike me, and I assured him that whatever was plaguing me was starting to pass.

"My fondness for you, against my better judgment, has grown, my dear. I'm considering extending my trip to stay in London so I can see you more. How does that sound?" he said, taking my hand on the table in his.

"Honestly, that is the best news I'd heard in a long time." I said, squeezing his hand back. "I don't want to deny the effect you have on me anymore."

He looked into my eyes with his deep amber browns, and it felt like home. His hand still clasped mine, and I liked that he wasn't in a hurry to let go. It was the closest we'd been to one another in nearly a month, and I wanted the moment to last forever.

"How did you know that you didn't want to get involved with Olive romantically," I asked him, knowing exactly why Olive didn't want to get involved with him.

"I told you that my heart isn't easily captured, Hazel. Olive would have had her work cut out to wrestle it away from you. You've got a tight grip on it, Miss Vincy. Tell me, what did you think of me when you first set eyes on me? We never discussed that on the ship."

"You were the handsome man with the newspaper. I remembered watching you for a while jealous of the newspaper because it got the full view of your face.

He grinned, "I wanted to talk to you so badly, but I was worried about offending you. You had a look of excitement about you. The world was your oyster, and you were ready to dive down to the ocean to get it. When you sat by me on the train to St. Louis, I felt as if a gift had been dropped in my lap."

We didn't talk about the man with the gold tooth—though the memory still clawed at the back of my mind. Watching that Rolls-Royce barrel into him was forever etched into my memory. I had never been so happy that something so awful had happened to another person.

Before he headed back to the chateau, he asked for me to maintain my air of quiet indifference to him. He wanted to tell his mother about our connection, but not until after the trip as he didn't want it to be ruined for her.

Nodding, I told him I had only kept away from him because marrying Olive seemed like the best thing for him. I could see him being the manager of an estate like Chaffinch Fields.

"That wouldn't be a bad life, but I think the best thing for me is you, dear Hazel."

We picked up right where we left off on the *Leucothea* during our remaining time in Paris. Meeting clandestinely at various cafes and boutiques, we began to fall in love. As we walked arm in arm through the streets of Paris at night taking in the sights and smells of the wonderful city, I felt like I never wanted to let him go. He kissed me atop the Eiffel Tower, and it was an absolutely perfect moment.

I never could get accustomed to French cheese or eggs, and ever since my drunken night with Olive's friends, alcohol made me quite queasy. However, my appetite got larger and larger. Italy was nearly as wonderful as France. Florence, or "fair Firenze" as the Duchess called it, was one of her favorite cities.

Despite some initial awkwardness, Olive and I maintained our friendship, and we continued to have some adventures together. I always made myself available when she grew tired of the society friends her mother insisted on her visiting.

The Duchess demanded that we dress one morning for a trip to the Boboli Gardens to take in the view of Florence from there. She insisted it was breathtaking, and it would be a highlight of our trip. My dresses were significantly tighter than they had been before. They felt like someone had shrunk them in hot water. I soon realized that, no, they hadn't shrunk. My waistline was growing. Overeating Italian pasta was catching up to me, and I didn't like the look of my figure. Catching sight of my fuller face, I resolved then and there to rein in my appetite.

At the Boboli Gardens, Olive and Felix first broke from our group. The Duchess had invited an old friend of hers to join us which left me with Mrs. Byerly. Now that I had been sneaking around to see Felix again, I felt a pang of guilt whenever I talked to her.

"Hazel, do you have any idea what's going on between Olive and Felix? I was certain a proposal was coming in Paris, but now... it's as if they've lost interest."

"They did wander off right away," I offered, hoping the obvious might stall her suspicion.

Worrying her dreams of retiring at Chaffinch Fields were vanishing before her very eyes, she smelled a rat. Felix and Olive, she suspected, were pretending to be in love to pull a prank on their poor mothers.

"A prank?" I asked before immediately regretting the comment.

"Yes, a childish prank. They are pretending to be enamored with one another. I fear we pushed them too much. If Felix goes back to his uncle, I cannot stay here in England. I'll be less comfortable leaving you here when our work is done. And you—you've no one waiting for you, do you?"

I promised that Olive had been such a kind friend to me, and she had already invited me to visit which seemed to assuage her fears. She made small talk about the highlights of our trip while we strolled. Once again, I thanked her profusely for her generosity, and I was going to savor our last months working together. The thought of her retiring still pained me.

My words struck her, and she sniffled as a tear escaped from her eye. She called me a good girl and patted my arm. After about thirty minutes or so of vigorous walking, she needed to relax in the shade. I offered to keep her company, but she beckoned me to go ahead and find Felix and Olive.

"Put the idea of marriage into their heads if you can, Hazel!" she whispered to me as I parted from her.

I combed the gardens looking for them, but they had been strolling much faster than me and Mrs. Byerly.

"Hazel," Felix called out to me from behind a rather tall tree, beckoning me to come over to him.

He offered me his arm as I reached him, and together we strolled, Florence unfolding like a painting before us. I put my head on his shoulder, and he pulled me in closer.

"I love you," he said, almost as if by accident.

I was startled, and I looked at him deeply. The shyness I'd discovered on the *Leucothea* was standing in front of me, worried about my reaction.

What *was* my reaction? Did I love him? Was it possible to build something real from a handful of stolen moments? The European backdrop certainly assisted with making it seem possible.

"Oh, Felix… why must you be such a bastard?" I said, laughing through my tears. "Of course I love you. I just wasn't ready to admit it."

He grinned and kissed my hands before we continued our stroll.

"You'll finish your work with my mother this next year, but perhaps, you could see yourself agreeing to an engagement when it is all over?"

I felt like crying all over again. He wasn't asking me to give up my work or mold myself to his life. He wasn't threatened or jealous about putting his plans for the future on hold for me. The love I felt for him was so overwhelming that I passionately threw my arms around him and pressed my lips to his.

A sharp gasp followed by the thud of a body collapsing tore us apart.

Laying on the ground just ten feet away from us laid his mother, Mrs. Byerly.

Chapter 10

The doctor confirmed our worst fears about Mrs. Byerly—it was heart failure. She stayed in the hospital in an oxygen tent for nearly a week, and the only person able to see her was Felix. She claimed she was nearly herself again, eager to return to Chaffinch Fields.

Privately, Felix admitted her prognosis was grim. She had hidden her worsening symptoms—shortness of breath, palpitations—for days, determined to keep up appearances. She had been pretending all was well ever since we stepped aboard the *Leucothea*.

She had overexerted herself entirely on the trip and was prone to any number of infections in her weakened state. The doctor recommended she stay in isolation, seeing as few people as possible for at least a month, but his mother insisted on traveling back to Chaffinch Fields as soon as possible.

Felix fought with her tooth and nail to stay in Florence to recuperate, but she refused. The doctor warned that upsetting her to this degree posed a greater risk than the journey itself.

True to form, she refused to stay a day longer in Florence. She threatened to sneak out in the night unless Felix arranged passage. Perhaps, she'd die on the journey. Perhaps, she wouldn't, but regardless, she wouldn't die in Florence. Felix feared she might will herself to death just to prove a point so the Duchess made our travel arrangements.

Mrs. Byerly stayed in her hospital room up until we left, and the Duchess had a private train car for her while making the long journey back to Calais. Consequently, I hadn't been able to see or talk to her since she had seen me in that compromising situation with Felix.

I dreaded her summons, bracing for the moment she would finally speak of the disappointment I was certain still lingered in her eyes. My concern for her health far outweighed any worry about how she felt toward me, and I only heard news of her condition during a few brief conversations with Felix, snatched in the rare moments he stepped away from her side.

Thankfully, I didn't have to worry that Felix had changed his mind in regards to me. He came to see me most evenings after she was asleep, assuring me that she was doing as well as could be expected given her current state of health. He was certain she'd make it back to Chaffinch Fields in one piece, but she was by no means out of the woods yet. A light cough developed on the train which she attributed to the dry air, but he wasn't so sure.

I asked if he had a chance to talk to her about what she witnessed, and he shook his head. He assured me that she loved him and me, and her approval would be forthcoming. As we were both very important to her, he felt quite certain that she would want us to be happy together.

He believed the entire scheme he had concocted with Olive had upset her more than our kiss ever did. She didn't like being made to feel like a fool, and he was certain that once she recovered, she would have some sharp words for him.

In retrospect, he should have been forthcoming with her about where his feelings lay, but he and Olive were having fun with the ruse. As I had acted like a petulant child for several weeks, he wasn't even certain there was anything to tell her until after we'd cleared the air.

I spent most of my time with Olive on the train while Felix and the Duchess fussed over Mrs. Byerly. Our friendship could have been awkward, but we decided that we liked each other too much to allow a silly misunderstanding to come between us.

Olive told me tales of Paris, Vienna, New York—of glittering parties, stolen kisses, and laughter that echoed across continents. The free spirit in her with enough wealth to turn whatever she fancied into reality led to some amazing stories. Some of the best times of her life were listening to the witty writers in the Algonquin Hotel. Her friend, June had dragged her there a couple years ago, and she spent the evening laughing more than she could ever remember.

"There was this one lady whose name I can't remember, but someone asked her to use the word 'horticulture' in a sentence. With a wicked grin, the woman had responded, 'You can lead a horticulture, but you can't make her think.'"

I laughed and laughed at her stories, and it dawned on me how my mother and Olive were like two peas in a pod. They would probably entertain each other endlessly.

We returned to Chaffinch Fields in triumph as Mrs. Byerly had made the journey looking no worse for the wear. Unfortunately, the cough persisted, and each day after we returned, it got worse and worse. She'd had the strength to take one stroll in the garden before being confined to her bedroom too weak for any activity.

The doctor said she had an inflammation of the lungs which was exacerbated by her heart failure, and our hopes of a quick recovery were dashed. If she were to recover, the doctor said that her lungs were so damaged that she'd not be able to walk for more than a few feet without feeling fatigued. A fever arose, and she spent her nights shivering, unable to find comfort. No visitors were allowed into her room with the exception of the Duchess and Felix.

Each night, her fever deepened. The house fell into silence, and I waited—helpless, heartsick—for the moment her strength would return, if it ever did.

Olive and I resumed our riding sessions, and she soothed me with calming words. I wasn't sure what the future held for me. Mrs. Byerly recovering enough to open up the WCO office in London was unthinkable, and Mrs. Schiff wouldn't trust me with the responsibility solo. The lease would be voided, and the entire project scrapped. With no job and no home, my hopes for the future all revolved around Felix Byerly.

In those days, Olive was such a good friend to me. The distractions she provided at Chaffinch Fields while Mrs. Byerly was bedridden saved me from my own anxiety. Often overcome with grief, I was faced with the prospect of losing Mrs. Byerly, and Olive was always there to offer comfort or a diversion. There was no way I'd ever be able to repay her kindness. She became the sister I never had—the one I always secretly wished for.

Felix was not taking care of himself. His eyes told me that he hadn't been sleeping, and I knew this was a sign that his mother wasn't recovering. I feared he was preparing himself for the worst.

"I'm just so angry at her," he said after one particularly rough afternoon in her sick room. "She may have avoided all this if she would have rested and gathered up her strength in Florence. She's a stubborn old fool."

"She is, and that is part of her charm," I said.

He looked back at me with a furrowed brow before he broke out into a rather large grin. "God help me, I love you," he said, kissing me before retiring to bed.

Early the next day I received a message summoning me to Mrs. Byerly's room. My pulse began to race, and even with Felix's assurances, I feared she was going to declare me a disappointment who took advantage of her good will.

The walk through Chaffinch Fields' main hall felt endless. I was torn about seeing Mrs. Byerly as I wanted her forgiveness desperately but feared that I'd never get it.

Hundreds of portraits lined the halls of Chaffinch Fields immortalizing the previous occupants. Olive had told me that the Powlett family could trace their roots all the way back to the Magna Carta, and she was quite possibly the last of her family. It seemed sad to me that all this history was ending with Olive as I knew that she had no desire to ever get married or have children of her own. The family and the dukedom would become extinct.

Waiting outside Mrs. Byerly's room for several minutes before bearing up the courage to enter, I softly knocked. To my surprise, the door was unlatched, and it swung open at my touch.

The room was bright and the open windows brought fresh air into the room. She was propped up with pillows, either dozing or too weak to keep her eyes open. It was obvious she was expecting me as her hair was neatly pinned up, and someone had applied rouge to her cheeks.

She was a proud, vain woman, and she would be to the very end. Seeing her fixed up gave me a little hope, but as I approached, I could see that the rouge couldn't hide the ashen pallor that lingered underneath.

Felix looked stoic at her bedside, and the corners of his mouth raised slightly upon seeing me. He greeted me by kissing my hand. I wasn't sure if he had slept at all last night, or if he'd stayed up listening to her cough and wheeze.

"Should I come back later?" I said, still unsure if she was resting her eyes or sleeping.

"Mother, Hazel's arrived," he whispered, breaking her from her reverie. Her eyes popped open as if she had been surprised at the news. She glanced between us before collecting her thoughts.

"Come sit here next to me, Hazel," she said softly but sternly. It was a tone of voice that I'd heard many times before. Quieter than normal, but it was no less intimidating. I'd heard her fire people with that voice, and it sent a shiver down my spine.

"Mrs. Byerly, can you ever forgive me?" I blurted out upon taking a seat next to her, hoping that my distress would soften her tone toward me.

"My son revealed to me that your little public display of affection in Florence was more than uncontrollable lust," she said, discounting my words completely.

Looking to Felix to see if his countenance held some clue to the speech that Mrs. Byerly was delivering to me, I felt as though I were being summoned for sentencing, and she already had the verdict.

"Furthermore, Felix tells me that you sometimes go by the name Rosamond Vincy. Do you mind explaining yourself?"

Felix had told her all about the man with the gold tooth who had harassed me, and I explained that after that unpleasantness, it didn't feel safe to give my real name to a stranger. I had absolutely no idea that Dr. Lydgate was her son, or I would have given him my real name in an instant.

"He also informed me that your mother was dead. Should I offer my condolences?" she asked, the tone of her voice cutting through me like ice.

I had no way of explaining it. It was a lie, but in some ways it wasn't. My mother was dead to me, but she was very much alive in all other respects. There was only one believable way to explain my words.

"My mother demanded I stay home and get married. We quarreled. She told me that when I left, I needn't come back so I told the stranger on the train that she was dead," I said, feeling somehow that I was betraying my mother by inventing such a mendacity.

Mrs. Byerly's face began to soften in an instant. Felix looked rather startled. We hadn't talked about marriage since the Boboli Gardens, and my explanation seemed like I was opposed to the idea.

"How dreadful!" Mrs. Byerly said before erupting into a coughing fit that ended with her handkerchief dotted with blood. Felix held a cup of water to her lips for her to sip. She weakly clasped my hand while she drank the water, allowing the coolness to appease her throat for a moment before signaling to Felix that she was finished.

"Have your thoughts of marriage changed at all, child?" she asked me.

I looked at her, and I looked at Felix. He had the most hopeful eyes looking back at me. From the moment that I met him, I had been fond of him, but the way he looked at me with those eyes made me feel like I was home again. Those were the eyes I wanted to look into for all the days of my life.

"Yes, as a matter of fact, they have."

Felix reached for my other hand and planted a tender kiss on it. He managed a real smile for the first time since I entered Mrs. Byerly's room.

"My dear, I'm an old fool. I was so blinded by the wealth and privilege that came with a marriage to Olive that I didn't see how well matched you would be for my son. For that, you must forgive me."

"Oh Mrs. Byerly," I said, my eyes welling with tears. "I should have told you. I'm so sorry."

"Yes, you should have."

She held up a hand to silence me from any more apologies. I hadn't set out to wrong her. Felix and I were following our hearts, and she couldn't reproach us for that. There was plenty of fault to go around especially when it came to her son and Miss Powlett for their little ruse. She understood that I had no part in that, and I had suffered from their cruel little game as well.

I looked at Felix whose ears had suddenly changed to bright pink. It seemed that his mother had already had her stinging words with him over that.

"Furthermore, I have discussed this with Felix, and I'm told I don't have much time. The pneumonia will likely take me. Oh please, don't cry, Hazel, this isn't brand new information. If the two of you think you will get married someday, I'm asking for you to do it very soon. I would like to see my son and the girl that I've come to think of as a daughter married before I die."

"But, you'll be fine," I said, my voice filled with utter distress.

Mrs. Byerly looked at me, and I knew that she wouldn't. Her weakened heart and lungs wouldn't survive more than a few days of the coughing fits that erupted out of her. I squeezed her hand again and stayed silent.

"Hazel, dear. Would you like to marry...oh I suppose that I'm stepping on Felix's toes a bit."

Felix moved around the bed in front of me. The smile that he gave me turned into an utter grin. I let out a faint gasp as he got down on one knee as he said, "Hazel Sutton, will you do me the honor of becoming my wife?"

"Yes!" I said amidst tears, "Yes!"

We kissed, and I was suddenly conscious of the effect the last kiss we shared had on Mrs. Byerly, but she was beaming from her bed with a glint in her eye.

"My heart is full," Felix whispered to me.

I couldn't look at him without crying. Most of the details of my wedding day were already taken care of. The Duchess had been hard at work managing all the affairs since this morning. The doctor had prescribed Mrs. Byerly a strong dose of laudanum for her to gather her strength to make it to the East Garden where the wedding would take place.

The guest list was short with only the Duke, Duchess, Olive and the mother of the groom attending. The lilies were in full bloom now so the backdrop of the wedding would be alive with floral delights. It would be a lovely little ceremony. When Mrs. Byerly was satisfied that I approved of the wedding preparations, I went back to my room and burst into tears.

The tears came so easily because I knew in my heart of hearts that I couldn't marry Felix. There was no way I could marry him without revealing to him the secret that I'd been carrying around since we'd arrived back in England. I was pregnant.

My body had known for several weeks, but my mind refused to consider it a possibility. I had ignored all the symptoms. My tiredness and food aversions, I assumed, were all related to traveling ailments. My courses were never like clockwork so when I missed them for two months, I thought it was simply the stress of travel and departing from my loved ones forever.

The moment of realization came after we returned to Chaffinch Fields. The Duke had acquired a new horse called *Arabian Gemstone* while we were on our holiday, and when Olive brought out the new horse for one of our morning rides, she just called it "Gem."

Hearing Harvey's pet name for me took my mind back to the evening I spent with him at the fishing hole where the thought of losing him was so overwhelming that I threw myself into his arms, and I begged him not to stop. Gasping out loud immediately, I startled Olive and the horse slightly. I feigned a sudden headache and returned to my room where I knew that all signs pointed to pregnancy.

Felix was a good man, but there was only so much he would be able to handle. He'd no doubt bow out of the engagement gracefully heading back to his uncle feeling nothing but relief at having dodged a bullet. However, there was a small part of me that prayed he'd accept me and my baby as his own as he did seem to really love me. Would he be able to overcome raising another man's baby?

This whole proposal and wedding was thrust on me in Mrs. Byerly's sick room. It was so unexpected that I couldn't refuse, but I also didn't want to blurt out that I was pregnant either. Felix and I getting married was a dying woman's last wish. How could I disappoint her like that?

My belly hadn't started to grow obvious quite yet. The worst part of me thought of marrying Felix and trying to convince him that the baby came early. Many, many months early. How would I explain to the tall, dark and handsome Felix that his offspring came out with pale skin and white blonde hair? I would always know that our marriage was built on a lie even if I managed to convince him that the baby was his.

That wasn't the kind of life I wanted to build. Felix deserved honesty.

As if she sensed that I needed her, Olive knocked on my door. She was such a welcome sight that I paused my weeping for a moment to nod to her. Surmising that they were not happy tears, she rushed to my side.

"Hazel, love! Is everything alright? The Duchess just informed me that you and Felix were getting married. I came to congratulate you."

The whole story came pouring out of me. My relationship with Harvey, the night we went down to the fishing hole, and how I realized that I was pregnant.

Olive was so worldly that little about my story shocked her, but she was quite grieved to find me in such an impossible situation. She asked if Felix declined to marry me, would Harvey take me back, and I told her that it was out of the question.

"Did you not love him?" she asked, raising an eyebrow at me, "or perhaps, he was lacking in another way."

"I did love him, and he was more than adequate. He's married to someone else now."

She looked at me suspiciously, "Harvey was so in love with you that he begged you to stay to be his wife, and then ran out and married another woman? It sounds like you weren't all that in love."

My cheeks flushed with offense. I had been in love with Harvey once, and even though those feelings were long gone, her words made what I had felt seem small and meaningless. That love had been real, and it had grown into something deeper and truer with Ruby.

"What cheek!" I said furiously to Olive realizing her language had rubbed off on me a bit.

"Did he marry this other woman to spite you, or did he see her on the side?"

I flamed with anger. Harvey would have never seen girls behind my back, and I told her that I resented the insinuation. She apologized immediately, but something didn't add up for her.

She looked at me with completely genuine concern, and I realized that if anyone in this world would believe me, it would be Olive Powlett. I took a deep breath to calm myself.

"I need to tell you something, and you must promise you won't have me sent to the insane asylum?"

This intrigued her. She raised an eyebrow and nodded.

I started with the rumors about the Gates of Hell and told her all the alleged stories of people from the past getting summoned by Satan. Mother's story of Eustacia Vye and her incantations fascinated her.

When I talked about the day that I prayed for guidance down at the Seven Arches asking for a sign as to whether to stay and marry Harvey or travel to England with Mrs. Byerly, her eyes widened. I described in vivid detail how I had spotted those three little hidden mushrooms, and the loose stone that I pushed back into place. She gasped when I told her the first words that Ruby ever said to me, "Are you from hell?"

She hung on my every word, and even if she didn't fully believe the story, she didn't think I was crazy.

"So there is a woman in this Milligan place married to Harvey and she looks just like you?"

It was hard for her to understand that it wasn't even a likeness, but we were the same person. I had somehow traveled out of my world into Ruby's. Olive couldn't understand how the two worlds were the same. She wanted to know who created it. Was there a separate God for each of the different worlds? Were there more than two worlds, or was it a back and forth situation? How was I certain that this wasn't hell, and it just looked like reality?

The questions she had were innumerable. Particularly, she wanted to know if the worlds were identical, how I came to leave my world, but Ruby stayed in hers. It was hard to explain that somehow Ruby didn't see the mushrooms, and we never really figured out why or how.

I had no answers for her because I had never really thought it through. Ruby and I saw it as the answer to our prayers, so we agreed—she would stay and marry Harvey, and I would come to Europe to begin a new life.

"If you're pregnant with Harvey's child, does that automatically mean that Ruby is pregnant with Harvey's child?"

That fact hadn't dawned on me. Would Ruby and I essentially give birth to the same baby? I didn't know, and I really didn't care. Not now. Not when everything else felt so fragile. Marrying Felix was all I wanted, and all I wished was for Felix to be the baby's father.

But the thought that Ruby and I would give birth to essentially the same child was unnerving. The world would have two Ruby Hazels, and in a few months, there would be their identical offspring.

I sighed as just the thought of it was overwhelming.

We discussed it much of the evening. Olive even had our supper sent up to my room so she could continue asking questions. My reading with Madame Leveau and *le chemin de l'esprit terrestre* brought a whole host of theories into her mind. She wanted to know who built the Seven Arches, why they built it, and what purpose did they hope it to serve. Had it truly been built as a bridge between these identical worlds?

These were all excellent questions, and ones that I had no answers to give. I gave so much credence to my traveling into Ruby's world as an answer to our prayers that no other scenario had dawned upon me.

Finally, I managed to steer her back to my dilemma with Felix. She agreed that I had to tell him about the pregnancy, and she would arrange for us to have a private conversation the morning before the wedding. I thanked her, but I had no idea how to tell him, especially after all he'd been through. Any day now, he was expecting to lose his mother, and it could be too much for him to handle.

Olive scoffed at this notion, "You don't want to marry someone that you have to babysit. Felix is a grown up, and he will be able to handle the news. I don't know what he will decide, but he'll have to handle it." She said it with such authority that I actually believed her.

"What if he doesn't choose me?" I said, Harvey's words echoing in my head.

"You'll stay here with me as long as you need, and if we become two spinsters raising a child together, that's what we're supposed to handle."

Relief instantly washed over me at her words. I'd been worried about the future from the moment that Felix proposed. If he rejected me after my news, I'd be destitute, but Olive had offered me a lifeline. It was hard to believe that I hadn't known her my entire life.

I told her that I didn't deserve a friend as wonderful as she was. She didn't say anything for a moment, and I feared she might walk out—but then she pulled me into her arms.

"Probably not, love." she said sarcastically as she left my room.

After a fitful night of sleep thinking about the conversation I would have to have with Felix tomorrow, my mind spun with dread and longing. Would he agree to marry me still for his mother's sake and divorce me immediately after she passed away? He could cancel the wedding altogether. It was completely possible that his mother would be gleeful that he avoided being saddled with another man's child.

Felix was a good man—the kind I'd never dared hope for—and I loved him. The question was, did he love me enough to accept this baby as his own even though it couldn't be his? I prayed he did.

Dressing before sunrise, I wanted to look the best I could to at least make the thought of leaving me a little more difficult. My dresses were all tighter, but they still fit even though I felt like they were cutting off my circulation. I only wanted to focus on Felix and what I was going to say to him.

There was a knock at the door that was so faint I had to convince myself that I didn't imagine it. There was no movement when I called for the person to come in. I moved to the door to open it myself and found myself face to face with Felix. The tears in his eyes told me that his mother hadn't made it through the night.

"Oh Felix," I said, opening my arms and letting him fall into them. I held him as tight as I could. Twice as hard as necessary, but I feared this would be the last time that I would be able to wrap my arms around him before he left me.

I kissed him hard on the lips, at first to offer comfort, but he responded as if he were in need of greater consolation. We kissed passionately, and my head felt light from his embrace. Before I knew it, he laid me down on the bed, and I willingly pulled him closer, fumbling with the buttons on his shirt.

He cupped my breasts, gently stroking them through my dress in a way that titillated my whole body. Instinctively, I let out a soft moan of pleasure which only encouraged him further. He relieved himself of his shirt entirely, and I admired his physique. He was not nearly as muscular as Harvey but leaner and more mature.

When he placed his hand between my legs, he felt my eagerness for him. I expected him to remove his trousers, but instead, he focused on me. When his tongue made contact with me underneath my dress, I put my own hands over my mouth to keep from screaming out. It was a sensation unlike any that I had experienced. He probed every part of me expertly until I writhed in pleasure, nearly locking my thighs around his head.

He removed the rest of my dress, and his own trousers next. I gazed at his manhood which stood fully ready to ravage me, and I was quite eager at the prospect. At first, he teased me by grinding over the quivering mound between my legs without entering me. At the same time, he massaged my nipples with his mouth, expertly towing the line between pain and pleasure.

He brought me up to a point where I couldn't take it anymore, and my whole body ached for a release. I boldly rolled over, holding onto his shoulders until I was on top of him. He smiled up at me as I kissed him before easing my body down onto his throbbing member. He rocked with pleasure as I moved slowly at first but increased the pace until I quickly exploded in orgasm on top of him.

Now, it was his turn to roll me back over, and there would be no more teasing. He rode me hard, and brought me to the brink of orgasm a second time when he asked if I minded if he finished inside as we weren't technically married yet.

I laughed, and I urged him to do what felt best to him. He kissed me and after a few more thrusts he let out a moan of pleasure and covered me with kisses once again as I recovered from my second climax from his touch.

"Dear Hazel, thank you," he said as he held his body tightly against mine, "I needed to feel loved after everything that transpired last night and these last few weeks. I would have felt utterly broken without you."

I told him the pleasure was all mine, and he let out a chuckle. We laid in bed together for several minutes just basking in the afterglow of our first time making love. It was so intense and so perfect. It was so unlike the fleeting minute that Harvey and I spent together out by the fishing hole. This had been the most erotic moment that I'd experienced in my entire life.

He recovered himself sufficiently to recount what had transpired the night before. Mrs. Byerly had coughed so much that she requested some of the laudanum to sleep. It hadn't helped, and she kept coughing herself awake.

Felix, utterly exhausted from nursing her, didn't stir. He wasn't sure exactly what happened. He supposed that she wanted more laudanum, but she didn't want to wake him.

She took the bottle off the nightstand and drank too much of it. He had only awoken an hour ago, and he found her to be cold to the touch. The laudanum bottle was more than half empty. She had been dead for several hours.

He broke down all over again, blaming himself for falling asleep. I wouldn't hear of such a thing. She was in pain which was why she took the laudanum in the first place. Instead of lingering in agony, she died at peace.

"She didn't get to see us married!" he said.

I shuddered, thinking it was possible that she wouldn't have seen us married if she had survived the night. I still needed to tell Felix about my pregnancy, but it would have to wait.

"Today, we grieve for your mother. The wedding was rushed for her, but let's not have the cloud of her death intertwined with the happiest day of our lives," I said, buying myself some time.

He thought about it for a moment, and he nodded his head. When his mother suggested that he propose so that she might see it, nothing felt so right to him. There was no reason to delay it more than a few days. We would marry at Chaffinch Fields, but first we would bury his mother.

"After the way you made love to me, the Duke and Duchess will need to post an armed guard outside your door if you make me wait too long to share your bed every night," he said, giving me a wink before he left the room.

The Duchess, Felix, Olive, and I spent the rest of the day in the parlor recalling stories of Mrs. Byerly. Felix had shared with me many stories of his mother as we got to know each other over these past few months, but the Duchess offered a new perspective. She had known how her cousin felt when she met Samuel Byerly, and they were like two magnets, hopelessly attracted to one another and with a single turn immediately repelled.

"They got into an argument within thirty seconds of marrying each other," the Duchess laughed.

"Sammy complimented the blue ribbon on her mother's dress, and Clarissa informed him that the color was cerulean. He didn't like being corrected, and soon they were nearly shouting at each other about what constituted the color blue! It was quite ridiculous, but the passion they worked each other into was unmistakable."

Felix quite enjoyed the story as his mother never talked about his father. All he knew he learned from his Uncle Enoch. His parents both were strong-willed with fiery tempers. He commented that it was probably a good thing that he ran away when he did, otherwise they would have murdered one another.

It felt good to share stories of Mrs. Byerly and celebrate her life. I was able to tell a few stories about her professional side. Everyone laughed when I shared how Mrs. Byerly had given a heart-felt speech to Miss Lowery urging her to retire, only to realize that the deaf old biddy hadn't heard a single word she had said.

The lingering cloud of death had darkened the halls of Chaffinch Fields ever since our return, and it was nice to laugh again. We celebrated the life of Mrs. Byerly well into the evening. The Duchess handled all the details of the burial so that Felix wasn't burdened about it.

Felix retired early as his exhaustion was catching up to him. I would have to tell him about the baby after we laid his mother to rest tomorrow, and I prayed that he loved me enough. I knew I tempted fate by giving myself to him earlier in the day, but I was glad I did as it could possibly be my only chance to be with him that way. As I was already pregnant, there was no risk of being ruined a second time.

It was hard to fathom that only a few months ago I didn't know Felix Byerly, and today I felt that my life would be empty without him. My mind thought about Harvey, and how I'd never quite felt that way about him. I loved him, but I was always more worried about his happiness than my own.

In the back of my mind, I always knew that I could bear it if Harvey left me, but I felt sick at the thought of hurting him.

With Felix, I wasn't so sure that I would be able to bear a separation.

We buried Mrs. Byerly in Chaffinch Fields the next day. In a way she got her wish that she would be able to retire at the glorious estate. There were only the Duke, Duchess, Olive, Felix, and myself present. Felix gave a heartfelt speech about his mother's love, the Duchess talked briefly about her dear cousin as a little girl, and the minister said goodbye.

Before they lowered the coffin into the ground, I took a moment to speak to Mrs. Byerly. I had so much that I wanted to tell her when she was alive that it seemed like my last chance.

"Mrs. Byerly, you changed my life by hiring me. Working for you will always be one of the highlights of my life, and I hope one day that I can tell my children all about the impact you had on me. Unfortunately, I'm not sure that there will be a wedding. I have some news to tell Felix that he may not like, and he may not want to marry me after it. I learned from you how to be forthright, honest, and never cower in speaking your mind. You have been my inspiration since that first interview when you demanded that I go by Hazel at the office instead of Ruby. I was put off by it at the time, but somehow, you knew what you were doing. Hazel fits me so much better. I better get back to the others, but I want you to know that I will miss you forever, and I love you."

Placing my hand on her coffin as I said those last words, it was as close as I'd ever be to her again. I wiped the tears that were pooling in my eyes, and in an instant, Felix was beside me to offer comfort.

Later that evening, we were strolling in the East Garden where our wedding was supposed to take place yesterday. All the lilies were in full bloom and honeysuckle perfumed the air as we walked arm in arm.

The previous night was the first that Felix had gotten a full night of rest, and it showed on his face. Under his eyes the gray circles had faded and his mustache was once again perfectly trimmed. He looked as handsome as the day we met on the train when his nose was buried in that newspaper.

"The Duchess has asked when we would like to formally be married. Tomorrow suits me perfectly, but I defer to my bride," he said, patting my arm which was linked in his.

There was a nearby bench flanked by flowering shrubs as a place for us to sit. I had to clear my conscience, and I had to let him go if he wished to be released from our engagement.

"Felix, I love you. I was engaged to a man before you, but you are the one who has shown me what it means to be in love. For that, I will be forever indebted to you."

He looked startled and grabbed my hands as if looking for some clue in my eyes.

"I need to tell you about the man that I was engaged to," I said, patting his arm back before beginning my story.

The whole love story that occurred between Harvey and me over the last decade unfolded. The way we had met as adolescents when I visited Aunt Nettie, and how we became reacquainted when my mother moved back to the little community where she grew up. He watched me carefully as I recounted the night before Harvey shipped out to fight in the Great War, and how I agreed to marry him when he returned. I described how Mrs. Byerly kept increasing my salary and promoting me so that I wouldn't quit working at the WCO, and then I told him about the last decision I had to make.

"I could either go on this trip and work for a year opening the London office, or I could stay home and marry Harvey. It was a gut-wrenching decision as I had put him off so many times. This time I couldn't ask him to wait for me so I set him free."

"That must have been difficult," he said, still clasping my hands and hanging on my every word.

Feeling a single tear well up on my cheek, I explained how I felt horrible for abandoning him, and I wanted to do anything to give him comfort so I gave myself to him that one evening by his fishing hole before I said goodbye to him forever.

I looked up into Felix's eyes, and I saw him with an expression of surprise, but it quickly softened. Those kind eyes looked back at me. He kissed me tenderly on the lips and held me in his arms.

"This all happened before we ever met. You loved him. I understand, and I am not angry," he said, "After what we experienced together yesterday, I wouldn't care if there were ten Harveys that were before me. I only care that I will be your last."

I was in disbelief. A lesser man would have become enraged. He would have cursed at me and called me vile names but not Felix. He was the man that I hoped he would be, and he did truly love me.

I jumped into his lap, elated that he didn't judge me or cast me aside from the choice that I had made.

"Oh, I love you so much, Felix."

"I'm no angel, Hazel. I've done plenty that I'm not proud of. I was married before, and Tabitha and I didn't wait until our wedding night either. And there have been others, but I'm a gentleman," he said, straightening his tie.

"I'm pregnant," I blurted out as if it were an afterthought.

He choked and coughed, and the kind expression on his face vanished in an instant. His kind eyes flared with anger and betrayal.

"You're what?"

"I'm pregnant, and I'm so sorry. I wish I could undo it, but I can't. I was hoping that you'd look at it with the same understanding."

"It is not the same thing at all! It is one thing to overlook an indiscretion you made before we'd even met, but it is something else entirely to give another man's child my name."

Foolishly, I thought he'd see the act of having sex with another man as a betrayal, and if he accepted that, he could accept the baby. I was disappointed to discover just how differently he saw it.

"Do you plan on telling the father?"

"No, of course not, he has married another woman since I left him. There would be no good that would come from him knowing."

He paced the garden while I sat on the bench, and I felt like he was slipping away from me.

"I lost my Tabitha in childbirth. I'm not sure that I can go through that again especially for another man's child," he said and left the garden.

As the sun went down, I cried alone on the bench. I cried as much for the pain that I caused him as I did from the relief of having finished the most difficult conversation of my life. The chill in the air and the sound of the crickets were my first reminders that I should retire to bed. Crying myself to sleep that night, I tried to keep a small sliver of hope alive.

I dreamed that night that I was kidnapped by Harvey, and instead of taking me back to Milligan, he locked me in a labyrinth with a dragon to guard me. The dragon was sleeping, and I heard Felix calling my name. I wanted to call out to him, but I was afraid. My heart leapt with joy when I saw Felix's shadow come around the corner, but the dragon suddenly awoke. He snatched me round the waist and pulled me deeper into the labyrinth, but Felix once again got closer. This time I called out to him, and the dragon turned into Harvey. He snickered at me, and I looked down and saw my belly swollen as if I was going to give birth at any time. I listened for Felix, but he was silent.

I awoke in a cold sweat. Getting back to sleep seemed all but impossible. I stared out the window from my bed and watched the sunrise. Somehow, I must've fallen back asleep because the next thing I knew the room was bright as if it were midday.

There was a knock at my door, and I thought immediately it was Felix coming to take me to the altar.

"Do come in!" I said as I tossed the covers aside to throw myself into his arms.

Olive entered the room looking rather gloomy. I was groggy from sleep and confused as to what she could possibly want from me.

"Where's Felix?"

She took a deep breath and said that he had a car take him to Portsmouth to journey back to America. A piece of paper that had my name written upon it transferred from her hand to mine. With dread, I unfolded it to read the words, "I'm sorry. I can't do it."

I dropped the note and collapsed back onto the bed.

"That fucking bastard," Olive said picking up the note and reading it as she sat beside me. She gave me comfort while I wailed away my heartache.

From Across the Pond, St. Louis 1915

Dearest Dora,

I trust this letter finds you well amidst the tumult of these trying times. It seems the world has been engulfed in a tempest of conflict, and I cannot help but think of you and your family across the channel. The reports of the Great War have reached even our humble abode here in St. Louis, and I find myself yearning for news from England, desperate to know how you fare amidst the chaos.

My dearest cousin, are you safe? Is your family sheltered from the ravages of war nestled safely in your glorious estate of Chaffinch Fields? I cannot imagine the hardships you must endure, the constant shadow of uncertainty that must loom over your daily lives. Please, reassure me of your well-being, and know that you are in my thoughts and prayers every day.

Regrettably, I must convey news of a disheartening nature, which weighs heavily upon my conscience. Our cherished Felix, whom I have watched burgeon from adolescence into a commendable young gentleman, has chosen to espouse the daughter of one of his academic mentors.

If it hadn't been for this infernal war, I know that we'd have already introduced our children to one another, and perhaps, together we'd be planning a grander wedding at Chaffinch Fields. Alas, the fruition of our longstanding aspirations for Felix and Olive's union has been thwarted by circumstances unforeseen.

Felix, that paragon of my hopes and aspirations, has taken it upon himself to entangle his fate with that of Miss Tabitha Chalmers, a creature whom I previously regarded as nothing more than a footnote in his social calendar. The revelation of their burgeoning romance has left me reeling, for I had harbored no inkling that such an inconsequential figure could captivate his affections.

Miss Chalmers, with her unassuming demeanor and bespectacled face, strikes me as the epitome of mediocrity, hardly a worthy contender for the esteemed position of Felix's betrothed. Though I begrudgingly concede her status as a respectable young lady, she pales in comparison to the luminous radiance of your beloved Olive.

In light of this news and the recent tragic sinking of the Luisitania, I regret to inform you that I must cancel my planned visit to Chaffinch Fields for Christmas. I am truly devastated as memories of our childhood Christmases together are amongst the fondest of all my memories. Recalling how we vexed your parents when we bested them at The Minister's Cat still brings a smile to my face. I miss the Venable Family Christmases of yesteryear, and I delight in your letters recalling how you, Olive, and the Duke keep up the tradition.

How is England holding up under the weight of such a monumental conflict? I can only imagine the sacrifices being made, the courage displayed by your countrymen in the face of adversity. It pains me to think of the toll this war must be taking on your beloved homeland, but I find solace in the resilience of the English spirit, knowing that you will endure whatever trials may come your way.

And what of the Duke? Will he be called upon to serve his country on the warfront? I shudder to think of the dangers he may face, but I know that he will rise to the occasion with the same bravery and honor that has always defined your descriptions of him. Please, convey to him my deepest respect and admiration, and assure him that he remains in my thoughts as well.

There seems little point now in hurrying to introduce Felix and Olive, as their paths have diverged, but the moment this infernal war has ended, with or without my son, I will be on the next steamer to see you again. In the meantime, I shall continue my work with the Women's Charity Organization, striving to make a difference in the lives of women in need.

Please know that despite this disappointment in Felix's matrimonial choice, my fondness for you and the memories we share remain steadfast. As the war rages on, know that you are not alone. Though we may be separated by distance, our hearts are united in solidarity and love. Please, write to me soon and ease my troubled mind with news of your safety and well-being.

With warm regards,
Clarissa

Chapter 11

Felix

I kept telling myself I'd made the right decision, though I wasn't sure who I was trying to convince—myself or her. Leaving Chaffinch Fields in such a rush to protect myself, I didn't even properly explain to her why I couldn't stay. The guilt was almost as crushing as the loneliness. From the deck, the Atlantic stretched endlessly—a hollow, gray expanse that mirrored exactly how I felt inside.

I was an orphan now and the last vestige of family I had was dear Uncle Enoch. He had aged quite rapidly in the last few years. My mother's decline had consumed my attention so I hadn't taken proper stock of his fragility, but I had to prepare myself for the fact that one day soon I would have no one else in this world.

The trip across the Atlantic a few months ago was filled with excitement and anticipation. As I was traveling to see Europe with my mother who seemed to be more healthy and robust since that illness plagued her last year, I dared to harbor hopes that she would live another thirty or forty years.

There was this fascinating woman, who I met on the train to St. Louis, and by some divine intervention, she turned out to be my mother's employee who would be traveling with us. She had plucked my long dormant heartstrings in such a short time that I was excited to get to know her better.

Loving Hazel had felt impossible—and then inevitable. I hadn't meant to, but there she was, dragging light into a heart I'd left shuttered. And now, I was right back where I'd promised myself I'd never return. I mourned Tabitha for years and years, refusing to even entertain the possibility of getting married again, but Hazel Sutton changed all that for me in a matter of months. Even when she was being spiteful and ignoring me, I was more and more smitten with her, but it could never be.

This trip back home had my heart feeling more vaulted than after Tabitha died. Happiness didn't feel like a possibility for me anymore. There was so much taken from me in this life so far that I wouldn't let myself fall in love again. It would only end in death or disappointment.

"I'm pregnant."

Her words still rang in my ears like a hammer smashing all my dreams for happiness. If Mother had lived and Hazel said those words to me that morning before our wedding, I was not certain what I would have done. It would have grieved Mother to have the wedding called off, and I wanted her last days to be happy ones. Fleeing from Chaffinch Fields like a thief in the night wouldn't have been possible if Mother were still alive.

Perhaps, Mother died in order to save me from that hasty marriage to a pregnant woman. I had to experience the pain of losing my mother to save me from the possibility of another loss that I was altogether too familiar with.

It was almost hard to believe that my mother was really gone, and I couldn't pick up the telephone to hear her voice ever again. Even when I had to call her to tell her that Tabitha and the baby died, she was comforting to me.

The darkest hours I'd experienced in my entire life still occupied my thoughts all too often. My spine tingled and my heart ached whenever a memory of that day plagued my mind. A single drop of blood could whisk me back to that room. It was everywhere. The mattress was soaked and my hands and arms were stained so badly it took me days to scrub the stains off my skin. The last bit of life that had existed within Tabitha colored the water in my wash tub a faint pink color.

Images of the blood still reared its ugly head in my nightmares sometimes. I would hear Tabitha screaming and couldn't get through the door to her. The blood seeped underneath, and her shrieks of pain grew louder and louder, while my fingers, bloodied with splinters, clawed at the door unable to get to her.

Blood flowed from under the door and increased to a gush, running out under my feet at a furious pace. Unable to find my balance, I slipped and fell as red stained everything I was wearing. Using the doorknob to keep from falling, I was slipping all over the floor. Tabitha continued to call out to me, and I heard the agony in her voice which faded as the life faded from her body. Finally, the door burst open of its own volition, and there was this pale blue light before me so bright that I could see nothing else. Tears fell down my cheeks as I awoke.

The dream was awful, but somehow the reality of that day was so much worse.

It was early in the morning when she went into labor. I had been overly excited, unable to find an outlet for my nervous energy. A picture of contentment, she had read all about labor, especially first babies.

She had been so methodical and thorough to the point where she felt no tension at the arrival of our child. The midwife had offered her advice on how to prepare for the birth. Relaxation was the key to a happy and healthy delivery, and Tabitha laid in bed reading as if the contractions were little more than a tickle in her belly. It promised to be an uneventful delivery, except it wasn't.

The labor was so slow. For more than forty hours she was confined to the bedroom. The midwife wouldn't allow me to even see her or offer support. There was only so much I could do to occupy my time. Games of backgammon with Uncle Enoch lost any appeal after the first few hours.

The waiting was endless, but I remembered Tabitha's calm demeanor when she first went into labor. She laid on our bed with her book in one hand and the other hand lovingly stroking her belly. This image calmed me, but then came her screams. They were so much worse than the waiting.

I walked around the block several times. Waveland, the town Uncle Enoch had called home my entire life, was a beautiful place, but tipping my hat to the few people I met on my walk made me even more agitated. I felt like there should be more that I could do for my wife. It seemed unnatural to do nothing for her when she was in so much pain.

Pounding on the door for news of her progress, I annoyed the midwife, but I didn't care. Uncle Enoch tried to give me brandy to calm me. Many women were going to hospitals now, and I frantically decided that I could drive her just to make sure she was in good hands. My uncle assured me that women had been giving birth for many, many years. The midwife in Waveland had delivered more than eighty healthy babies, and from the sounds of the screams, it was far too late to leave for the nearest hospital.

It drove me crazy. I moved the rocking chair outside our bedroom door to wait for news. I heard the moment she started to push, and I steeled myself that soon my child would be arriving into the world. Earning the moniker "dad," I would wear it proudly.

"All right, Tabitha! You're almost done. Give me one more big push," the midwife said through the door. I smiled, knowing that all this agony was almost over, and our child would be crying and ready to be soothed by his mother.

The cry never came. I waited and waited for the cry to come, but it didn't. The sound of slapping was all I heard. It was soft at first, but it got progressively louder until I heard the midwife shriek.

My heart sank as I knew there was something wrong with the baby. I pounded on the door, and privacy be damned, I stormed in. The midwife was smacking the baby over and over again on his backside. He was blue and hadn't drawn a single breath. To my horror, the limp object didn't respond to the slaps. It was a stillbirth.

I stood at the door in utter disbelief. The vision of that blue child destroyed the hopes I had quietly nursed these past few months. Uncle Enoch had asked about starting a trust fund for him, and Mother sent weekly gifts for her grandchild. They would both be beyond devastated. My clouded brain tried to process what had happened when I saw that lifeless child.

The oddest thought struck me as I took him in my arms. The color of blue that tinged my boy's skin was so lovely even though it represented the end of him. It was a color that I would dream about for the rest of my life.

Laying the little boy in Tabitha's arms, we wept together as a family. She said that he looked just like me, and I kissed the little mop of curls that he had inherited from her. We wept for a long time while we said goodbye to him.

When she suddenly went to sleep with our lifeless child in her arms, I thought that the act of giving birth had exhausted her. Savoring the only moment I would ever hold my wife and child together, I wished it had all been different.

I kissed her on the forehead to give her a moment to rest when I heard what sounded like dripping water. The basin and the water cups were undisturbed. The sound seemed to be growing louder which was perplexing. Out of options for where to look, I got on my hands and knees where I saw the blood dripping from the stained crimson sheets of Tabitha's bed. I tore the sheets away, and the room exploded in red—more than I thought a body could hold.

She hadn't fallen asleep. While we said our goodbyes to the child we would never raise, life had quietly slipped from her too. Screaming in utter agony, I begged her to stay with me as the midwife rushed back into the room.

Stirring barely, she said dreamily, 'I'm sorry I'm dying too,' before slipping away forever. I fell to my knees, lost in a grief so vast I could hardly breathe. How was it possible to lose my wife and child within an hour of each other?

Begging her to wake up, the blood smeared on my hands and arms. With violence, I shook her to revive, and I pleaded with her not to leave me. The light had already gone out of her. My bloody arms wrapped around her lifeless frame, and I wept. I couldn't believe how quickly it had all happened. It felt as if my light had burnt out as well.

Time eventually passed that day, but it was irrelevant to me. Uncle Enoch pried me away from the embrace of my dead wife and child. There was a washtub ready, and I scrubbed and scrubbed myself raw before I fell into the bed. Vaguely recalling the sun rising and falling during various points of wakefulness, I didn't leave the confines of my room. Everything in the outside world was too painful to think about. When I slept, I could pretend that Tabitha was reading in the next room.

I couldn't imagine going through that again. How could I? No. That memory—the unbearable silence, the blood, the look on her face—was why I'd written the note. "I'm sorry. I can't do it." I meant it. Leaving Chaffinch Fields for Portsmouth, I climbed aboard the first boat headed to America.

Running was the only instinct left to me. If I stayed, I'd shatter. Uncle Enoch and I would continue as we had since Tabitha died, and I would pretend that Hazel Sutton didn't exist because I'd be damned if I could go through that again. My mother's death was still so fresh, and I refused to lose another wife and child a few months later. My soul could barely handle that one time. If I had to go through that again, I'd die with them.

The child Hazel was carrying wasn't even mine, and it bothered me only a bit. I wish I would have told her that before I left. There was no way for me to prepare myself for her giving birth in only a few short months. The blood would be everywhere, and I would throw myself off a building, leaving Uncle Enoch all alone.

I pictured blood in my wine glass instead of a port as I swirled it around and around—circling like a whirlpool drowning my wife and son and leaving me to bear it all alone yet again.

Eating my lunch in the dining room late to avoid a crowd, I didn't wish to meet any new acquaintances on the journey back home. I only wanted to get to Uncle Enoch's house to mourn my mother and put this whole unsavory mess behind me.

There was a hole being burned in the back of my neck while I stared at the food on my plate. When I turned around, I saw two young ladies staring at me, giggling like a pair of schoolgirls. I turned back to my port quickly, but it was much too late. The color was rising in my cheeks as they beckoned me to join them. I was almost always resistant to meeting new people when I was alone, especially the type with too much money and too little sense.

I couldn't stop the color from rising in my cheeks as I introduced myself to them. "Good afternoon, ladies. I'm Felix Byerly. May I be of some assistance to you?"

They had traveled to England with their mother for the social season and found it to be a complete and utter waste of time. American men, they said, were much more to their taste. They were attempting to flirt with me, and I was more annoyed than flattered at the prospect. One was so vapid in her interests that I forgot her name the moment she mentioned it, and the other had such a squeaky voice that I hardly understood a word she said.

"English men are so reserved. You never know if they have any regard for you, or if they're simply being polite," the vapid one explained as if I had any interest in the subject.

I attempted to extricate myself from their conversation, but they were insistent that I amuse them while they lingered over their lunch. Their mother had a case of seasickness, and they had no one to entertain them.

My stupid sense of honor, instilled by my mother, prevented me from telling them that I was in no mood to join their conversation, but I did my best to make myself seem like a completely unsuitable dinner companion.

"I assure you that Indiana rich is New York poor, ladies, and I'm a widower who has experienced loss much too recently to be good company for anyone."

They peppered me with questions—where I'd stayed, who I'd met, what parties I'd attended—utterly unmoved by my disinterest. I made the mistake of telling them that my distant cousin was the daughter of the 5th Duke of Cleveland, and they were immediately fascinated by me.

"Whyever didn't you marry her?" one asked after I had half-heartedly relayed my mother's hare-brained scheme to wed me to Miss Powlett.

"She didn't love me, and I didn't love her. We were better suited as friends."

Both the girls laughed at the notion of love. They could get all the romance they needed out of a Jane Austen novel, but that wouldn't dress them in furs or adorn them with jewels.

"I suppose that my notion of love makes me more middle class than my uncle's modest fortune."

"Are you saying you'd marry a poor girl, say a lady's maid, if you had romantic feelings for her?" squeaked the sister with the irritating voice.

I nodded. My own parents had married because they had an overwhelming passion for one another, but it fizzled soon after, leaving only hatred in its place. I didn't think they ever actually loved one another, and it was quite possible neither of them ever experienced what it was to be utterly devoted to someone else.

Tabitha and I had love, and I begrudgingly thought I'd found it with Hazel as well. I'd never settle for anything less in a wife. Love transcended any sort of social class in my opinion. I'd rather break my back in a field and come home to a woman I loved than spend one day in luxury with someone I couldn't stand.

They both found this notion to be ridiculous, and I both hated and felt sorry for them. Neither one of them could have ever been in love or they wouldn't be so flippant about it. I sighed and thought of Hazel's baby. It belonged to another man, and we had never even talked about children. As I never expected to fall in love again, I had resigned myself to not having children. Hazel probably wanted children. I never asked. I was too consumed with wanting her to even think about the future.

I bid the silly girls a good day, and I wandered the ship, recalling how heavily losing my wife had affected me.

The weeks after Tabitha's death were difficult. Mother demanded that I travel with her back to St. Louis after the funeral for an extended stay to heal away from the constant reminders of my wife and lost child, but I didn't want to go. Uncle Enoch's house was the last place I had hope for the future, and that meant something to me. At the time, I thought that I owed Tabitha and the baby daily visits.

We had buried them together, and I visited their grave often at Maple Ridge Cemetery. It bothered me that we never named the boy. We had discussed naming him after Uncle Enoch, but Tabitha had wanted to wait to see if the name suited his face. Their headstone said, "Tabitha and Baby Boy Byerly."

The first few times that I visited, I called him "boy," but it didn't feel right to call my son just "boy" as he could very well be the only child I'd ever have. I asked Tabitha what she thought he looked like in heaven. A fit of tears overcame me, and I dug into my pocket for a handkerchief.

When I looked up, there was a blue jay perched on the headstone. The bird's feathers reminded me of the boy's color when I saw him. It felt like Tabitha had sent me a sign that I should name the boy at least for my sake. From that point on, I started referring to him as Jay whenever I visited.

I grieved for months in seclusion, supping with Uncle Enoch every day, otherwise, not seeing anyone. While I mourned, I had taken a step back from Uncle's business dealings. Mother continued to harangue me for a visit, but I put her off, opting for an extended Christmas holiday with her instead. My uncle eventually beckoned me back to business as he was getting closer and closer to the age when he wanted to retire.

My daily visits to the cemetery gradually became weekly visits, and I felt that Tabitha and Jay were telling me that I still had more life to lead. I simply had to figure out what that meant. As I had no desire for any romantic entanglements, I threw myself into Uncle Enoch's investments, and the people he was cultivating to run them.

Mr. Lucas was an ambitious young fellow chosen by my uncle to run the Waveland Telephone Company in which he was a majority shareholder. Lucas was a graduate of Wabash College, which immediately raised his esteem in my uncle's eyes, and he had recently married.

We were the first guests of the married couple, and it was my first social call as a widower instead of a married man. I agreed to go because I understood how much my uncle esteemed Mr. Lucas, and he wanted his new wife to feel at home in the town of Waveland. It was my fervent hope that I could endure the call without being overcome with emotion.

Mrs. Lucas was a short, wiry woman who looked as if she was made mostly of sinew and muscle underneath her homespun house dress. She had grown up on a farm not far from our little town, and it was immediately obvious that she all but dominated her new husband. I could tell that Uncle Enoch did not take a liking to her the third time she scolded Mr. Lucas for his poor table manners.

Lucas seemed to run his marriage like his business relationships as he was ingratiating and worked his utmost to keep the other person happy even at the cost of her personal dignity. Mrs. Lucas was quite a loquacious woman. She had heard about the loss I had suffered recently. As her mother had lost two sons growing up, she understood how terrible the grief could be.

The questions she peppered me about Tabitha were invasive, and I tried my best to change the subject. Reliving the death of my wife and child during my first social visit was to say the least not enjoyable. Uncomfortably, I answered her questions, but Uncle Enoch finally cut her off. Realizing that she'd been too forward, she apologized.

The rest of the evening she stayed silent, making sure we had our dessert and coffee while Lucas and my uncle talked about the future of the phone company. My mind wandered from their conversation while I watched Mrs. Lucas flitting around their little home cleaning up. I hadn't been around a woman with the exception of our elderly housekeeper in the months since Tabitha died. I liked to watch her work, and she whistled a little tune, "Rock of Ages" I believe, not thinking that anyone was listening to her.

When she saw that I was staring at her, we both colored. I could feel the pink in my ears rise. She wasn't a particularly handsome woman, but she did stir small feelings of lust inside me that hadn't crept out since I'd lost Tabitha. Ashamed at what I was feeling, I listened to Uncle Enoch and Lucas talk about expansion of lines until it was time to go home.

The next day Uncle Enoch traveled out of town for a few days to visit his friend Mr. Clyde, an old business contact from his Muncie years. Mr. Clyde had been my uncle's closest friend ever since I could remember, and they traveled to see each other frequently. I visited Tabitha and Jay for a few hours that morning, and upon my return, I saw Mrs. Lucas with a basket in her hand. She had made biscuits to apologize for her behavior and inappropriate questions from the previous night.

I thanked her for her kindness, and even though I knew better, I invited her inside for a cup of tea. When I got the kettle started, she explained that her husband had been mortified at her curiosity involving my wife, and she wanted me to know that she sincerely meant no harm. The habit of occasionally sticking her foot in her mouth was a family trait. Her mother didn't believe in tact and always said whatever was on her mind, no matter the level of discomfort it caused.

I readily forgave her, feeling awkward at how I had eyed her lasciviously after dinner, and told her that talking about Tabitha and my son would never be easy. It was a part of who I was, and I had to get used to it.

"It's so beautiful that you were so devoted to her," she said, touching my hand tenderly.

My pulse raced slightly at her touch, and I could tell by the look on her face that she was being overly friendly to serve a purpose which was not at all chaste.

"Thank you," I said, slowly attempting to pull my hand from her grip but being unsuccessful.

"I suppose the nights are the hardest for you," she said looking up at me with her doe eyes and her hands still clasping mine. "I saw how you were looking at me."

I coughed and sputtered, but I couldn't deny it. Apologizing to her over and over again, I hoped she knew that I meant no disrespect. Since my wife died, I hadn't even seen a woman in many, many months. Hoping she hadn't read too much into it, I begged her pardon.

"If I hadn't read anything into it, I wouldn't be here in the first place," she said smiling.

My eyes must've doubled in size when I looked at her. She explained that Gerald Lucas was a fine man and an excellent choice for a husband, but there was no love between them, not yet at least. Her mother had arranged the whole thing as she would not have a spinster for a daughter. Her two older sisters were married years ago and had seven children between them.

I was quite sorry to hear that she was in an unhappy marriage, but surely, she'd have to work that out for herself.

Apparently, I misunderstood her as Gerald Lucas was a wonderful husband, and she was perfectly happy with him in almost every way. There was one small department where he lacked, and she thought the way I had looked at her the night before that I could help her.

Sputtering for a moment at her audacity, I saw how amused she was by my awkwardness. She didn't want my heart by any means, only my body. Since I was a widower, she felt that I wouldn't fall in love with her either.

She planted a kiss on me, and I pushed her away. I couldn't imagine what she was doing. Bursting into tears, she accused me of leading her on. While her behavior flabbergasted me, my chivalrous instincts were to comfort her. The kiss reminded me how much I longed for the feel of a woman in my bed, and even though she was nothing like Tabitha, my body betrayed me in wanting her.

"I don't want to divorce Gerald as I care about him, but I am only occasionally overcome with an itch that he is unable to scratch." she said, the tears seemed to have magically faded away.

The impertinence! I couldn't believe that it was filling me with lust. She kissed me again, and this time I didn't push her away. My body needed the release, and she was offering me an outlet with no hope of a romantic entanglement. Deep down I knew it was wrong, but I didn't care.

We had sex over and over again that morning, and I needed to put my hand over her mouth several times to stop her from screaming out. She was insatiable, and I had never been with a woman quite like her. Her nails would dig into my flesh until I pushed her to the edge of pleasure. It was electric, but there was no love in it. It was animal, nothing like the reverence I'd felt with Tabitha — so different, in fact, that guilt never found me.

Meeting several times a week, we could not get enough of one another. If Uncle Enoch was out, it would be at my house. If not, we'd have sex in her marital bed. It felt dirty, and I was ashamed. She had some power over me which I hated. The urge to pleasure her was more than my own need.

Months went by, and the excitement of it all began to fade. We met less frequently, and when we did meet, it wasn't the same as it had been. At our last meeting, she announced that she was pregnant. She never meant to be so careless, and it made her feel overcome with guilt.

"The baby could be his," she said, as if the possibility was so slim that she had to convince herself of it.

I nodded, and I told her that I would be leaving for St. Louis soon to stay with my mother for several months. We agreed to part ways forever but on friendly terms. In a lot of ways, we had helped each other. She helped me remember that I was still a man with urges, and the guilt over our affair made her realize how much she had grown to love her husband. While I regretted the cuckolding of Gerald Lucas, I did not regret my time with her.

We didn't speak again for more than five years. Waveland being a small town had us seeing each other occasionally from a distance. Curtly nodding in acknowledgment of one other if we crossed paths, we never exchanged words. Mr. Lucas always sent his wife's warmest regards when he came over to the house to talk business with my uncle. I occasionally felt a tinge of embarrassment at the mention of Mrs. Lucas, but by and large, I forgot about her.

I was buying a newspaper for my train ride to St. Louis to escort my mother to New York then onward to England when I collided with Mrs. Lucas and her children for the first time since our affair ended. Her five-year-old son, running ahead of her and his baby sister, collided with my leg as I rounded the street corner.

"Sorry, Mister," the little voice said and when he locked eyes with me, I gasped in shock. Mother had a portrait taken of us when I was five years old. She sat in her best dress with a garish hat full of ostrich plumes. I stood to her right in my short pants and black bow tie, my thick brown hair tamed with petroleum jelly. This boy before me was identical to the boy in the portrait.

Astonished, my fingers twitched involuntarily, longing to touch his face. Mrs. Lucas boxed her son's ears for running away from her, and she nervously glanced towards me, unsure whether enough time had passed for us to consider speaking. The boy wailed, and I bent down to get another look at him.

"What's your name, little fellow?" I asked him.

"I'm Jerry Lucas, just like my daddy!" he said, a smile forming on his lips, erasing his tears.

The boy's mother could see my struggles. Jerry looked exactly as my Jay might have, had he lived. Grief washed over me. I wanted to pick up the boy and squeeze him tightly as if he could somehow bring Jay to life for me.

"Jerry, we need to go. We had a lot to get done if we're going to visit Grandma, Grandpa, and Uncle Harvey this evening," she said.

She urged him forward, but I instinctively grasped her arm. Our eyes met, and whatever softness had once existed between us hardened into annoyance. I silently pleaded for acknowledgement, but she refused to yield. It vexed me, but I wouldn't press the issue.

"Good day, Mr. Byerly," she said, peeling my hand off her arm and continuing on her way.

"Penelope," I nodded, letting her go with her little family.

As I watched them continue down the street, it occurred to me how unfair life could be. My little Jay was wanted so terribly and prayed over by his mother and father. He died before he even entered this world, and Little Jerry Lucas' mother must've spent countless nights in prayer hoping that her son would resemble her husband in some small way. Neither one of our prayers were answered.

A few hours later I was on the train headed toward St. Louis. I had purchased the newspaper because of the investment advice I had given my uncle, but I was still agitated thinking about that boy. My boy would never know I was his father—named instead for Gerald Lucas. It felt like my family had been stolen from me.

Agitated, I flipped rapidly through the newspaper until she caught my eye: Hazel Sutton.

My mind immediately left behind the image of little Jerry Lucas and focused on any way to overcome my shyness and speak to her.

I found myself smiling at the memory of first seeing Hazel, and I snapped back to reality back on board the boat. I managed to successfully avoid the girls that plagued me for the last few days of the journey. It meant spending a lot of lonely hours in my berth reading novels, but it was a small price to pay to avoid those insufferably vapid gold diggers.

I couldn't help but think about Gerald Lucas raising my son, believing he was his own blood. Would I have been able to do that with Hazel's child if I hadn't known? But I did know. Every time I looked at the child, I would search for signs of his father. The man that Hazel had loved before me. I knew that she chose to leave him for a life in Europe rather than marry him, and I knew she wanted to marry me. She did love me. So why did everything have to be so damn complicated?

Loving Tabitha was so much easier. She was two years older than me, and the daughter of my business professor at Saint Louis University. Uncle Enoch and my mother had butted heads over where I would attend school. Uncle Enoch thought I should go to Wabash like my father had, but my mother was completely opposed to the idea. When Uncle Enoch reminded her of the agreement to send me to live with him when I was grown, Mother countered that she had been in charge of my education, and she saw this as including college. Keeping me in St Louis while I attended college meant she would release me to live with Uncle Enoch after I graduated.

"Of course, I'll want to take him on a holiday to England to visit my dear cousin Dora and her daughter before he makes the move to that little wilderness you call home," my mother had said, already trying to hatch her plan of marrying me to Olive.

Professor Chalmers often entertained students over at his house to discuss economic theories and even occasionally novels. On the evenings when novels were discussed, his daughter Tabitha was always present to join in the conversation.

She wasn't classically beautiful as she had a rather flat nose and wore her hair up in a tight bun. The little round spectacles that she wore made her seem a decade older than she actually was. If someone had taken the image of a school marm out of my brain and made a person, it would have been Tabitha Chalmers. I think the fact that she was rather plain made it easier for me to talk to her.

Tabitha loved books, and she had strong opinions on characters as she looked beneath the surface to find some fascinating criticisms of novels that were usually lauded. She called the ending of Great Expectations, where Pip and Estella met at the ruins of Miss Havisham's house, "pure romantic drivel." Dickens' original ending to the book, she believed to ring much more true. Estella had been trained to be an utter shrew to all men from a very early age.

The idea that love could undo all that, she felt, was complete nonsense. A foppish little fellow named Hollis Grimsby spoke out of turn and she put him in his place when he intimated that women were swayed by emotion not logic.

"Ah and we all know that you're the expert when it comes to women, Mr. Grimsby," she said, raising an eyebrow and causing him to go red in the face.

She often got worked up making her point no matter what novel we were discussing, and there was a hint of redness that rose in her cheeks which I found to be beguiling. Soon she had me reading the classics to have excuses to argue with her. As the youngest daughter of my professor, she was the last one he had at home. He and his wife never expected Tabitha to get married as they thought she'd live with them forever as an old maid.

So naturally, they were gratified when I started visiting under no other pretense than to see her. She called herself "Mommy and daddy's little spinster" which horrified them to no end. I loved her wit, and she taught me how to use dark humor to both disarm and delight people in conversation.

We traded playful barbs and light insults with each other, and it was obvious to me that I wanted to marry her when we read Wuthering Heights together. The passion that Heathcliff and Cathy shared had me extolling their virtues, but she put a stop to my line of thinking immediately. "They're assholes, Felix. Those two make everyone they come in contact with miserable."

I proposed to her on the spot, and she accepted. A few days later we made love for the first time while her parents were on an overnight trip to Columbia to visit her sister. That night while I held her in my arms, she cried.

Because she never thought she would get married, she had told herself that she never wanted to be a wife. Although she loved her father, he still ruled her mother. It bothered her to imagine spending her whole life in a man's shadow. But with me, it was different. I made her feel complete, but she insisted that she had always been a whole person without me. Somehow, I managed to complement her perfectly in a way she never expected. She hoped that I felt a little for her as to what she felt for me.

"Actually, I just wanted to see what you looked like with your glasses off," I said, making her roar with laughter.

"Your humor is part of it," she said when her giggles subsided, "Felix, that connection with you was nothing that I'd ever felt before. That first night you laughed when I told mother that her little spinster would answer the door, I knew. You captured my heart, and that had never happened to me before."

It hadn't happened to me before either, and it hadn't happened since until…Hazel.

The afternoon of passion we had spent together was reminiscent of my time with Tabitha, but somehow, it was even more powerful. I was much more well practiced with how to treat a woman in bed after marrying Tabitha and my time with Mrs. Lucas. Hazel and I connected on a deeper level that I had anticipated, and I would never recreate that with anyone else ever again.

I was a fool as I had found someone who I loved as much as Tabitha, but I had let her go for a fatuous reason.

Suddenly, I recalled the pride that Little Jerry Lucas had in his voice when he told me he was named after his father. Little Jerry Lucas would be devastated to know that I was his blood. The man he put on a pedestal—the man who had raised him since birth was his dad. Blood would never matter to Jerry if he knew the truth. His father would always be Gerald Lucas.

Penelope didn't die giving birth to little Jerry or his sister. What happened to Tabitha was harrowing, but it didn't mean it would happen to Hazel. I could demand to be with her the entire time of the birth, and I would have ten doctors looking in on her if need be. What happened to Tabitha, I could prevent from happening to Hazel. If I didn't go back to England and try, I'd lose her anyway.

"You were an asshole for leaving her," I could hear Tabitha's voice whisper in my ears. It made me grin. They would have gotten along swimmingly.

The ship was ported in New York, and I narrowly avoided another encounter with the girls as they were disembarking.

I hurried to the ticket office, booking passage back to England on a ship leaving within the hour.

Before boarding, I quickly sent telegrams, one to Uncle Enoch, explaining my change of plans, and another to Chaffinch Fields, begging Hazel's forgiveness. The ship that I would arrive on, which, in a stroke of poetic irony, was the Leucothea—the ship where we'd first fallen in love. Smiling, I hoped that it was a sign I was in fact making the right decision. Hazel had every right to reject me for my fear and cowardice, but I hoped that she wouldn't.

We steamed away from New York, and I felt a sense of hope that I lacked on my voyage away from England. This ship, where I had fallen in love with Hazel, would take me back to her.

I spent a lot of time on the journey imagining what life would be like with Hazel and our child. Would it be a boy like Jay, or would we be blessed with a little girl? Looking out on the water, I pictured my life with a smile permanently fixed upon my face.

I frequented a lot of the spots on the ship where Hazel and I spent our time getting to know each other, and I reflected on how each morsel of information she fed me made her more lovely in my estimation.

The journey seemed to be eternal, but I endured it for six days, knowing that in less than 24 hours I would set foot back in England to claim my bride if she would have me. I lingered over breakfast at our table in the dining room, recalling her exploits and expertise in hunting mushrooms.

A faint scent of smoke lingered, which I initially dismissed as a grease fire from the kitchen—until alarm bells suddenly erupted across the ship.

"Fire! Fire!" I heard a call, followed by the screams of passengers everywhere.

Leaping from the table, I rushed onto the deck. A thick plume of black smoke towered above the Leucothea. Something was dreadfully wrong.

"Abandon ship! Abandon ship!" rang out followed by mass hysteria and chaos.

Chapter 12

"That fucking bastard." Those words still echoed in my mind days later.

He left me to rot. The love that sprang up between us in Europe seemed strong enough to weather any obstacle, but it wasn't. Because I was carrying Harvey's baby, he stopped loving me. Everything that led to this baby happened before I'd even met him, but it didn't matter. Felix Byerly wasn't the man I needed—he ran away like a coward.

The days that followed his flight from Chaffinch Fields all ran into one another. My emotions ebbed and flowed like the tide before a hurricane. I'd spend hours completely indignant that he couldn't face me before he'd left.

Cursing his name, I vowed to spit in his face if I ever saw him again. Later I would cry that I'd never be able to hold him again or smell the sweet musk of aftershave on his neck after he returned from the barbershop.

There was one inexplicable hour that I felt thankful he left me so he wouldn't suffer odd looks from strangers about the little blond head in a brood of dark-headed children. At one point, I made myself laugh maniacally when I realized that I was the hands-down winner of the saddest person game we'd played on the train to St. Louis. Now and then, I roused myself to read, but I couldn't focus on anything but the hopelessness of my predicament.

Mostly, however, I just missed the man that I loved. I had gotten used to seeing him every day. Learning about his behaviors and eccentricities brought me unexpected joy. He always yawned before taking a drink of his first cup of coffee, and he got a little twinkle in his eye when he'd talk about his mother's feistiness. Butterscotch candies were always in his coat pocket as he popped one in his mouth whenever he felt bored. A green tie would reveal flecks of amber in his brown eyes, but the best thing of all, I learned what it was to be completely in love with someone.

Coping as best I could with my loss, I told myself that Felix couldn't raise Harvey's child as his own because he didn't love me enough. These thoughts made the sting of losing him less devastating as I loved him more than he loved me, and that was not my fault.

My situation called to mind Madame Leveau's tarot card reading. The first card had been The Fool which I obviously was. The second card discussed how unlucky I would be in love. I had attributed it at the time to Olive and Felix, but now it took on a darker meaning. The final card was the Tower. She said it was an unexpected change, but she wouldn't say whether it was good or bad. Felix running away from this pregnancy wasn't exactly unexpected. It was, however, bad.

The only appetite I had in those days was foisted upon me by the growing child in my belly. I wanted to hate the baby as it had cost me so much, but it was absolutely innocent of any wrongdoing. All he or she wanted to do was exist which was obvious by the food it demanded.

It should have been easy to hate Harvey, but deep down I knew this child's conception wasn't his doing alone. All too well, I remembered that evening by his fishing hole. The blame for my condition lay squarely on my own shoulders.

My guilt for leaving Harvey behind had created this child. I gave myself to him, hoping the memory of our lovemaking would make him wait another year for me. In hindsight, now that I was no longer in love with Harvey, it almost felt transactional. My body was offered in exchange for patience. It made me an imbecile, and I was paying the price.

The uncertainty of my future was the only thing I could be certain about. Olive assured me that Chaffinch Fields could be my home as long as I wished, but her parents might have other ideas in mind once they found out I was pregnant. This was the ancestral home of the 5th Duke of Cleveland, not some charity home for runaway girls.

I couldn't even imagine the embarrassment the Duchess would endure if her society friends knew she was harboring a fallen woman. Assuring me that she hadn't told them about my condition yet, Olive only mentioned that Felix got cold feet about our abrupt wedding and absconded back to America.

One good thing that came out of Felix leaving was the Duchess' disappointment in him. She vowed to never try to find her daughter a husband again as it was obvious that she was a poor judge of character when it came to young men in this day and age.

I couldn't hide my pregnancy from them forever, and even if I could, telling them the stork arrived and dropped a baby down the chimney wasn't likely to fool them either. Olive had her work cut out for her to convince them. My only connection to their family was Mrs. Byerly who the Duchess was still mourning as she wasn't receiving visitors yet.

The Duke continued on conducting business as usual, riding his horses and visiting tenants on his property. He dined with his daughter every day and asked how I was bearing it all. There was only so long I could stay cloistered before he saw my growing belly.

The Duke would naturally assume that Felix had gotten me pregnant, and he would call him a scoundrel for putting me in this state and abandoning me. I wouldn't be able to drag Felix's honor through the mud so I would have to admit that he wasn't the father of the child, but there was another man. He would no doubt believe there was more than one other man, and he'd demand that Olive break ties and cast me out of Chaffinch Fields like the harlot I was.

The road ahead was quite bleak. Virginia Rappe's future was brighter when she was introduced to Fatty Arbuckle. Several days after Felix left, I still hadn't come to terms with what I was going to do with this baby after it was born. The WCO didn't employ married women, much less unwed mothers. I couldn't go home in shame to my mother as it would throw the whole community in upheaval with Ruby's presence.

I couldn't go to Milligan without traveling through the Seven Arches to go back to where I came from. I shuddered at the thought. With Mrs. Byerly's death and Felix's desertion, I had begun to think that they were the cursed Gates of Hell. If my life wasn't hell at this moment, I didn't think that Satan could make it much worse.

Returning to Milligan with Ruby still there would be a risk even if I would disappear through the arches soon after arriving. I had agreed that I would never go back, but I also had no idea at the time that I was pregnant. It would be nice to see my mother and Ray again. Familiar faces outside of Chaffinch Fields were not a luxury I had anymore. Pregnant and alone, I hadn't realized how incredibly much I missed my mother until I needed her.

When I walked through the Seven Arches, I never considered what happened in my world. Time surely didn't stand still when I left. Had I simply vanished from their lives? I felt incredibly selfish for never considering that possibility. What would Mother and Ray do without me? Four months had passed. They had probably given me up for dead. Ruby and I believed that I was a blessing, an answer to her prayers, but it was looking more and more like I was a curse, the curse of the Seven Arches.

If I had indeed vanished from my world the moment I entered Ruby's, there was the possibility that everyone was better off without me. Roscoe had seemed to hit the big time in St. Louis. Mother and Ray didn't need my paltry dollar a week to stay afloat.

Harvey dodged a bullet as he deserved a woman who wanted to commit to him, not one that would go off and flit around Europe. There was always a long line of women waiting for Harvey to wake up and notice them when I was in St. Louis, and I was sure he had by now. I'd known his mother had paraded an endless amount of girls from Milligan, Judson, and Waveland in front of him over the years.

My heart sank. Felix lived in Waveland, and Felix from my world wouldn't know me at all. Sadly, he wouldn't be the same Felix that I fell in love with. We'd have no shared experiences. He'd be easy enough to avoid, but I knew that I'd be tempted to see him if I went back.

If there was indeed a curse surrounding the Seven Arches, I might be able to set everything right by returning to where I came from and filling the void that I'd left. The thought of seeing and hugging my mother warmed my heart as I had only been able to hug her in my dreams.

If I were to stay in this world and there was no Felix, I had no other options open to me except for charity homes for unwed mothers. The bitter irony was that Mrs. Byerly and I had planned to open charity homes in London through our WCO office.

Going back through the Seven Arches was worth a try. If anything, I felt like it gave me an opportunity to set right what went awry when I came through. It would be a long journey, but I still had months before the baby would arrive. If I returned after the baby was born, I could try to pass off the child as a charity case that I adopted in Europe. No one would believe it, but it would at least help me save face in Milligan.

I considered marrying Harvey if he were still single in my world. Ruby was surely insanely happy with him as a husband in this world. Could I recreate that happiness in the world I left behind? My nose wrinkled at the prospect. I didn't love Harvey anymore, and even if I did, it was unlikely he would believe that this was his child. Too many months had passed. I truly hoped he'd found happiness with someone else.

When Olive entered my room, I still hadn't come to a final conclusion of what I would do. She started chattering on about how my mourning for that rat bastard was over, and she was chasing all the gloom away.

A book was under her arm when she entered the room, and she promptly set it down on the table before throwing open curtains and windows. I sat up in bed actually feeling like the sunlight would do me some good. Focusing on what I needed to do in the future made my present seem a little less miserable.

I was about to ask her opinion on what I should do when she began to speak first, "I'm taking you to London for a few days. We need to air out Chaffinch Fields of that man's stench. Dear Hazel, you only have a scant amount of time before you are tied down with motherhood. We need to live at least for the next few weeks."

She wouldn't take no for an answer, dismissing any objections before I could voice them. The way she quickly took charge of everything surprised me, and my mouth was agape for longer than I realized.

Close your mouth, dear. You don't want it to get stuck that way," she said, laughing warmly, "You're the one expecting, and I'm the one talking like a mother."

We laughed. It felt good to laugh with Olive again, and I had no reason to object to a few weeks in London as it might clear my head and give me perspective on the impossibility of my future. Besides, I came on this journey in the first place to make memories in Europe. Going back to Milligan seemed silly without first seeing London, curse or no curse.

I jumped out of bed and hugged her. Her gentle prodding was just the push I needed, and her unwavering care warmed me deeply. Patting my arm, she told me to wash up and get dressed as she wanted to take a stroll in the garden. The book she'd laid on the table was once again in her hands.

"We have much to discuss," she said, raising an eyebrow. She placed the book under her right arm and left the room.

Intrigued by her parting words, I wanted to stop her, but a quick smell of my bedclothes served as a reminder that I had not washed up or dressed in several days. I smelled of salt and despair—not exactly a pleasant fragrance.

In the West Garden, hostas bloomed brightly amid freshly trimmed hedges, offering a comforting contrast to my inner gloom. The sun peeked out from behind the clouds for a moment or two helping to wash out the gloom that had settled in my bones. We strolled arm in arm for a while. I wanted to ask her about the book, but her mind seemed to be elsewhere.

"Hazel, I want you to stay with us in Chaffinch Fields when we return from London," she said, breaking the silence.

It was too kind of her to offer, but somehow, I knew in the back of my mind that she would. Even though we'd only known each other a short time, Olive always seemed to put my needs ahead of her own. I loved her for it, but it made me feel like an imposition.

"That sounds wonderful, but what about the Duke and Duchess? I can only hide this pregnancy from them for so long. If it got out that your family had a connection to a ruined woman like me, wouldn't it cause a scandal?"

A ruined woman? Hazel, it's the 1920s, not the 1820s," Olive chastised gently, "Quite frankly, I don't care what anyone thinks, and I doubt the Duke cares much either. It is my mother who is obsessed with status, and I'm certain she is only obsessed because she still harbors this notion that, perhaps, I'll marry one day."

I knew of Olive's proclivities, but even I wondered at times if she'd endure a husband to continue her family line. I knew she didn't want to anytime soon, but she had such a rich family history. I assumed she'd feel obligated to eventually have a child.

The dukedom ends with my father. I can't inherit it, and frankly, I don't give a damn about titles. Also, no offense dear, but the thought of growing a baby inside me gives me that willies."

Laughing, I agreed that it was an odd sensation at times. She looked as if she was going to say more, but my curiosity regarding the book was too much to put off any longer.

She apologized for keeping me in suspense, but while I was bemoaning my future, the library at Chaffinch Fields occupied many hours of her time. Her father and his father before him had been a bit of a collector in religious texts which I had noticed, and she thought it was worth a try to see if there was any information on *le chemin de l'esprit terrestre*.

There was an anthology of religious texts from the 16th and 17th centuries. It was full of religious poems and sermons from abbots, priests, nuns, and religious philosophers. I was bristling with excitement, and she realized that she left the book in the library.

We scurried back inside, and she opened up the book to the page she had found. I scanned down the page and my eyes popped when I ran across the sermon she had discovered.

Heavenly Worlds Upon Worlds
from *Le Chemin de L'esprit Terrestre by* Père Dieudonné Suivant

The Path of the Earthly Spirit is our march toward the Lord Almighty. He has given us free will and with each choice we forge a new path to him. In God's house there are many rooms, infinite rooms prepared for all the ways we reach enlightenment in our journey toward heaven.

To borrow a phrase I'd heard the Duchess use a few times, I was absolutely gobsmacked. It astonished me that she'd discovered this text. The sermon went on for a few more pages, and it seemed to retell what Madame Leveau had said to me when I visited her l'atelier. What Olive had discovered that was most exciting was a priest named Père Dieudonné Suivant who had written an entire book all about *le chemin de l'esprit terrestre.*

She told her father about our interest in this book because of Madame Leveau as he had plenty of contacts that would help him track it down. She said with any luck there would be a copy at Chaffinch Fields when we arrived back from our excursion to London.

We ambled back to our discussion of my future at Chaffinch Fields, and I told her that I wouldn't feel comfortable staying with her if the Duchess were dead set against it. Feeling incredibly lucky to have a friend in Olive, I didn't want my presence to upset everything and cause a rift in her family.

The Duchess would be difficult to convince, she admitted, but I had become quite necessary to her. While she was so terribly sorry that Felix had left me, a small part of her was happy because I would stay with her longer. We decided to leave the matter of my future unsettled until after our return from London.

The next morning, it felt as though the sun was finally shining just for me. I had experienced the loss of Mrs. Byerly and Felix in quick succession of one another, and any form of happiness had eluded me for the past several days. Looking out at the lavender-scented West Garden from my window, I felt a fresh wave of hope for the first time in days.

I had eaten and enjoyed my robust breakfast that morning for the first time in a while. The prospect of packing my trunk for a few weeks in London was an exciting one until I realized that all my dresses were too tight, or they showcased the little child that I still wanted to hide for a little while longer.

I went out in search of Olive to lament my situation when a servant stopped me to place a telegram in my hands. Examining the outside carefully, I had no idea who would be sending me messages at Chaffinch Fields as the only person from the outside world who knew I was here was Ruby.

The prospect of the telegram coming from Ruby was frightening as she had already insisted we break off communication with one another. If something was wrong with Mother or Ray, she might send me a message. A feeling of foreboding suddenly overcame me as I tore open the message which was from Felix.

My heart raced as I reread his words, desperate to confirm I hadn't imagined them. He was coming back! He wanted forgiveness! He still wanted to be my husband! A giddy yelp escaped my lips as I found the nearest chair to fall into, reading the telegram for a third time! I couldn't believe it!

I hadn't been wrong about him and the love we shared. He realized that he did love me enough to raise this child as his own. It was so overwhelming that I wanted to dance. As quickly as he had turned my world upside down, he had turned it right side up again!

"Hazel, are you ill?" Olive said as she stormed into the room, "The maid said you'd received a telegram, and I heard you cry out!"

Laughing still with joy, I handed the telegram to her to read for herself. She snatched it from my hands and greedily read all the words out loud for me to hear. It was true. He was on his way back to me and aboard the *Leucothea* no less.

"That fucking bastard actually came through," Olive said with a delighted smirk. "I'm going to pout and be impossible to live with until you leave me."

I giggled. She picked me up out of the chair and hugged me. My wedding would be at Chaffinch Fields after all. Suddenly, my fixation on the supposed curse of the Seven Arches seemed foolish. Life was always a gamble, and I had been on a losing streak. However, happiness was returning to me.

Olive was a little upset that Felix's return would ruin our trip to London, but she quickly decided we could spend a few days there. His ship wouldn't be in for at least five days. I quickly agreed, rattling off all the spots that I couldn't wait to visit. She made no move to hide the rolling of her eyes.

"I'll play tourist with you for a day or two. I want to take the car one day to Stonehenge. After your description of the Seven Arches, I want your opinion on it," she said.

Still giddy about Felix's telegram, I became twice as excited about the trip to London. It all sounded wonderful almost as if it were a dream. Quickly recalling my reason for seeking Olive out in the first place, I told her all about my dress problem.

"I went through a fat phase a few years ago. I've got the perfect dresses to cover your, um, generous proportions."

We left for London the following morning and arrived in the city to overcast skies and a gloomy fog hovering over the ground. It was absolutely perfect! I'd read about the London fog, and I was so happy to be able to experience it.

Almost all the books I'd read set in London had the fog settling in, and I recalled Harvey's memory of the city from his time in the war. Olive thought it was quite ridiculous to be impressed by fog. The men in bowler, trilby, and top hats walking through the train station completed the effect. Only Sherlock Holmes walking down the street to 221b Baker Street would have made me more excited.

"Yes, how exciting," Olive said dryly, "especially considering he's fictional." I gave her a peevish look, and she returned it sourly. "I said I would play tourist with you. I never said I'd like it."

The Duke and Duchess kept a house in London all year so we sent our bags there directly and began exploring immediately. The chimes of Big Ben could be heard reverberating through the streets as we left the train station.

I looked to Olive with a huge grin on my face, and she directed me toward Parliament for our first stop.

"I'm going to regret this, aren't I?" she said to which I tartly responded, "Probably."

She called me impossible several times as I enthusiastically pointed out details of the clock tower. The words written below the face were in Latin, and I tried my best to pronounce them, "Domine salvam fac reginam nostram Victoriam primam. I wonder what it means."

"O Lord, keep safe our Queen Victoria the First," Olive responded looking supremely annoyed, "The Duchess saw Latin as a requirement in my schooling."

The mention of the magnificent queen overtook me, and I regurgitated all the facts I learned about her in the history books, especially the love between her and her Albie. Olive didn't even attempt to hide her eye roll when I told her about rumors that she later loved her personal assistant so much that she secretly married him.

She laughed out loud at the insinuation and told me if I were to repeat such a story too loudly we may be escorted out of Parliament by an armed guard as no one in England is allowed to besmirch the reputation of the King's grandmother. I felt scandalized and shut my mouth immediately.

We managed to get in a lot of sightseeing before the day was done. At Westminster Abbey, I got to see the grave of Charles Dickens, one of my greatest heroes. The Tower of London was majestic and where I gushed over all the people who had been imprisoned there: Guy Fawkes, Lady Jane Grey, even Queen Elizabeth I for a few months during the reign of her sister, Mary.

The last place I dragged her was the building that Mrs. Byerly had leased for us to open the London office of the WCO. It was the fourth floor of a modest building. With no desire to go inside, I only wanted to see what it looked like. Imagining what my route would be to get to work every day was enough. After seeing all the sights in London, I was overwhelmed by my reaction to it.

I had expected this place to be the first office that I would run for the WCO. Poised to be a working girl in London for the next several years, I was a bit sad seeing it. Standing before the building, I felt a pang of sadness for all the dreams that would never be realized within its walls. It represented what was supposed to be the end of Mrs. Byerly's career and the beginning of mine.

If Mrs. Byerly had lived, we would have opened the office here, and I would have married Felix after we had finished. My career as a working woman would have ended on my terms instead of with the death of Mrs. Byerly and the realization that I was pregnant. That life seemed a million miles away, and yet Mrs. Byerly had only been gone a few weeks.

"Damn, I miss her." I said to Olive who found this adventure far more interesting than the tourist places I'd dragged her to.

"I can tell," she said as she placed her hand on my shoulder to comfort me.

That evening Olive tried to drag me out to a pub to meet with her London friends, but I was much too exhausted from the day of sightseeing. Begging her to go out and see her friends, I only wanted to take a bath and consider all the things we saw that day.

My mind turned from the sights to Felix as I reclined in the bathtub. I'd had time to prepare myself for his return, but it still didn't seem real for some reason. Olive booked me a room at an inn in Portsmouth the day before the *Leucothea* was expected to dock, and I could hardly wait to set eyes on him again.

It felt like years since I had seen him instead of days. I found it hard to come to terms with losing him and getting him back. My emotions were in such a state of upheaval that it was easy to be giddy but hard to be happy. I tried to imagine his face when he would see me waiting on him to walk down the gangplank. I could almost picture his half-cocked smile when we locked eyes.

I was prepared to take him directly back to the inn and recreate when we discovered each other's bodies for the first time. The memory of it still titillated me and I closed my eyes to relive the whole experience while I soaked in the tub.

The next day I dragged Olive to Buckingham Palace and the British Museum, where she constantly complained. Later, we met a couple of her artist friends for dinner where I learned a lot about the island of Lesbos and some interesting symbolism involving a waterfall.

On the third day rain poured down so we delayed our trip to Stonehenge. The site was about a two hour drive from the Powlett townhouse. With Olive behind the wheel, we made excellent time, and I found myself petrified out of my mind. The steering wheel being on the wrong side of the vehicle should've been easy to get used to, but I found myself constantly looking for a phantom brake pedal. Honestly, it was almost as unnerving as driving anywhere with my mother.

I had seen a few photos of Stonehenge in picture books of British History, but they didn't quite do justice to the awesome architecture that had taken place thousands of years ago to erect such a structure. It did seem like a primitive version of the Seven Arches but on a massive scale. Part of me wondered if the seven keystones in the

Seven Arches were somehow inserted into Stonehenge if it would have the same power.

Olive explained that scholars believed that Stonehenge was once a full circle, and I wondered if it could possibly be related to *le chemin de l'esprit terrestre*. With the Duke, Olive had been to Stonehenge more times than she could count as it was centered around the pagan festival of the summer solstice. Her father had studied many pagan religious rituals, and he had told her all the stories over the years of the rumors and theories about this mystical place. It was difficult for her not to talk to him about the Seven Arches as she knew he would be fascinated by it.

"It does feel like the same energy," I said, "I realize that it is hard to understand if you haven't been to both places. The Seven Arches was always a peaceful place for me, and I get that from here as well."

I ran my fingers along the stones, almost searching for a little jutting stone that would serve as an activation to it. The absence of color was in stark contrast to the Seven Arches. The eye was always drawn to the magnificent keystones that seemed to always glow in the daylight as if they were inviting anyone to journey through them.

"Tell me what you were thinking when you went through?" she said with her arms outstretched, pantomiming an airplane as she weaved in and out of the arches.

"No, you have to understand that I didn't think anything of it. I saw those three mushrooms, and there was that loose stone. I pushed the stone in, and nothing happened, at least nothing seemed like it happened. I walked through the first arch with only a slight sound that seemed to gurgle in the horizon. About the second arch, I felt like it was going to rain because I could hear a sound like distant thunder. The sound got louder and louder, but I had no idea what was causing it. I couldn't even concentrate because my brain was foggy. I was focused on getting through to the end, and when I did, I immediately passed out. It wasn't for more than a few seconds because Ruby called out to me."

We'd talked about it all before but it still fascinated her. While we'd been in town, she had stopped in a few libraries to ask about *Le Chemin de L'esprit Terrestre by* Père Dieudonné Suivant, but she hadn't any luck. I suggested that as the book was French an English translation may not exist.

"It makes me wonder if this Père Dieudonné Suivant saw a link between *le chemin de l'esprit terrestre* and Stonehenge, or if the person or people that built your Seven Arches knew something he didn't," she said.

We made no real progress on the mystery, but it was fascinating to ponder. For all we knew the path of the earthly spirit had nothing in common with Stonehenge other than looking vaguely familiar. I was a bit sad to see the state the historic site was in. There were initials carved in it as well as places where people had chiseled away fragments to keep, I suppose, as souvenirs.

It was peaceful, and we spent several hours there together with no one else around. Stonehenge was as nice a place to reflect as the Seven Arches. I thought to myself over and over that Felix was coming back to me, and by this time tomorrow, I'd be barreling toward him on a train to Portsmouth.

When we arrived at the train station the next day, Olive offered to accompany me to Portsmouth as she was a little concerned about me traveling alone. She knew about my introduction to Felix on the train to St. Louis, and how I had handled that man with the gold tooth. Reminding me to keep my time with Felix chaste as she didn't want me to get in trouble, I flattened my dress to my burgeoning belly, and said, "That ship has sailed."

"Tramp!" Olive said, giving me a wink as she kissed me goodbye.

The seaside inn where Olive booked me was much more luxurious than I anticipated although I should have expected the very best as she had spoiled me every day that I'd known her. The air was damp, and there was a small fire in the room to dry it out. I was perfectly cozy there my first night.

Having grown up in the heartland of America, I hadn't been to the sea until I was an adult with Mrs. Byerly. I had a love affair with the ocean. There was something about it that called to mind all the possibilities that lay beyond the ocean. I could buy a ticket and be bound for America, Norway, or Morocco in a matter of hours.

The ocean represented endless opportunities as did the Seven Arches which were nowhere near the ocean. I had considered the Seven Arches a curse when Felix left me, but I had to consider it a blessing now that I knew he was coming back. There was some magic in the universe that brought us together, and I would be forever grateful for it.

The following morning I roused myself early to stroll along the seaside. I was captivated with the ocean and the idea that Felix was getting closer and closer by the moment. If they hit a strong current, it wasn't out of the realm of possibilities that the *Leucothea* could dock a day early.

As I walked, I wondered if I was forgiving him too easily. He left me in misery for more than a week before I received his telegram. Yes, I'd given him shocking news, but did he really have to flee an entire continent to cope? On the other hand, I wouldn't be quite as anxious to marry him if he announced that he'd gotten another woman pregnant.

I wished I had Mother to prattle on to as she always cut through to the heart of the matter. She would have said, "It only matters that he's coming back. I don't give a damn how long he had his head up his ass."

Maybe I could pout like a coquette and demand jewelry until he begs forgiveness—a performance that would surely make him laugh. He would most likely be amused as I tried to act as a tease and a gold digger, two archetypes of females that I knew he loathed.

I chastised myself for being so silly. Felix was making enough sacrifices for me without piling onto it. He was willing to raise Harvey Cleghorn's child as his own. How could I ask for more? The first time I set eyes on him I won't be able to stop myself from throwing my arms around him and kissing him hard and long. It would be a kiss that will put all our others to shame, a kiss that belongs in the hall of fame of kisses. I wanted him to drop to his knees and thank God that he came back to me.

The next morning the *Leucothea* was set to arrive as I woke with the sun. I was so excited and brimming with anticipation to see my love, my groom, that I had a fitful night of sleep. It didn't matter. Nothing would matter until I had Felix's arms around me.

The morning the ship was set to arrive, I ventured down to the sea, hoping in vain to catch a glimpse of the *Leucothea* off in the distance. It felt poetic that the ship that had brought us together all those months ago was bringing him back to me once again.

Back in my room knowing that a watched pot never boils, I tried to read, but my lack of sleep suddenly overcame my nerves. I fell asleep in the armchair with dreams of Felix's embrace rocking me softly.

I roused myself in a panic with no idea how long I'd slept, but I didn't even bother with my shoes. If I missed the moment he stepped ashore, I'd never forgive myself. When I got to the docks, the *Leucothea* wasn't in port, and I breathed a sigh of relief. Relieved that I hadn't missed him, I inquired as to when it was expected as I was certain it must almost be within sight.

"The *Leucothea*?" His expression softened into pity. "Miss, she sank yesterday, off the coast of Ireland. It was in last night's edition.

My pulse raced as my heart sank, and I could feel my eyes filling with tears.

"Were there survivors?" I asked shakily as the fear was dislodged from my voice and replaced with full-fledged panic.

"Yes, I believe another ship, the *Amphitrite* was dispatched to collect the survivors in the lifeboats. There was a nasty fire that broke out on board when one of the boilers overheated and exploded."

"Do you know how many died?"

My heart was beating outside of my chest. I wasn't even sure I wanted to know the answer to that question. I only cared if Felix was alive. My Felix. My hands shook uncontrollably as my mind flooded with visions of him dead or dying. I couldn't handle it. I had only recovered my hope for happiness.

"They won't know until the survivors can be cross checked with the passenger logs. I'm sorry if you had a loved one aboard."

My life was shattering with every step I took away from the docks. I became absolutely certain that Felix had died aboard the *Leucothea*. I wanted to do something dramatic like throw myself into the ocean to be with him.

Somehow, I needed to stop this pain I was feeling. Crying didn't seem to even curb the agony. My hope of a happy life with the man that I loved was dangled in front of me only to be snatched away by a boiler explosion.

I wandered up and down the seaside for a while, pausing to weep every few yards. He had to be alright. He had to be. I had to push the bad images out of my head. They were a knee jerk reaction. Felix had survived. He might have been injured, but he was alive. There was no other option. As a survivor, he was aboard the *Amphitrite* coming to reunite with me.

By the time I fell into my bed I was completely numb to everything, I slept for a long time and awoke with a clearer head. More convinced than ever that Felix had survived, I was so damn mad at him.

If he hadn't abandoned me in the first place, we'd be happily married, perhaps honeymooning in Scotland at this very moment. When I saw him get off the boat, I would hug him for a long, long time, but I would slap him hard. He had no business making me fret like this. It was so selfish of him.

I knew he was one of the survivors. There were shipwrecks that had almost no casualties. One of the boilers had exploded. That was beneath the ship, and Felix was most likely a first or second class passenger. He would be far away from the danger.

I bought a newspaper to see what was reported, but there was little in the article that the man hadn't told me at the docks. A boiler exploded causing a fire to break out and the passengers had to abandon ship. There was no news on survivors or casualties.

Sleep wouldn't find me that night. I was so angry at Felix that I wanted to spit nails in his face. It was his fault. All of it. If he would have been sensible and listened to reason, he never would have left for America so hastily.

We would have worked it out, and he would have realized that he loved me almost as much as I loved him. He was such an idiot that I wished he had gotten hurt. Nothing serious, but like a sprained ankle, to make sure he learned his lesson.

The next morning my anger faded, and I began to consider the possibility that he hadn't survived the shipwreck. I prayed and prayed to God to make sure he was alright. I promised that I would live to be a better Christian as I recalled the lust that I had succumbed to with both Harvey and Felix. I swore my next intimacy would be as a properly married woman, if only God would spare Felix. I would also abandon an outdoor wedding in the gardens of Chaffinch Fields for a church wedding if God would make sure that Felix got back to me.

I ran down to the docks to await the arrival of the *Amphitrite* with my heart in my throat. Unlike the *Leucothea*, the *Amphitrite* arrived right on time. Watching the haggard group of survivors file off one by one, my body felt like it was made of glass. The first class passengers were let off first, and they didn't seem to be much worse for wear. There was a man with a bandaged arm, and a few faces smeared with soot. My heart sank as Felix was not among them.

Calling out his name as the second class passengers funneled off the ship, I noticed they looked a bit worse than their predecessors. There was no one that remotely resembled Felix. Anyone that would stop, I asked if they knew of a man named Felix Byerly on the ship, but they all shook their heads, more exhausted than I was.

I began to lose all the hope that I mustered as the third and fourth class passengers made their way down the gangplank. The smell of smoke from them was overwhelming. Shouting "Felix Byerly" over and over again, I couldn't get anyone to hear me. They'd all been through a harrowing ordeal, but I needed news about my Felix. Why wouldn't anyone answer me?!

A woman stopped me in the midst of my despondent cries. She was only a few years older than me and wore a tattered dress. Her wild hair had almost completely come out of the bun she wore. The expression on her face was care worn, and her eyes were red from crying.

"Did you ask for Felix? Felix Byerly?" she said.

"Yes, yes! You know him. Is he still on the boat?!" I asked, grabbing her arm so that she could not get away from me.

Quickly describing his size and build along with his perfectly trimmed mustache, it was obvious she had talked to my Felix. She had seen him on board the boat, and everything was going to be alright.

After taking a deep breath which evaporated all my hope with her exhalation, she began her story.

"Felix Byerly saved my daughter's life," she said softly. "He was a hero."

He rescued her from the hold of the ship where she was trapped after the explosion by carrying her out on his back. Smiling at her, he said there was one crew member still trapped down below. Once he got that boy out, he'd meet the woman in the lifeboat, and they'd swap life stories.

"Then he winked at me and went back down below. The ceiling collapsed, closing off the stairway not more than a minute later. I searched for him on the rescue boats vainly hoping a miracle had saved him, but I couldn't find him. I'm sorry, but I don't think he could have made it out alive."

My glass frame shattered, and as darkness closed in, I fainted from shock.

Clarissa's Gambit, St. Louis 1923

After years of delays and flimsy excuses, Clarissa Byerly was finally getting her wish: her son was going to accompany her to England.

Of course, it took her nearly dying last winter to make the plans come to fruition. Felix was incapable of breaking a promise—especially one made at her sickbed.

Dora's last letter confirmed that she was making arrangements for a trip to Paris, Florence, Rome, and Scotland for Clarissa and Felix. She thought it would be best to spring the trip onto Olive at the last minute as she would likely make plans to be away if she were given too much notice.

Both Dora and Clarissa were dutiful mothers, having each given birth to only one child. Dora had longed for more children, but fate had intervened, leaving Olive as her only daughter. Clarissa knew the moment that Felix was born that he'd be her only child.

Olive and Felix were strong-willed and defiant, a Venable trait they assuredly inherited from their mothers.

Felix pleaded for a summer departure date—'Mother, the damp will kill you'—but Clarissa refused. A promise, once extracted, stayed extracted

He'd returned to his dreadful uncle a week ago, but he promised that he'd return at the end of March for their journey across the Atlantic.

In her heart of hearts, Clarissa knew that the trip had to be now or never. The illness last winter had nearly killed her, leaving her frustratingly weakened and painfully aware that time was no longer on her side. Her doctor told her that she was in incredibly delicate health, and he recommended her immediate retirement.

She had dismissed his advice without hesitation. Retirement wasn't an option—at least not yet.

At the WCO she had worked endlessly to seize the Director of Outreach, and it had finally been awarded to her a few short years ago. She and Hazel had opened up the Nashville Office with aplomb, and she returned home when that damn flu got her. What she expected to be an illness of a few weeks ravaged her heart and lungs. She had been at death's door, but with Felix's dutiful nursing, she recovered.

She left for San Diego the day after Felix left for Waveland to prepare a room for her at Uncle Enoch's. She wrote him a letter telling him that her doctor insisted the climate in California was better for her health at this point than anything.

After the opening of the Atlanta office later that year, she knew that Hazel was more than ready to leave her. It was likely time, and Clarissa reluctantly made plans to start retirement.

Almost as a pipe dream, she finished her long delayed proposal of opening up an international office in London and laid it on Mrs. Schiff's desk. Never in her wildest dreams did she expect to get the green light, but the successes in Nashville, San Diego, and Atlanta made it all possible.

Clarissa had been stunned. After years of wrangling with Eudora Schiff over every penny, the sudden generosity seemed nearly suspicious.

Mrs. Schiff assured Clarissa that she was in her right mind. The decision to open up an international office in London met unanimous approval with the board of directors, and it was all due to Clarissa's business acumen and savvy fundraising. The WCO was becoming a household name after being on the verge of collapse before Clarissa took hold of the finances.

The only thing left to do was the uncomfortable part. She couldn't do anything anymore without Hazel, and Hazel had planned on marrying that farmboy for the last few years since he returned home from the war.

She couldn't do this without Hazel—her protégé, her confidante, and the only person she fully trusted to see things through.

It would be such a joy to take the girl to Europe on the tour with her and Felix. She had grown up in such a sad household. Abandoned by her father and helping support her mother and delicate brother, Hazel deserved to live a little before she was saddled with taking care of a husband and a brood of children. Clarissa doubted such a life would ever bring her any happiness.

But Clarissa had promised almost a year ago that it would be Hazel's last year with the WCO. She'd dangled opportunities in front of her to make her choose work over marriage. She knew how much it pained Hazel to choose between once in a lifetime opportunities and her future husband.

She knew however that if Hazel wasn't on board. It wouldn't happen.

The girl's contract was up in May. Opening up the office in London would take at the very least twice as long as Nashville which took four months. It would be six months to a year overseas. If she didn't agree, the London office would never happen.

The trip would be a gift to her, and they would be able to continue their work in London when it was over. Clarissa hadn't told Hazel that she would retire when the girl left her, but it was inevitable especially with her health.

Hazel ambled into her office that morning with a fresh-faced smile. Clarissa was struck with the beauty of the girl. If she hadn't been saddled with that farm boy, she would've been a suitable match for Felix if dreams of him running an estate in England never came to fruition.

"Hazel, dear sit down for a moment."

She laid it all out for her. The surprise move by Mrs. Schiff approving the opening of an international office in London. The six months to a year it would take to open it up, and she even sweetened it by inviting her on the sightseeing trip with her and Felix.

Hazel initially reacted with indignation, torn between excitement and dread at the prospect of disappointing Harvey once more.

Clarissa emphasized that she never ever thought that Mrs. Schiff would approve the idea. She had dreamed it up last year when they were opening up the San Diego office. It was as much a ploy to write off much of the voyage as business expense as it was a serious venture. The idea of an international office had monopolized her thoughts off and on over the years, but she figured it was at least five years off.

"I can't disappoint Harvey," Hazel maintained.

He had covertly come to St. Louis a few months ago just to see her as she didn't get home between the opening of the San Diego and Atlanta offices. He had missed her, and he was so excited to marry her.

Clarissa sighed dramatically. "Say no more, Hazel. I'll tell Mrs. Schiff the whole venture was ridiculous. Better to cancel it altogether."

"Cancel it? Why would you cancel it? You could take one or two of the other girls."

"No dear, I'm not as spry as I once was. I will never open another office without you. It's hard work. I'll either organize the opening from the home office, or maybe I'll just quit."

Hazel was as indignant about Clarissa quitting as she was about being asked to go to Europe.

"Think of the women you've helped, and all the women that can still benefit from your help, Mrs. Byerly. You're not quitting."

"I'm not going to open up the first international office of the WCO without you."

Hazel's eyes softened with that familiar glimmer of resignation, and Clarissa knew the battle was won.

Felix would go too, and he'd fall madly in love with Olive Powlett.

Life, Clarissa decided, was finally falling into place.

Chapter 13

I wasn't sure how long I had lain on the floor after that woman told me Felix was dead. It couldn't have been too long, but I was surprised at the amount of eyes staring down at me when I came to. The people looking over me asked if I was alright, and all I could say was, "No."

They offered to call for a doctor, but I shook them off. Physically, I was unharmed—but internally, I had shattered into a thousand pieces. The poor woman that gave me her account of Felix's death looked especially concerned, and I apologized for upsetting her. She threw her arms around me in bitter earnest, apologizing for the loss of a great man, but I couldn't even hug her back.

I stood limp while she squeezed my body. The crowd eventually dispersed when it was determined that I wasn't in any danger.

The numbness I felt at first was a blessing because it got me back to my room at the inn in one piece, and although no one would have faulted me, I was glad I didn't make a public spectacle of myself by sobbing uncontrollably.

I stared at the fire in my room for several hours, knowing that my love had died. He wasn't simply on another continent; he was now trapped forever beneath an endless, unforgiving sea.

Silent tears fell down my cheeks for I don't know how long. I wasn't even conscious that I was crying as I stared at the fire wrapped up in a blanket, mourning him and not knowing if anything in my life would ever be good again.

The memory of every interaction we'd ever had poured through my mind starting from the train stop in Milligan and ending with the bitter separation in the East Garden. I clung desperately to these memories, knowing they were the only pieces of Felix I'd ever hold again.

It wasn't until hours later when I could appreciate that he died a hero. If he hadn't been aboard the *Leucothea*, that woman's daughter would have died. His death hadn't been totally in vain. The curse of the Seven Arches may have taken my Felix, but he had saved a little girl.

Somehow, that didn't soften the blow any. He was still dead. I'd never be able to hug him again to feel his mustache against my lip. The scent of aftershave mixed with butterscotch candy would never again linger on my clothes when I'd spent more than an hour with him. All my hopes and dreams were turned to ashes once again.

Olive appeared later that afternoon without being asked, the grim news clutched tightly in her hands. She took one look at me and silently helped me pack. In the short time of her knowing me, Olive had already seen me at my worst several times.

Still numb from losing Felix, I should have been grateful by how she looked out for me, but I couldn't even recall if I properly thanked her for rescuing me.

We returned to Chaffinch Fields, and I fell back into bed for several days. This time Olive didn't leave me for days to stew in my depression. She found and read an Agatha Christie mystery novel to me even though I was only half listening, and the windows were open for a few hours a day to let in fresh air.

In those agonizing days, I tried my best to be polite to her, but wallowing in my own pity was all I wanted to do. If I had anywhere to go, I would have left Chaffinch Fields for a place to totally escape the world, but I had nothing, not even money for a return ticket to America.

Life looked bleak for me and the baby. It seemed so frivolous to wonder if Hercule Poirot would uncover who really killed Emily Inglelthorp.

When I begged her to stop reading to me, she looked like she would get huffy, but a smile spread across her face. She agreed not to read to me anymore, and I thought it odd that Olive Powlett would fold that easily.

An hour later, she burst into my room with two servants and ordered them to set up a movie projector I could watch from the comfort of my bed. I nearly laughed at her audacity, but I still didn't have it in me. Her stubborn insistence on protecting me from despair warmed me, even if I lacked the strength to show it.

We watched several movies every day and ate popcorn together. I caught a few movies in St. Louis over the years, but I never in a million years thought I'd experience the decadence of watching a movie in bed. There was no lively piano music playing, but we didn't seem to miss it.

A few days later, I apologized to Olive for not being more grateful to her for help in coping with the loss of Felix. She assured me that it was her pleasure as she knew how much I'd come to love him.

The Duchess now knew that I was having a baby and had given her blessing to deliver the baby at Chaffinch Fields. It was a relief to hear that I wouldn't be cast out any time soon. The news that the Duchess had ordered a monument for Felix to be erected next to his mother's grave in the family cemetery was a bit emotional, but I took it in stride. The monumental highs and subterranean lows of my relationship with Felix had left me all cried out.

The four of us had a small service for Felix when the stone was ready. It felt real to see his name on the monument with the year of his birth and death written across it. His headstone matched his mother's perfectly.

I nearly laughed aloud—darkly amused by the absurdity—that only weeks ago we'd stood here, grieving for Mrs. Byerly. I imagined Felix's sardonic voice: "Christ, we're dropping like flies."

When I rejoined the household, my belly had grown exponentially in my seclusion, and the baby had started to kick. It helped rouse me to know that the baby was strong.

The Duchess pulled me aside one day, and she told me that Olive had explained all my fears to her. She wanted me to know that this baby is her dear cousin's legacy. Felix was coming home to me, and in her eyes that made us married. She would not give a fig if anyone wanted to create a scandal out of something so beautiful.

I opened my mouth to correct her, to clear the confusion, but an unexpected wave of longing silenced me. In my heart, this child was Felix's in every way that mattered. He was going to be a father if he had lived. Nothing had changed in that regard. This child would know Felix Byerly as its father no matter what. The Duchess offered me a maternal hug, and I thanked her for the kindness of her family.

I visited Felix and Mrs. Byerly in the cemetery almost every day as my belly grew larger and larger. Sometimes, I talked to each of them together and sometimes separately. It seemed kind that Mrs. Byerly wasn't without her Felix in the afterlife for long. Her headstone read, "Here lies Clarissa Venable Byerly, Devoted Mother and Employee of the Women's Charity Organization." She had wanted her two proudest achievements etched on her eternal resting place. She was a damn good woman.

My anger with Felix lasted for a long time. If he had only come to the conclusion that we belonged together before he foolishly left me, I'd still have him. He'd argue with me from the grave that the little girl he saved would be dead. I tried to argue that I didn't know the little girl. She could be a terrible person, and I imagined him laughing at me and saying, "Touche."

As the long days of summer faded into the crisp days of fall, Olive and I resumed our daily walks on the grounds of Chaffinch Fields. I sometimes watched her ride her horse, but I could not return to the sport until after my pregnancy.

Olive wondered if I had thought about staying after the baby was born, or if I would try to go back to America and through the arches. Ever since I got the news that Felix had perished, I hadn't worried as much about my future. I told her that I was open to any advice she had as I had decided to focus on nothing but the baby until it was born.

Awkwardly, she started to prattle, and it was odd to be on the receiving end of it from her. She said things like she had been considering it for a long time, and she almost told me about it when we didn't know if Felix was coming back. Unsure as to how I would react, she assured me it would not be an act of charity. It would simply be a way to secure the future of Chaffinch Fields with someone the family trusted.

Unable to endure her fumbling another moment, I stopped her abruptly. "Olive, please—what are you trying to say?"

She took a deep breath, met my eyes, and spoke plainly. "We wish to name your child as my heir."

"Surely, you must be joking."

Her father was an only child as well. His distant Powlett relatives were all in debt and would mortgage their ancestral home into the ground to cover their bon vivant lifestyles. Her mother had family in America, but she didn't speak to them. Mrs. Byerly was the only relative she ever liked. It was all but settled, and her parents were in agreement that making my child her heir was an excellent decision. She only wanted me to agree to it before she had the papers drawn up.

What could I say to such generosity? She informed me that I only had to say "yes" so I did. Before I left for Europe, I dreamed of meeting an eligible Duke or Earl, but I had no idea that I'd give birth to a child who would one day inherit an estate quite the magnitude of Chaffinch Fields. **Lord, what would my mother say if I could tell her? No doubt, she would retire from washing clothes and spend her days languidly while a servant fed her grapes and bon-bons.**

The idea of the Seven Arches curse faded as the blooms from the chrysanthemums gave way to the approaching winter. After Felix died nothing horrible happened to anyone else. My pregnancy progressed normally, and my belly stuck out to an embarrassing degree. Olive said she saw the pregnant woman glow with me, and I told her it was only sweat from lugging around the extra weight.

I spent a lot of time that autumn and winter considering my baby's future. What more could I dream of for the child than an entire estate? It seemed almost poetic that Mrs. Byerly's grandchild would inherit the estate she wanted for her son.

I had made some personal decisions as well. My heart knew there was no room left to love another. I'd tasted a depth of feeling few ever experienced, and marrying anyone else would feel like a betrayal. The rest of my life would be devoted to raising my child in much the same way that Mrs. Byerly had devoted herself to Felix. The love of two great men had blessed me at a rather young age, and I knew that any other man would be a disappointment in comparison.

Harvey taught me what it was to love, and Felix showed me what it was to be in love. He had never wished for me to give up anything to marry him as he only wanted me to be with him, and I missed him every day. The baby would have the name of Byerly to honor the man who would have been his or her father.

The Christmas season at Chaffinch Fields was a wonderful event to behold. The Duchess had five trees decorated and set up in different rooms of the house. Some were trimmed with gold and red ribbon. Others were covered with silver tinsel and ornamental balls.

Walking into different rooms of the house gave me a whole new perspective on Christmas. Even much of the artwork was swapped out for portraits of the nativity as well as Father Christmas. She even had some holly and mistletoe decorating the various bedrooms.

Olive confessed that she and the Duchess had an addiction to Christmas, and while she was mostly reserved and sarcastic, the Christmas season had her humming carols and sleeping with visions of sugar plums dancing in her head.

There were teas, parties, and celebrations, and while I attended none of them due to my confinement, I was treated to the confections and dinners the kitchen prepared for them. In the last few weeks of my pregnancy, I had no desire to get out of bed, much less converse with the Duchess' snobby friends.

Olive, who usually complained of the society snobs, went on and on about the charities that they were donating for during the season of giving as well as the games they played to celebrate the season.

She later admitted that Christmas was always special because it was the one day of the year where her family was totally devoted to one another. It had always been that way ever since she was a little girl. The three members of the Powlett family celebrated Christmas Eve alone without any servants waiting upon them.

They had oyster stew and mincemeat pie for dinner, which she and the Duchess always prepared together. The labor of cooking her own meal made Olive feel middle class, and she adored it. I couldn't help but laugh at the sentiment. After dinner they sang Christmas carols around the piano, drank hot cider, and played the Minister's Cat until it was time for Father Christmas to arrive.

"I've talked it over with the Duke and Duchess, and we want you to join us this year," she said.

I protested that it was their family tradition, and I didn't even believe that I could stay up that late as I was due to give birth to this child any day now. She was quite insistent and even dragged the Duchess into my room to plead her case so I joined in with the Powlett Family Christmas festivities.

In the kitchen, watching Olive and the Duchess prepare the meal, I'd never seen them get along so well together. They were usually arguing with each other about what was proper and what was unseemly, but not during the preparation of the Christmas Eve dinner. They were laughing with each other and singing carols. Even if they didn't always share the same opinion, they did indeed love each other.

Before dinner, it had been a tradition of the Duke to give each of his girls a Christmas Eve gift, and I was gratified to be included. He had chosen jeweled brooches, and all three were beautiful. The Duchess had a diamond encrusted lily. Olive had a horse made out of rubies, and I had stork made of pearls which was indicative of the baby I was about to birth.

It was absolutely gorgeous, and I didn't believe all my thank yous were quite sufficient because the Powlett family essentially adopted me for the holiday. I supposed the cost of the brooch to be more than I'd made in all my years of working at the WCO.

We sat down to dinner, and it was nothing like the other meals I had experienced at Chaffinch Fields. There were no servants, no ceremony, just a table filled with food and people talking over one another. It reminded me of meals with my own family, where formality gave way to familiarity. Watching the usually composed Powletts laugh freely and share stories, some of them surprisingly bawdy, felt oddly intimate. It may have been out of character for them, but I loved it. For once, it felt less like tradition and more like togetherness.

After dinner, the Duke opened an old, beloved copy of 'A Visit from St. Nicholas,' his voice rich and comforting. As he read, I felt the gentle embrace of belonging—a sensation I'd long missed.

The Duchess even made an insinuation that it would be wonderful to read to a child the next year. I colored with embarrassment, but I was happy to bring any sort of joy to this family who had welcomed me and my unborn child as one of their own.

It was nice to be a part of a family again as it was the first Christmas that I was away from Mother and Ray. I wondered briefly how they were celebrating. Did Ruby spend Christmas Eve with them or the Cleghorns?

But, it didn't really matter to me what Ruby did. These people were my family now, and they were the best Christmas gift I could have ever asked for. The Duchess made a few tears erupt from my eyes when she whispered that I was the sister that she'd always hoped to give her Olive. I hugged her for her kind words, and she called me a blessing.

When it was time for carols, the Duchess sat down at the piano. She began to play "What Child Is This?" and we all sang along. The Duke and Olive walked up to the piano, but as I was ensconced in a comfortable chair, I would need help getting up. Rubbing my belly expectantly, I sang rather quietly as I knew that I couldn't carry a tune to save my life.

Halfway through the song, Olive gasped audibly, and it awoke me from a reverie regarding my soon to be son or daughter. I looked at the expression on her face, and I couldn't imagine what she was seeing. The Duchess continued to play and sing alone as her back was to the door as was mine.

I studied Olive's face for a clue, and she shook her head as if she could not believe her eyes. Struggling to get up, the Duke saw that I was in need of assistance and helped me.

"Merry Christmas, dear," he said as I turned around and saw Felix Byerly in the flesh standing at the doorway.

My breath seized sharply, my legs weak beneath me. Felix stood in the doorway—impossibly alive, his familiar half-smile daring me to believe my eyes. He couldn't be real. I felt like I was hallucinating, but that cocksure grin that I loved didn't disappear into thin air as I expected. It endured, and I took my first step toward him.

My pregnant belly swung as I approached, and I could tell he was surprised to see just how big I had gotten. A smile spread across his face, and he began to slowly limp toward me. He looked like he hadn't slept for weeks, but nothing else mattered because he was alive.

The Duchess finally stopped the music as Olive directed her attention toward Felix. There was a long silence in the air as we stood face to face with each other.

My voice shook with disbelief. 'Felix, is it really you?' I whispered, terrified that if I reached for him, he'd vanish like a ghost.

"I am. Did you forgive me?"

"I did."

We embraced awkwardly, laughing and crying at the absurdity of it—my swollen belly pressing gently against him, his weary arms straining to hold me close. It wasn't the kiss that I planned on all those months ago, but I was so overcome with emotion and shock that I didn't know quite what to do with myself.

I automatically started crying tears of joy once we parted. In my most desperate prayers, I had never dared ask for this miracle. Yet here he was, Felix Byerly, back from the dead—my perfect, impossible Christmas gift.

With some assistance, he sat down and relayed to us the hardships he had undergone when fire broke out on the *Leucothea.* He helped all the women and children he could into the lifeboats and managed to save a little girl still trapped in her cabin near the hold of the ship. A crew member pleaded to him for help as his leg had been pierced by a broken rafter which pinned him to the wall.

The little girl was handed off to her mother, and he went back to help the young man. Just as Felix freed the crew member's leg, the ceiling splintered and crashed down, engulfing them both in darkness. When he awoke on what he thought was a floating door, he was shocked to be alive.

The crew member he had saved was lying beside him, and he quickly realized that the man wasn't breathing. The blackness of his face suggested that he'd died inhaling too much smoke. Felix believed that the man had saved his life after he'd freed his leg.

The makeshift raft drifted helplessly, caught in a swift current that carried him far beyond sight of the Leucothea's lifeboats, leaving him utterly alone on an endless, empty ocean. He realized fairly quickly that both his legs were broken, and there wasn't much he could do for himself to survive. Drifting aimlessly on the vast, indifferent ocean, Felix wondered bitterly if the quick mercy of smoke inhalation was preferable to the slow agony awaiting him.

The ocean carried him for two or three days as the pain in his broken legs took him in and out of consciousness. He resisted the urge to drink the water, but he eventually had to say goodbye to his companion's corpse which had started to smell. As despair began to consume him, a distant cry broke through his delirium. A weathered Icelandic fishing vessel appeared like a mirage, and hands reached down, pulling him back from the brink.

He developed a bad infection due to one of his injuries, and he was delirious with fever for several weeks. Somehow, he survived again, and it took several months for him to recover and regain the use of his legs. The first chance he got he boarded a Danish fishing ship bound for

Copenhagen to work his way back to England as he had no money.

The plan was to make it to Chaffinch Fields by Christmas, hoping that I was still there because seeing me again would be the best Christmas present he could dream of.

"Felix," I whispered, tears threatening again, "you returning to me will go down as the greatest Christmas gift ever received."

"Well, no gifts next year then," he said with a wink.

The Duchess arranged for the wedding to take place the very next day on Christmas. Olive made me a beautiful bouquet of poinsettias and the altar was decorated with holly as well as red and green bows. It was absolutely perfect. The Duchess herself lovingly altered the dress I'd bought at Rice Stix—transforming a garment once associated with fear into a symbol of joy and hope.

Wearing the dress purchased from the twisted fortune of the gold-toothed man felt strangely symbolic—as if fate had used even darkness to bring Felix and me together. The Seven Arches had also brought Felix and I together, and I wondered briefly if the gold-toothed man could be alive in all the other worlds. It made me shiver, and I quickly forgot it to focus on my wedding.

The wedding night was a bit awkward and not something me or my husband ever pictured in our wildest dreams. I was nearly nine months pregnant. He was still stiff from his injuries and hadn't completely built his strength.

We laid with one another for a while. He cupped my pregnant belly in his hands and cradled it lovingly, and he said that he didn't think that I'd ever looked so beautiful. The kisses he laid on my neck and the gentleness as he caressed my body sent waves of pleasure over me. It bore little resemblance to the passion of our first encounter, but this was deeper—an intimate communion, gentle and profound, sealing our bond as husband and wife. My world seemed complete again.

We spent the next week not ever being separated from one another. He and I were at each other's side like we were physically connected by a tether. I didn't want to take any chances of losing sight of my Felix ever again. Olive even brought the projector back into the room, and she watched a few movies with us. Neither of us were too mobile as Felix was still building strength from his injuries, and I was so pregnant that any movement was uncomfortable.

A little after midnight on January 2nd, I went into labor. Felix paced anxiously, his eyes wide with worry, fussing over my every breath until I gently squeezed his hand and whispered, "Felix, I need you calm, for both of us."

A doctor and a whole team of nurses were on hand to see to my every need. They didn't think it was proper for Felix to be in the room with me, but that became his one concession. He would sit with me throughout the birth.

The moment our child was born a strong, determined cry filled the room, shattering our tension. Felix burst into joyful tears, repeating in disbelief, "He's here. He's healthy. He's perfect."

Within minutes, I was holding the baby. He was as pale as Harvey was, and I could tell I had a little towheaded angel. I asked Felix if it bothered him that the baby was likely going to be fair in complexion, but he was just over the moon that we were all happy and healthy.

He wanted to name the boy Jay for sentimental reasons to honor the child he and Tabitha had lost. The name fit the little child's face perfectly. The little boy looked exactly like a Jay to me. We got a bit stuck thinking about a middle name.

"Do you like the name Samuel after my father?" he asked when it was just the three of us in the room together.

I laughed softly. "We can't do that. Your mother would climb out of her grave and come knocking at our door."

"And she is right outside," he laughed, gesturing to the window toward the cemetery.

He agreed that there should be an ocean that separated them from his mother's spirit before we named a child Samuel.

I asked him what he thought about naming the baby after her.

"Clarissa?" He asked.

"Clarence," I said softly, looking into Felix's eyes. "To honor your mother and all she's meant to us."

"Jay Clarence Byerly," he said with finality.

I kissed him, and we sat together as a family on the bed for a long while. Together, we held our son, a family made whole by miracles. Felix, Hazel, and Jay Clarence Byerly—against all odds, finally united.

Chapter 14

A few months had passed since little Jay Clarence Byerly was born. Felix embraced fatherhood with quiet wonder, as if Jay's birth had finally filled a part of his heart that had remained empty since losing Tabitha and their child. In the years since the tragedy, he wasn't sure he'd ever get the chance. The baby made him realize what he would have missed if I hadn't come into his life.

Felix quickly came to regret naming our son Jay, feeling that the name, meant to honor the child he lost, unfairly burdened our little one with echoes of grief. I suggested that a nickname would help. Laughing that Jay was basically one letter, he didn't see how I could shorten it further.

"What about Jaycee? We'll just add another letter," I said.

He smiled, "Jaycee Byerly. That's a wholly original name."

The nickname made him feel better about the whole affair, and the entire Powlett family felt it was the perfect moniker for our child. There hadn't been a child that graced the nursery at Chaffinch Fields since Olive had been a baby. The Duchess wished that she and the Duke had been able to give their Olive a sibling, but it wasn't meant to be for them.

She was over the moon at having a child to snuggle. The Duchess spoke quite lovingly to Jaycee about how she was keeping house for him until he was all grown up. Her similarity to Mrs. Byerly gave me a glimpse as to what Felix's mother would have been like with her grandchild. I wish she had gotten to see either Jay or Jaycee Byerly. She would have melted at the sight of the child, and she'd immediately make plans for his future.

The Duke was quite smitten as well. He leaned over the Duchess often when she was holding the baby, and he talked about how he hoped the boy took to horses as he had. Olive would insist that her heir keep up the family legacy of breeding polo and racehorses he said jovially.

Despite the blond hair and pale complexion neither the Duke or Duchess seemed to suspect that the child was not biologically Felix's. If they had counted the months, they'd know, but Olive assured me that they had better manners than that. They'd never embarrass themselves or me by pointing out something so gauche.

Olive was probably the biggest surprise of all as she took to little Jaycee Byerly the way that bread takes to butter. She enveloped Jaycee in fierce affection, scooping him into her arms whenever she entered the nursery, her earlier protests about motherhood forgotten in the joy she found simply holding him. It was quite comical after all the comments she'd made about pregnancy.

I wondered if seeing my son in the flesh might have had an unintended effect on her. If his birth had awakened some maternal feelings, I wasn't sure if she wanted Jaycee to still inherit the estate. Originally, the baby and I were going to stay at Chaffinch Fields forever, but since Felix was alive, we'd return to America. It felt awkward to ask her, and I enjoyed watching her bond with my son.

I struggled after my little Jaycee came into this world. He was a strong baby, but my milk supply didn't fully come in right away which stressed me out. It made me feel like a failure as a mother from the very beginning. The Duchess took it upon herself to hire a wet nurse for him in those early months, and she said that a wet nurse was the most natural thing in the world. Some women didn't produce as much milk as others. Mothering capabilities had nothing to do with it. When I could, I still nursed Jaycee, but the wet nurse did alleviate some of the stress that I felt.

Felix noticed fairly quickly that I had trouble bonding with the baby. He stroked my hair, and he told me that I was probably just nervous that the baby didn't look much like her handsome husband. He managed to make me smile, but there were some bad days when I felt almost unable to get out of bed. On those days, Olive and Felix arranged for the projector to come into my room, and we'd watch movies together. It helped me feel loved even though inside I felt wretched.

Sleepless nights blurred into anxious days, leaving me fragile and tearful. I would lie awake in restless silence, overwhelmed by a nameless dread I couldn't shake until Felix's comforting presence soothed me back into calmness. If he hadn't been there advocating for me, I could have easily spiraled away. Always listening, he'd pull me into his arms if he heard me crying in the night. It brought me so much comfort as he was forever my rock.

It was the wet nurse that told me about the baby blues. She'd had four children of her own, and she had the baby blues with them for a few weeks. Apparently, it was an effect of birth and my body readjusting itself. Reflecting on those challenging first months, I felt profoundly grateful for the kindness and unwavering support that surrounded me. Certain that without their compassion, I might have lost myself entirely.

Felix and I were also surprised by the arrival of his Uncle Enoch at Chaffinch Fields who traveled with his companion from Muncie, Mr. Clyde. I had suffered so much while believing that Felix was dead that I didn't even consider what effect it had on his dear uncle.

Having only known Mrs. Byerly, I was taken aback to see just how much Felix resembled the Byerly side of his family. He definitely had his mother's eyes, but his nose and jawline were quite similar to his uncle. The man's hair was completely white, but it was still thick and full. A part of me was gratified to believe that Felix might always have his thick, wavy hair that complimented him so well. I thought it was adorable that Felix and his uncle had nearly identical mustaches.

Mr. Clyde and his uncle had been lifelong friends, and his uncle spent much time in Muncie visiting the old rapscallion. Uncle Enoch was a confirmed bachelor, and Mr. Clyde had been a widower for the last twenty years. They seemed to enjoy each other's company ever since they were young men. Mr. Clyde was a shorter man than Uncle Enoch, but he had a charming face and bright smile.

Felix had kept in regular contact with his uncle regarding the deterioration of his mother's health and her eventual death. He had sent his last telegram to him in New York before he boarded the *Leucothea*.

Uncle Enoch heard about the sinking of the ship, and he was informed that his nephew had not been among the survivors. He was devastated beyond measure and withdrew from much of his business dealings while shutting up most of his house in Waveland.

A new headstone for Tabitha and the boy was erected to include Felix's name on it. He had gone out regularly to talk to the little family he'd hoped would be his legacy. Mr. Clyde had accompanied him on many of those trips, and he relayed that poor Enoch was quite inconsolable. Felix embraced his uncle tightly, reassuring him that their shared legacy was safe, bringing visible relief and tenderness to the older man's weary eyes. It brought him endless amusement to know that he had not only one headstone but two.

"I'm the alivest dead man that's ever been," he said with a chuckle.

Uncle Enoch didn't quite have the dark humor that Felix and I shared, and he scoffed at the insinuation. He was on the verge of making a new will to leave the entirety of his estate to the town of Waveland, but he received the telegram that Felix was alive the day after Christmas.

He and Mr. Clyde wasted no time making travel arrangements to see that his boy was alive with his own eyes. The gentlemen arrived about six weeks after Jaycee was born so I was only beginning to come out of the baby blues, but Uncle Enoch was not the type of man to worry about formalities.

Kissing my cheek, he thanked me for my years of service to his sister-in-law, the old battle ax. Then he winked at me, and I could see how strong the family resemblance was. Absolutely thrilled to be a great uncle, he seemed to not ask any questions about how little Jaycee looked like Felix either. Commenting that the boy had good strong lungs, he said the child was a Byerly through and through. Uncle Enoch was a good man, and I could tell that Felix's happiness in life was his happiness as well. If Felix loved Jaycee and me, then he did too.

"You wouldn't by chance be the daughter of a man named John Wesely Sutton, would you?" Uncle Enoch asked me once when he ran across me one day rocking Jaycee in the nursery.

Startled by his accuracy, my heart jumped—how could this man from Felix's world speak of my estranged father with such warmth and familiarity? When Felix told him my maiden name, he was startled by how much I reminded him of his old friend. My father had evidently been employed as a blacksmith in Waveland several years ago before my parents had eloped. Uncle Enoch tried to lure him back to Waveland once, but it never panned out.

He'd not met my mother, but he recalled my father telling him that the woman he was going to marry was a bit of a spitfire. She wrote to him several years ago, telling him that my father was dead.

There were plenty of stories about my father's prowess when it came to shoeing horses and making almost anything that Uncle Enoch could dream up out of iron. It was thirty years later, and he still had a set of outdoor seats at his home in Waveland that my father had made for him when they worked together. I had no idea that my father was ever a blacksmith in Waveland. I vaguely recalled him as a laborer on a farm in O'Fallon, but he disappeared when I was only eight.

It was so odd to hear someone who had loved and respected my father so much speak so highly of him. I could hardly believe it as there wasn't a single person I'd ever met besides Mother and Ray that seemed to have a kind word to say about him.

By the time Mother and Ray moved to Milligan, all my father's siblings had left the area. Outside of a few letters, I'd never conversed with anyone in my father's family.

Thinking of him only as a louse that abandoned his family, I hadn't considered that others like Uncle Enoch would have a different opinion of him. To Uncle Enoch, John Wesley Sutton was this talented entrepreneur. The surprise that Mother had written Uncle Enoch about my father's death was fascinating, especially when she'd never told us that he had died. Roscoe was certain he had seen him in Texas years ago so it seemed unlikely that she knew the truth.

Somehow the man that Uncle Enoch talked of with such alacrity didn't reconcile in my head to the rogue who left his wife and kids to fend for themselves while he wandered the country.

Listening to Enoch's fond recollections, I realized with a pang that my image of John Wesley Sutton had been shaped entirely by his absence, leaving me ignorant of the complicated man he truly might have been. He may not have been the awful man that I built up in my head. It was quite likely that he was a flawed human being like everyone else on the planet.

The whole conversation with Uncle Enoch made me wonder what truly happened to him, and if I would ever find out. Is it possible that he was still out in the world somewhere? I shuddered at the thought that I had disappeared through the Seven Arches into Ruby's world. What if the same thing had happened to him?

Jaycee was three months old when Felix approached me about the prospect of returning to America. Before I walked through the Seven Arches, I'd only planned on staying in England for about a year.

I could hardly believe that an entire year had passed. It felt as if I had lived an entire lifetime in that single year. I couldn't help but wonder about the happiness Ruby had found in Milligan. Surely, it must've been filled with a lot less drama than my year.

Our Jaycee had grown into quite a happy baby, and he was much more aware of his surroundings. He had laughed out loud a few times when Felix would hold him, and it irritated me to no end that I couldn't make him laugh no matter what face I made.

Felix had put on some of the weight he had lost during his harrowing experience after the sinking of the *Leucothea*. Daily exercise in the garden had reduced his limp to only slightly noticeable, and he assured me that he only occasionally needed aspirin to deal with the pain.

I had recovered from the birth and my baby blues sufficiently so we were all three healthy enough for the voyage. Mr. Clyde and Uncle Enoch departed the week before we were scheduled to leave.

They had talked for years about taking in the sights of Europe and seeing his nephew, grandnephew, and new niece-in-law seemed like the perfect excuse to finally take the trip. Uncle Enoch said it would also give us time to adjust to his home in Waveland without him lumbering about.

"Darling, I want you to change whatever in the house doesn't suit you! It has been far too long since that old place has seen a woman's touch."

I thanked him kindly, but inside I was terrified. The thought of living so near Ruby tightened my chest with dread. I had promised her we'd stay apart, and now fate was pulling me dangerously close to breaking that vow. It had been a year, but I most certainly would get recognized as her especially since Harvey had relatives that lived there. If I moved to Waveland, I felt like I was breaking a promise to Ruby. Last year, it seemed ludicrous to think that I would fall in love and marry a man who lived one town away from her.

But, we had been separated for a year. She had lived her life as Harvey's wife, and I was certain she rarely went to Waveland. There was a chance we'd never run into one another, and if we did, what of it? People who were unrelated often resembled one another.

It was probable that Jaycee would also have a lookalike at Cleghorn Farms, and that coincidence would be a bit more difficult to explain away if they encountered one another. On the other hand, by the time that Jaycee was old enough for school, we would want to send him somewhere prestigious especially if Olive really intended on him to be her heir.

Olive eventually assured me that she was still adamant about Jaycee Byerly one day running Chaffinch Fields for her when he came of age as she loved the boy. She made it clear that was still not inspired to motherhood in the least bit. There wasn't a scenario she could imagine where another child could usurp the place Jaycee Byerly held in her heart.

As our departure date from Chaffinch Fields got closer and closer, she made more frequent visits to the nursery to hold the boy she considered to be her nephew. She refused to use baby talk with him and spoke with him the same way she'd converse with an adult. When asking pointed questions about his disposition, she listened intently as if he were responding. It was mildly amusing to see her so playful.

The thought of leaving her thoroughly choked me up. At one point, I expected to stay with her forever at Chaffinch Fields, and now I wasn't. I was elated that Felix was alive and my husband, but a small part of me regretted that an ocean would separate me from dear Olive.

Olive and I had come from two very different worlds, and I couldn't even imagine what she'd think of the places that I had lived growing up. She was always understanding which was part of the reason I loved her. One day, she promised that she would come see the Seven Arches.

We debated about whether or not I would tell Felix the whole truth about the arches. I was concerned that he would think that I was mad, but she countered that Ruby Cleghorn would be all the proof I needed. If he was still skeptical, she said I could drag him through the Seven Arches myself and introduce him to a Felix Byerly from another world.

The idea that the arches carried a curse with them seemed so silly to me now. All my problems vanished the moment that Felix made it back to me. If I hadn't walked into Ruby's world, I may have chosen to stay behind with Harvey. I never would have met Felix, and that thought was too difficult to bear.

Felix was quite necessary to my happiness, and after fearing that I'd lost him twice, I never wanted to be parted from him ever again. Ruby may have claimed this as her world, but I felt very strongly that I belonged here too.

I sat him down and told him the whole truth as to why I was apprehensive at returning. He listened to me carefully waiting on the punchline, but I shook my head in earnest. I explained that I had told him my mother was dead because she was dead to me and alive to Ruby.

She never would have insisted that I marry a man I didn't want to. It sounded ludicrous to him, but he trusted me more than anyone else in the world so it must be true.

"It would be so easy to disprove if I didn't believe you, wouldn't it?" he said with a smile.

I agreed. He suggested that I should get a haircut if I was concerned about being mistaken for Ruby, and we'd stay away from a farm in Milligan, Indiana. Not familiar with a family by the name of Cleghorn, he wasn't concerned about crossing paths with them.

Olive didn't think a haircut would alter my appearance enough if I was worried about being recognized as Ruby. She found me a wig that I could wear for going out in public. While I was wearing it, she thought I looked almost like Lillian Gish, an actress from some of the films we had watched while I was pregnant. I asked her if she had purchased this wig because she had a thing for Lillian Gish, and she told me to mind my own business.

Felix held my face tenderly, looking deeply into my eyes. 'You will always be my Hazel Byerly. Ruby's life is hers, but you belong with me."

The announcement that we had gotten married had most likely been spread all over town by Uncle Enoch anyway.

When he saw that I was still apprehensive, he promised that we'd look into moving outside of town if need be. He hated to disappoint his uncle, but these were very unusual circumstances.

The relief I felt after I'd been able to unburden myself to Felix was great, and I was gratified that he was understanding about something that was so out of the ordinary. He only winked at me and told me that he wanted a wife that would keep his life interesting.

I packed Olive's wig and considered writing to Ruby about my return to Indiana as Mrs. Felix Byerly. However, she had been insistent that we no longer communicate. With any luck, we wouldn't cross paths for several years, and by then, we'd have our own circles established.

It was hard to be certain if I was doing the right thing by going back, but I thought with the wig I would be able to get by for a few months. Olive and I prepared my backstory. My parents had died of the Spanish Flu, and my father was British. I came across the pond to find my English relatives, but I found Olive Powlett instead and became her social secretary. Felix arrived with his mother a few months later, and we were instantly smitten with one another.

My trunk was once again packed for travel. It was emotional leaving Chaffinch Fields and Olive behind. I told her that I wished to put her in a trunk and take her with me. She stepped into my trunk, then stepped out with mock indignation. 'Absolutely not. My dear, I only travel first class.' Her playful dismissal filled me with laughter, masking the ache of leaving her behind.

We shared that last laugh together, and she once again insisted that she was quite serious about Jaycee being the heir to Chaffinch Fields after her. Felix and I would have to have another child to inherit the business holdings in Waveland.

Jaycee, after all, was a British citizen being born in England, and he would call Chaffinch Fields home when he came of age. Felix laughed as it was reminiscent of the agreement his uncle and mother hatched when he was still in short pants. She was resolute that Felix and I bring Jaycee for a visit every year.

Felix and I had a long talk with his mother at her graveside, and it was surprisingly painful to leave her behind as well. We knew that spending eternity looking down over Chaffinch Fields, the place she dreamed of her son inheriting, was the best place for her.

Clarissa Venable Byerly lived a remarkable life—from debutante to devoted mother, from turbulent wife to tireless advocate for women. She embodied strength, grace, and resilience, leaving an indelible legacy in her wake.

The voyage across the Atlantic and the train ride to Waveland was blessedly uneventful. Felix masked his unease with humor, but I could see the tension in his eyes each time we stepped on deck, memories of the Leucothea's sinking lingering beneath his calm exterior. Jaycee seemed to love to travel. I had expected him to be sick for a while as he adjusted to the motion of the ship, but he was completely unaffected.

I wasn't sure exactly what to expect when we arrived in Waveland. Felix jokingly told me to keep my expectations in check after staying for nearly a year at Chaffinch Fields. As long as there were stables, a solarium, and my own wing of the house, I told him that I'd be perfectly content.

The house in Waveland took my breath away—a striking three-story red-brick home, dignified yet inviting, promising a future filled with memories waiting to be made. Jaycee would have his choice of six bedrooms when he got a little older. It made me wonder if we could stay here. I didn't want to wear that wig forever, but still, it seemed a shame that this home would not be filled with our family as it had housed Felix and Uncle Enoch for many, many years.

It was nice to be able to move around and learn about the house at my own pace without anyone but Felix and Jaycee. Uncle Enoch had telegrammed that he and Mr. Clyde were enjoying Paris, and we shouldn't expect them to return for another month.

The kitchen was a decent size, and Felix said that he and his uncle took most of their meals out. However, he was quite adept at making breakfast. There was the awkwardness of realizing that my husband had more culinary skills than I did.

Realizing with embarrassment that my husband outmatched me in the kitchen, I sheepishly confessed I barely knew how to scramble an egg. It was the first time I'd felt truly inadequate in our marriage, and Felix's teasing laughter only made it harder to maintain my dignity. It never occurred to me that I'd need to learn how to cook as I wished there was someone who could give me lessons.

We managed as well as we could. Felix had purchased a smoked ham and bread for us so we had a lot of sandwiches in those first few days. He made us breakfast every morning as he had done for Uncle Enoch in the years since Tabitha had passed away. He taught me how to cook an egg over easy as the runny yolk was very necessary for his happiness.

It took several tries for me to get it right, and he complained that he should have inquired about my domesticity before sliding a ring on my finger. I tartly replied that it was much too late for that as I wasn't going anywhere.

Jaycee adjusted well to the new house. When the stress from my baby blues was gone, my milk supply came in which was more than enough to adequately feed him. I missed the nanny who the Duchess employed to change Jaycee's diapers, but I'd always known I'd wanted to be a hands-on mother just like my own.

The realization hit me hard—I was only a short drive from my mother, yet still impossibly distant. An ache settled in my chest, knowing she was so near yet entirely unreachable, a mother's advice forever just beyond my grasp.

As I had worried so much about living close to Ruby, I never considered that I would live close to my own mother. She was only a short automobile ride away, but I couldn't go and see her. It seemed unfair that I wouldn't be able to get advice from her on anything. I hadn't realized that living this close to her would sting.

A few days after we'd arrived, Felix announced that he would go out and observe some of his uncle's local investments like the Waveland Telephone Company. Uncle Enoch would be pushing Felix to take over for many of his day to day business when he returned, and a visit to Tabitha and his son's grave was warranted as he'd been gone for so long. He also wanted to see his second headstone and wondered if it would be as impressive as the first one.

"I might announce my resurrection to Tabitha and Jay with a bit of religious humor," he said softly, eyes distant. I understood his need to make this pilgrimage alone—to gently close one chapter before fully opening ours.

He wanted to take me to see it someday, but it felt odd. It was silly, but he wanted to tell her about his new family before I visited. Assuring him that his devotion to her was heart-warming, I completely understood. While he was out, I said I might take Jaycee on a walk around the block, and he smiled before disappearing for a moment.

He reappeared with a beautiful red baby buggy, smiling gently. "Uncle Enoch bought it when Tabitha was expecting," he said softly.

I touched the handle, moved by the thoughtfulness of an uncle's stubborn hope finally realized. Felix smiled and said that his uncle was wise beyond his years, and he kissed me and Jaycee before walking out the door.

Adjusting my wig and wool cloche hat nervously, I stared at my unfamiliar reflection, silently praying my disguise would hold. Each step outside felt precarious, a test of my ability to live unnoticed in Ruby's shadow. Jaycee happily laid in the buggy. Looking in the mirror, I gave myself the once over before leaving and decided that I was disguised enough. Even if I ran into someone who knew Ruby, they'd certainly second guess themselves when I ignored them.

It was a nice April day with the sun shining brightly over our heads. The weather took a little getting used to after we had adjusted to the many overcast, rainy days in England. Jaycee loved the warmth of the sun, and I felt a pang for Harvey Cleghorn and his straw hat. Jaycee would likely love the outdoors, but he would be prone to sunburn. He was gurgling up at me most of the time that I pushed him, and it was impossible not to love my beautiful baby boy.

My predilection for prattling didn't relent even though my son could barely lift his head let alone carry on part of the conversation. I had grown used to the silence with Harvey over the years so I was comfortable talking to Jaycee out in the streets of Waveland. We mostly talked about plans for landscaping the outside of the house. I was shocked that it was April and there wasn't a single daffodil in Uncle Enoch's front yard. That oversight would be rectified before the next spring.

I took little notice of the people we passed on the street. Lost in plans for spring flowers, I nearly collided Jaycee's buggy into a mousy little girl who appeared around the corner so suddenly she seemed conjured from thin air. We both froze, eyes wide with shock.

The plain girl who I couldn't imagine was more than fourteen years old looked at me quite shocked. I tried to apologize to her, but our collision had upset my son.

"Quiet down, Jaycee," I said absentmindedly, while trying to ascertain if the girl I had bumped was alright. She nodded oddly at me, refusing to speak.

"I'm Hazel Byerly, what's your name, miss?" I said, while Jaycee's wails increased in volume.

I didn't even wait for an answer as Jaycee's cries were getting more and more concerning. He was suddenly in hysterics, crying as loudly as his little lungs would allow him. Wishing her a good day, I began pushing him back home, hoping the movement would calm him.

He was still so upset that I had to pick him up out of the buggy before we got halfway home. Jaycee's hysterical cries grew increasingly frantic, piercing my heart with panic. I clutched him tightly, murmuring reassurances, my nerves frayed as we hurried on our way.

By the time he fell asleep, I was nearly in tears myself. I held him tight against me with one arm while I pushed the buggy back home with the other. I left the baby buggy on the front porch as we entered the house. The poor thing had tired himself out with all the crying and was fast asleep.

I laid him gently in his cradle upstairs, then lingered a moment, debating whether to make a cup of tea. I filled the kettle, set out a knife and cutting board, and eyed a jar of blackberry jam that seemed to beckon from the shelf. But before I could slice the bread, I changed my mind. A few pages from my new book sounded more appealing. The tea and toast could wait until after Jaycee's nap. I barely made it through ten minutes of reading before sleep overtook me.

The clock in the parlor told me that I had been asleep for over an hour when I roused myself. I turned on the kettle for my tea and ran upstairs to see Jaycee still happily enjoying his afternoon nap. He looked perfectly content. The redness in his face which he had worked up with his crying had faded away.

I dreamily walked downstairs while imagining some new artwork hanging on the stairway and wondering if Felix would be coming home for lunch soon. Stepping into the kitchen, my heart stopped. Leaning casually against the counter, eyes cool yet piercing, stood one person who could unravel everything I had built: Harvey Cleghorn.

Rosamond Vincy, St. Louis 1923

As Felix Byerly exited the train station in St. Louis, the exquisite figure of Rosamond Vincy lingered in his thoughts.

From the instant Felix glimpsed Rosamond Vincy across the train car, her presence captivated him so completely that even the burden of his secret son momentarily faded into oblivion. The newspaper became his camouflage on the journey as he knew he'd be caught staring if there were no barrier between them. Over the years, he'd half-heartedly noticed other attractive ladies on the train, but there was something different about her.

When she ended up sitting next to him on the train to St. Louis, he thought he was dreaming, but the ruffian that was pursuing Miss Vincy quickly snapped him out of his reverie. The brute was easy enough to frighten away, but the gall of that man harassing a defenseless woman set Felix's temper ablaze. It was his anger at the man which caused him to be so terse at first with her.

Anxiously, he recalled saying "You're welcome" to her very abruptly before she'd had an opportunity to thank him. He was all set to apologize, but before he could, she flashed biting words back at him. The byplay between them was so much fun and so resonant of his Tabitha that he nearly forgot that it was unmannerly of him.

Now, she was gone, most likely forever. Felix silently cursed his own restraint, wishing he'd pressed gently for more details. He'd been too careful, too mindful of propriety—and now the intriguing Miss Vincy had slipped through his fingers like smoke. She insisted that they had simply been strangers who had met on a train and had a wonderful moment together.

Tabitha had been gone for nearly five years, and he hadn't seriously ever considered another woman in a romantic fashion. After his months with Penelope, he'd turned to celibacy largely because of the lingering shame he'd felt during his time with her.

What was it about Rosamond Vincy that stirred so much inside him? Feelings Felix had buried with Tabitha were suddenly alive and undeniable again, bringing both excitement and guilt. Rosamond Vincy had effortlessly revived something within him that he feared was lost forever.

He got off the streetcar less than a block from his mother's house, caught up in daydreaming about her the entire way.

Why was she supposed to cross his path at that particular moment in time? Was there a lesson in it for him?

Pondering the great mysteries of the universe was a favorite pastime of Felix Byerly, and the strong attraction he felt to Rosamond Vincy told him that their story wasn't finished quite yet. They had been thrown together by a chance encounter, and it had been magnetic. He would find her again, and there was no convincing him otherwise.

He arrived at his mother's house with an urge to scour St. Louis in search of the elusive mystery woman that he'd practically fallen in love with upon sight.

Mother and son had barely greeted one another before he asked her the best way to find someone based solely on a description. At first, his mother was concerned and demanded an explanation for haranguing the police about a woman on the train.

The whole story came out, and Clarissa knew that it would never do. Felix was on the verge of meeting his future bride and inheriting an English estate. This Rosamond Vincy would ruin all her plans if he somehow managed to find her.

She felt a surge of protective urgency—she had worked too long and too hard to let some beguiling stranger unravel her carefully woven plans. Felix must be whisked away immediately, before his romantic impulses derailed everything.

Clarissa Byerly was nothing if not a master at thinking on her feet. She explained to Felix that she would have no time to help him in his search for his mystery woman as they were departing for New York that very night.

"I thought you had some last minute preparations for the trip to work on with your secretary?"

"There have been a change of plans as I want you all to myself for the next couple of days, and New York is a perfect excursion for us. I admit it is a little last minute, but who needs an itinerary for everything?"

The two argued briefly, but now that the introductions between Felix and Olive were imminent Clarissa was not going to let some captivating social climber like the fictional Rosamond Vincy ruin her hopes for Felix.

"Mother, I can't simply walk away," he insisted, his voice tinged with desperation. "It's absurd, I realize, but something inside me feels that this was no mere coincidence. I must at least try."

"Felix," Clarissa retorted crisply, "'If it were truly meant to be, do you honestly believe she'd have chosen Rosamond Vincy as her alias? Have you forgotten Middlemarch entirely? Rosamond and Lydgate married in haste and lived in regret. Do not romanticize what was merely a charming coincidence."

Felix was a bit crestfallen at the prospect of leaving early, but his mother was persuasive in her ability to make him see just how ludicrous it was to start a search for a woman that he barely knew and hadn't even gotten her real name.

With practiced subtlety, Clarissa guided Felix's memories away from regret toward introspection, carefully steering him through gentle but pointed questions about Miss Vincy's appeal. As Felix recounted their interaction, she nodded knowingly, planting just enough doubt to temper his desire to chase a shadow.

As their train pulled away from St. Louis that evening, Clarissa felt a surge of triumphant anticipation. Felix was finally ready to love again, and she was certain Olive Powlett—not the mysterious Rosamond Vincy—was the woman destined to capture his heart.

Chapter 15

"Ruby," Harvey's voice was cold, brittle with hatred, his pistol gleaming ominously at his side.

It had been more than a year since I had seen Harvey Cleghorn, and I remembered awkwardly pulling him to the ground by Mother's cedar tree to feel him against me one last time. The fact that this was the same Harvey standing before me with hate and disgust in his eyes seemed unbelievable. I couldn't even begin to fathom what he was doing here or how he had found me.

"No," I protested, "I'm not Ruby."

"I'd sooner put a bullet in your head than call you 'Gem' ever again."

My heart plummeted as I realized Harvey truly believed I was Ruby. I wasn't Ruby or Gem in any sense of the word as I hadn't been in Harvey's life in over a year. The man staring me down didn't know me. It was difficult to believe this was the man I'd left behind when I got on that train to St. Louis. Panic flooded me—why was he here, and how had he found me? He held up the wig that I had thrown aside when we returned from our walk.

"This wouldn't fool anyone," he said, flinging it at my feet, "I want my son."

"I don't know where your son is? Dammit, I'm not who you think I am."

"Don't play games with me," Harvey growled, his eyes lifeless and merciless. "You took my son, Ruby. You'll give him back, or I'll make you regret ever being born."

"I don't understand why you're here. Where is your wife?" I said.

"I'm here," he said, repressing a rage, "to collect my son. The one you stole after you tried to kill my mother and ran away."

"Ruby ran away?" I said, completely confused.

His eyes narrowed at me as if I were speaking a foreign language. My mind raced. Ruby trying to kill Mrs. Cleghorn made no sense—but Harvey's eyes burned with conviction. What horrible chain of events had brought us here? Mrs. Cleghorn had never been a kind woman, but I didn't feel like Ruby was capable of cold-blooded murder. What could have possibly provoked her into doing such a thing?

"Harvey, can you tell me what happened?"

"I didn't come here to play games. You know perfectly well what happened. I have no idea why you thought you could hide out here in Waveland of all places, but I'm thankful you did. Now, I want my son," he said, slowly raising the pistol at me.

We stood stock still, each one waiting for the other one to make the first move when the sound of the front door came open.

"Hazel, darling!" Felix called cheerfully from the doorway. "Your devoted husband—" He froze, his smile dying instantly as his gaze landed on Harvey's gun aimed squarely at my chest."

Harvey redirected the gun straight at Felix, and he cocked it. The kettle hissed quietly at first, the soft whistle rapidly climbing to a piercing shriek that mirrored the rising terror in the room.

"I only want my son back, you can keep the whore," Harvey said, not moving the gun an inch from Felix's chest.

Taking a step toward Harvey, I intended to shut off the flame from the whistling kettle, but he took a step back and pointed the gun at me again. The sound of the kettle was ear-piercing at this point, but he didn't dare take his eyes off me to turn it off.

He backed toward the stove, the gun wavering between me and Felix as if he were deciding who to shoot first. When he reached the burner, he clearly didn't know how to lower the flame. Refusing to look away from us, he fumbled with the kettle and burned his hand badly. Instinct took over—he dropped the gun in surprise, clutching his injured hand with the other.

I lunged at the floor where the gun hit, but he was quicker than me. Felix was able to clock him in the side of the head before he recovered himself. The gun once again went flying through the air as Felix landed on top of Harvey on the floor.

Felix and Harvey grappled desperately, tumbling violently across the kitchen floor. I watched helplessly as Felix's injuries betrayed him, Harvey quickly gaining the upper hand. Harvey was younger and stronger than Felix, and he hadn't recently had both his legs broken. It was obvious that Felix wouldn't be able to hold him off for long.

I picked up the gun, turned off the gas stove, and I pointed the gun directly at Harvey's head. He thought quickly and grabbed the knife off the counter, holding it to Felix's neck. He sneered at me from behind my husband, and I knew he could be violent if he felt cornered.

"I'll kill this bastard, Ruby. I swear to God," he said with the knife at Felix's throat, "Put down the gun."

If I put down the gun, Harvey would take my son to God knows where. Ruby and her baby had disappeared so everyone would believe my son to be his child. Even though he was Harvey's biologically, Jaycee didn't know this man at all. He wouldn't understand what happened to his parents. I was at a loss for what to do, and I could see that Harvey was getting agitated. He had been in the war, and even though he had never talked about it, I knew he was capable of killing if he felt it was justified.

I wouldn't be able to live with myself if anything happened to Felix so I set the gun down.

"No!" Felix cried, but Harvey kidney punched him, and he dropped to the floor.

Harvey smiled that sinister smile at me, and I prepared for the worst. He picked up the gun that I had placed on the counter and pointed it directly at my head.

"I should put a bullet in your brain for what you did to my son and my mother," he said, pressing it against my forehead. I hadn't expected him to want revenge on me, and I broke out in a cold sweat.

He held the barrel of the pistol on me for what seemed like an eternity. I closed my eyes as it felt like the end was near. I thought about Felix losing another wife in this house, and a tear welled up in my eye. When Jaycee began to cry from upstairs, I did as well.

I flinched as Harvey's arm jerked suddenly, expecting the gunshot—but none came. Harvey's face twisted in confusion, eyes widening as he reached behind him, fingertips brushing against the knife Felix had plunged into his back. His arm fell to his side and the gun to the floor. He turned around and saw Felix behind him. Attempting to grab the knife out of his back, he lost consciousness too quickly. The blood began to pool around the knife after he had fallen to the floor.

I stood completely still for a few seconds unable to believe what had just happened. After I stared at Harvey's limp body, I looked at Felix. We were both in shock as to what happened and how quickly it happened. Jaycee's cries continued, and I finally snapped back to reality.

While I was running up the stairs to get him, I tried to figure out what Ruby had done. She and her baby had run away from her husband. If Harvey had become abusive, she may have run. Judging from that man's cruelty, it didn't seem like it was that far of a stretch. Mother would have helped her run away in an instant if he laid hands on her. Somehow, Harvey tracked me down thinking I was Ruby. Now, he lay dying on the kitchen floor.

He was convinced that I was Ruby, and I had a baby that was identical to hers. No one in Waveland or Milligan would believe I wasn't Ruby, nor would they believe that Jaycee wasn't Ruby's baby. Felix and I would go to prison for murdering Harvey Cleghorn. The jury would see us as adulterers who cuckolded Harvey. Even if Uncle Enoch took the stand in our defense, no one would believe him either.

I realized the only safe thing to do was run away, or we would risk losing Jaycee. Chaffinch Fields with an ocean between us and the protection of the Powlett Family would be the perfect place to hide out until Ruby resurfaced. What if we were caught on our way to New York? We needed to get away from here and fast. For all I knew the entire Cleghorn Family was waiting on him down the street.

We couldn't stay a moment longer. Panic surged as I realized no one would believe us—Harvey's blood on our hands condemned us. We had to run, and fast. With the baby in my arms, I told Felix we had to get in the car. He listened without a moment's hesitation. He drove out of town as fast as he could without attracting attention while I sank down in the car with the baby in my arms to avoid detection. I gave him directions to the Seven Arches.

He didn't want to leave without explaining to his uncle. There wasn't time for it now, but it was possible that we could come back and get word to Uncle Enoch before he returned from Europe. Time was of the essence now, and he agreed.

"My God, Hazel—I've killed a man," Felix whispered, the stark realization trembling in his voice.

"We had no choice," I said, holding Jaycee extra tightly.

The most important thing to me was getting our son safely away from Harvey's family. If Ruby had indeed tried to kill her mother-in-law, there wasn't a doubt in my mind that they'd try to send me to prison for her crimes. It was no longer safe for me to live anywhere near Waveland in this world, and I felt awful that Uncle Enoch's dream had been destroyed because of Ruby Cleghorn.

We abandoned the car along the side of the road and went as fast as we could down through the pasture to the Seven Arches. My mind raced as we rushed to our destination. How I would explain my absence let alone Felix and Jaycee to my mother, I did not know, but there was no time to ponder it. The Byerlys only needed to get out of the world where they would be charged with the murder of Harvey Cleghorn.

A terrible thought entered my mind that I hadn't considered in the chaos of Harvey's attack. When I was in trouble, my first thought was to go through the Seven Arches to escape it. I feared that it was also Ruby's first thought. Had we both traveled here to get away from trauma caused by Harvey Cleghorn? We had been the same person at one point, and I knew that our personalities couldn't diverge too much in a year. Was it possible that she was there as well? The thought scared me.

Felix was a bit dumbfounded when the arches came into sight for the first time.

"I believed you," he said, "but seeing this and knowing what it does is incredible."

Nodding in agreement, I took a deep breath and pushed the activation stone. Each keystone ever so subtly glowed in response. Seeing the anticipation in my husband's face as he held our child in his arms made the frightening prospect of leaving behind a world we knew in exchange for one filled with mystery a little exciting.

"Are you ready?" I asked.

"I've got everything I need," he said with a wink.

I took the child from him, and we made our way through the arches with the blood of Harvey Cleghorn still fresh on our hands.

The strain the arches caused on my mind, which led to me passing out the first time, was lessened considerably my second time through. I was able to stay conscious the entire time, but Felix, unfortunately, swooned as we walked out. Shouting in vain to keep him awake was of no use. Jaycee was still in my arms, but I managed to help Felix fall more softly to the ground.

I exhaled for the first time since I encountered Harvey Cleghorn in the kitchen which oddly couldn't have been more than an hour ago. Felix regained consciousness as I took in my surroundings. My heart seized with dread. The Seven Arches—the lifeline I'd relied upon—lay in ruin, reduced to crumbling rubble and dust. There was no going back.

There was nothing but rubble and stone. They had been in perfect working order when we walked through, and it felt almost as if our journey had destroyed them. What could have transpired here that had left them this way?

To survey the damage, I handed Jaycee back to Felix when he found his legs again. There wasn't a single arch left standing, but I found what looked to be a chip off one of the pink keystones. For the most part the colored stones were gone or ground into dust.

"We're trapped here," I whispered, despair overwhelming me. Tears blurred my vision as I realized the life we'd built was lost forever.

Felix took my face gently in his hands, steadying me with calm determination. "My love, we've faced worse. As long as we're together, nothing is truly lost."

His mouth fell open. Uncle Enoch. The Duke and Duchess. Olive. Dear, dear Olive wouldn't know us here. Jaycee wouldn't be her heir here either. Our lives were in the other world, and we had nothing here. There was even a second Felix here who would be his Uncle's heir. We had less than nothing.

"Darling, it wouldn't be us if there wasn't a bit of a struggle, now would it?"

He kissed me and reminded me all over again how easy it was to fall in love with him. With his kiss, I knew as long as we had each other that we'd never be unhappy a day in our lives.

"But, I would like to inquire as to what our next move might be?" he said looking around at the open pasture after realizing that we had no one in this world.

He made a classic Felix Byerly face of mock disgust when I suggested it was time for him to finally meet his mother-in-law.

"Oh, she's going to love you," I said, rolling my eyes.

Chapter 16

When we made our way back up the road, Felix was still a little surprised that our car wasn't parked where we left it in the other world. Explaining this without sounding condescending proved trickier than expected—especially when Felix eyed the empty space where our car had just been with baffled frustration.

"Because that car is likely in Uncle Enoch's garage in this place. Everything may look similar here, but there's no telling what is different. The most important thing is that we didn't kill anyone here," I said, patting his arm.

"You've had a whole year to grow accustomed to this bizarre circumstance. How about giving your husband a few days?"

I smiled tenderly and began to lecture him on the fundamentals of *The Path of the Earthly Spirit* when a figure stepped suddenly from between the trees, and recognition hit me like a bolt of lightning. It was Harvey Cleghorn. I gasped sharply, nearly screaming his name before Felix stepped protectively between us.

"We don't want any trouble from you!" he said, totally prepared to defend his family to the death again if he had to.

I peeked around Felix to see Harvey looking thoroughly confused. Harvey's brow furrowed deeply, confusion rather than anger shaping his familiar face. He looked genuinely startled by our presence. I'd seen all faces of Harvey Cleghorn over the years, and I knew that he was not the enraged monster we'd battled one world over.

"Harvey, my name is Hazel," I said, taking a chance.

His face went completely white for a moment.

"As I live and breathe," he said, "I never thought I'd meet you in a million years.

His face erupted into a wide smile, and he reached out his hand to Felix's. "I'm Harvey Cleghorn. Delighted to meet you."

"Felix Byerly. I suppose you know my wife Hazel, in a manner of speaking."

Harvey laughed out loud. It almost startled me, but then again, this Harvey had no idea that Felix had stabbed his counterpart in the other world. I was relieved that he meant us no harm. He was, however, still the natural father of my son, and I didn't want to acknowledge it in front of Felix.

My husband eyed me suspiciously. It was all so surreal. Somehow this Harvey was practically unrecognizable to the one we'd likely just killed. Felix and I both seemed to be waiting for the other shoe to drop.

"I thought it was so strange to see my Gem, pardon me, I mean Ruby, walking up the road when she just left with Bernice to go into town."

A cold shiver raced down my spine. Ruby was here—and suddenly everything about the ruined arches made terrifying sense. Had she destroyed them herself to prevent any return to that nightmare? Was that something I would have done if I'd endured a life with that monster that tried to kill me just an hour ago?

Realizing that I'd soon be reunited with the same Ruby, the future felt uncertain. The two of us, it seemed, had managed to make a huge mess in the other world, and now, we were trapped in a new one. I spent so much time since Felix returned convincing myself that there was no curse of the Seven Arches, but now I wasn't so sure.

I had so many questions, but Harvey had a lot of farmwork to tend to. He wasn't the one I wanted to talk to anyway, especially considering what had just happened to us, but he promised to relay to Ruby that he had seen us when she returned from town.

When we arrived at Mother's house, the anticipation to see her again after a long year nearly got the best of me. I fought the urge to run into the house and shout for her, but I was afraid that she'd be scared out of her wits.

She'd know I existed if Ruby had already been back here for some time, but still it made me feel like I was an imposter all over again. Jaycee was being the best baby boy, and Felix stood quietly beside me, a shy half-smile on his face as he nervously smoothed his hair, clearly anxious about impressing his new mother-in-law.

He admitted that he was a bit nervous about meeting the in-laws as he never thought there would be any to meet. I assured him that he'd do fine, and I wiped his chestnut bangs out from his face.

Before I had a chance to knock, the front door swung open, and Mother surveyed us silently for a moment.

"Ruby? Is that you?" she said almost as if she didn't know me.

"I go by Hazel nowadays," I said hopefully.

She nearly fainted when she realized who I was.

Mother's arms wrapped around me tightly, and the long-awaited embrace flooded me with relief. I clung to her as if I were a child again, tears streaming freely as the weight of our year-long separation dissolved between us. I never thought I'd be allowed to see her again, and here I was back in her house. Part of me never wanted to leave again.

There were so many times in Europe where I had wanted her love and guidance that to have her in front of me was bliss. She cried too as this had been the world that was missing a Ruby for more than a year.

She'd been without a daughter for a year's time, and now within a few weeks of each other, Ruby and I made our way back to her.

Mother filled the kettle for tea while I prattled on about her grandson, Jaycee Byerly.

Mother's eyes widened dramatically before bursting into hearty laughter. "Ruby. I mean, the Ruby that arrived here before you, brought a baby boy to meet me as well. His name, if you can believe it, is Justus Frederick Cleghorn, but we call him J.C."

"Jaycee is a nickname for this bundle of joy as well. It is short for Jay Clarence."

It was funny, and a little crazy to realize that both our sons would be identical and share the same nickname.

Mother laughed out loud again. She began to prattle on about how she managed to get a pair of twin girls without having to go through the agony of birthing two at a time.

While Mother snuggled her second grandchild, I introduced her to my husband, Felix Byerly. She stared at me in consternation for a moment and asked if I had married my boss' son. I replied that I had and told her in a twist of ironic fate that he was living in Waveland all along.

"Wait, are you related to Enoch Byerly of Waveland?" she asked.

He smiled and confirmed that Enoch was indeed his uncle.

"Uncle Enoch told me that you wrote him a letter years ago informing him that my father had died," I said.

She nodded, "I did put that in the letter as an introduction, but the reason I wrote him was to ask if he had a job for you."

"What?"

"Yes, you wanted to work and be independent. I didn't have any connections in O'Fallon or St. Louis, but Mr. Byerly employed your father before we eloped. John Wesley always talked highly of Enoch Byerly, and I hoped that he could help you find employment."

"Of course, I remember it now." Felix said, stepping in to add to the story, "Tabitha and I were visiting my mother at the time, and Uncle Enoch wrote to her about a young lady he knew looking for work and he asked if my mother had any openings at the WCO."

With a twinkle in his eye recalling his mother, he said that she nearly tore up the letter and threw it in the fire as she would rather eat nails than help a friend of Enoch Byerly. It was Tabitha that convinced her to give me an interview.

I looked at Felix incredulously, and he promised that he hadn't connected the dots until now. His mother had employed many girls over the years. What were the odds that I was the one that his uncle had asked a favor for?

The news embarrassed me a little bit, and I wasn't sure why. It seemed that I had my father to thank for his acquaintance with Uncle Enoch, and Tabitha for pushing Mrs. Byerly to meet with me.

Mother poured us tea and explained all that Ruby had endured with Harvey and Mrs. Cleghorn in the world where we came from. My initial anger softened as Mother told me about Ruby's baby blues sinking her into melancholy, and how Mrs. Cleghorn had used it to drive a wedge between her and Harvey.

I squeezed Felix's hand, silently vowing to cherish every moment with him. After all he'd carried me through, no words would ever be enough to repay his kindness.

She explained how Harvey here had pined for Ruby when she disappeared, and they had married after connecting. Ruby and Harvey had none of the bad blood whatsoever between each other here.

Felix mentioned that we had run into Harvey on our way here, and he had nearly frightened the dickens out of all of us.

Mother assured us that Harvey meant us no harm. The major bad influence in his life was his manipulative mother, and here, they didn't have contact with Mrs. Cleghorn. Harvey didn't think he would ever forgive her.

Felix and I looked at one another knowing that we would have to tell the story as to why we ended up here when we were more than happy in the other world. We tried our best to brace Mother for the story, which after seeing how different the two Harveys were would be hard to believe.

We told Mother all about how Ruby's disappearance from the other world had affected us. She was shocked that the Harvey in the other world could be so vicious and cruel as to hold us at gunpoint. She hoped that we wouldn't be angry with Ruby as she assumed I was living and working in

England, none the wiser of her struggles with the Cleghorns.

I thought back to the one letter that I'd received from Ruby when I was in England. She said it was too dangerous for us to communicate, and I wondered if her troubles had started almost immediately after I left.

Felix and I relayed our own love story when Ray arrived home, shocked by our presence as well. Seeing him again after a year was emotional as I never thought he'd look so happy and healthy. I commented that I barely recognized him as he wasn't the Ray that I remembered, and he joked that he actually wasn't the Ray that I remembered.

He told us all about his own adventures through the Seven Arches regarding the Ray that lived in this world, and his own responsibility in Ruby's inability to sniff out mushrooms.

With some trepidation, he explained his theory about the Seven Arches, and how I had belonged in the other world so my life had turned out well. Ruby's life progressively got worse as the world tried to push her out. In his theory, it was almost as if the universe tried to self-correct by making Ruby so miserable that she would leave.

It had worked, but the ripple effect had also brought Felix, Jaycee, and I here too. It was dark and ominous to consider especially when we were trapped.

No one seemed to know who destroyed the arches here. They had been destroyed several months prior to Ruby ending up here. Ray seemed to think this was the only world where the arches were in ruins.

A cold shiver traveled down my spine as my brain refused to consider what happened here that would have motivated someone to destroy the arches. Ray had no idea how we would begin to repair them, but I knew that we would have to try.

Felix, Jaycee, and I belonged in the other world. It was a world with Uncle Enoch, the Duke and Duchess, and dear Olive. They were our family there, and we couldn't imagine never seeing them again.

I told Ray and Mother all about my adventures with Madame Leveau in Paris, and how she explained to me *le chemin de l'esprit terrestre*. I told them that a book existed somewhere, probably in French, written by Père Dieudonné Suivant.

It was a possibility that Olive had already tracked it down in the other world, and we didn't quite have her resources here in Milligan. If I was right about the Seven Arches being related to *le chemin de l'esprit terrestre*, then there had to have been someone who knew about the book that was living in Milligan at some point in the past.

We all agreed that our family had to try to get back to the other world because there were now two Felixes and two

Jaycees in addition to me and Ruby. If this world didn't want an extra version of me, what level of tragedy would be unleashed on the three of us? A tense, chilling silence fell over Mother's parlor as Ray's words sank in. If the world had rejected Ruby, what fate awaited Felix, Jaycee, and me?

"Well, this has been delightful," Felix remarked drily, breaking the tension. "Most fun I've had since my mother's funeral." His morbid humor caught us off guard, releasing our anxiety into relieved laughter.

Later that day as Ray and Felix set up the chess board and Mother contentedly rocked Jaycee in her back parlor, I stole back down to the ruins of the arches. Felix, Jaycee, and I were surrounded by my loving family for now, but for how long?

Would the universe reject us too, pushing us toward tragedy just as it had Ruby? Every shadow and crack in the ruins seemed to whisper that we no longer belonged here.

I had been brought to tears when Ray told me how Ruby had been shot in the other world. What was in store for us? I could accept anything that happened to me, but not Felix or Jaycee. They were innocent. This was all because of Ruby and I.

It was all overwhelming, but the ruins were still my place of peace even if the arches no longer stood here. There wasn't any other place in the world that I had found from St. Louis to San Diego to London that rivaled the Seven Arches for me as a place to think.

The secrets of the arches needed to be unearthed because it needed to be repaired somehow. Felix, Jaycee, and I had to return back to the other world or perhaps face deathly consequences. If we stayed for even a few months, I would wonder every time I stubbed my toe or Jaycee got a runny nose if the arches were trying to push us out of this world.

"Who built you?" I asked the ruins as if they would answer me.

There were so many questions, and I only had so much time to answer them. I looked for the activation stone and couldn't find it in any of the rubble. In fact, I couldn't find more than remnants of the keystones. Was this pillaged after it was destroyed, or simply ground into dust? The person that destroyed this place had never wanted anyone to repair it.

Why had they destroyed it? Did they wish to trap us here, or did it have absolutely nothing to do with us? It didn't make sense, but I supposed it could be an outrageous coincidence.

My meditations were interrupted by an all too familiar sight. Ruby came walking down the hill. I recognized her immediately. We hadn't seen one another in over a year when our paths wildly diverged. Even if it had taken a while, we'd separately found happiness. Her with Harvey in this world, and me with Felix in the other.

Stiffening a little as I saw her approach, I felt at least partially responsible for her getting shot. It was me that Mrs. Lopp saw on the train stop and watched pull away from Milligan. If I had stayed hidden or not drawn so much attention to myself, Ruby's entire life might have been different. I didn't know how to apologize for that, but then again, she unintentionally unleashed a vengeful Harvey on us.

"Hello Hazel," she said, "I suppose it isn't that strange that we are both still drawn to this place."

The silence between us was heavy with unspoken history. We were no longer reflections of each other but separate souls, shaped by divergent paths of joy and suffering. The year and the abuse she suffered made her look older to me, but I supposed that I probably looked older to her as well.

She had gone through so much with Mrs. Lopp and the Cleghorn family. The Harvey that held Felix and I at gunpoint had been unrecognizable to me, and she had lived with him as her husband. It was hard to understand how she had survived at all.

"It's odd to think that I might have stayed behind and married Harvey while you went off to Europe," I said, breaking the silence that had grown up between us.

She grinned, "I was just thinking that."

It recalled to mind our first meeting with one another, and how we had been unable to speak at first without saying the exact same thing at the exact same time. That was a problem we no longer experienced.

We began to talk about our experiences when we had been out of each other's lives. Ray and Mother had filled me in some, but Ruby largely knew nothing about my time with Felix. She could hardly believe that I had married Mrs. Byerly's son.

I learned how she felt so incredibly lucky when she was walking to the Cleghorns from the train stop on that fateful day we met. She had dreamed about marrying Harvey for so many years. Even though she was a little jealous of my trip, she was more excited about starting her new life with Harvey.

I told her all about the gold-toothed man stalking me on the train and in St. Louis, but he somehow led me to Felix like it was all predestined. She was surprised at how quickly I had fallen for Felix, and I agreed. It was the shock of my life to discover he was Mrs. Byerly's son, but it made our connection seem so much deeper. I talked for a long while about my best friend in the world, Olive Powlett, and how Olive was mad to meet her someday.

Our lives had diverged in almost unrecognizable ways. Ruby was a housewife adept at cooking, cleaning, and homemaking while I learned nothing except how to ring the bell for a servant at Chaffinch Fields. She laughed and offered me cooking lessons someday soon. We decided that we were more like sisters than the same person, and as long as we lived in the same world, we didn't have to avoid each other totally. There was no big secret we needed to keep. We were wholly two different people now.

As twilight fell softly over the ruins, we realized our conversation had gone on for hours. We exchanged a final, gentle embrace. Turning away, we each walked toward separate horizons—she headed back to her home with Harvey, and I walked back toward Mother's house where my own family waited for me.

Our paths clearly heading in opposite directions.

The Aftermath, Milligan 1924

Milligan buzzed like a kicked hornet's nest.

Two months ago, Ruby Cleghorn had vanished in broad daylight—child in arms, mother-in-law concussed by a frying pan. Posters papered the post office. Search parties combed the woods. Police from St. Louis to Indianapolis were on alert.

The Cleghorns called in every favor they had. But Ruby was gone, and no one could say how she'd disappeared so completely.

The town was still raw from last year's horror: the brutal decapitation of Mrs. Elmira Lopp. Her killer, Justus Cleghorn, was behind bars, but the wound hadn't healed. Whispers spread that Ruby might be next to turn up dead, buried in a cornfield or dumped in the river. The troubles with her in-laws had never been a secret.

Suspicion turned to her family. Ruby's mother and brother were hounded, threatened, dragged into questioning. But they held firm—said they hadn't seen her, didn't know where she was. A full search of Mrs. Sutton's house turned up nothing. No child's blanket. No worn out copies of Jude the Obscure.

Then came Harriet Lucas.

She claimed she'd seen Ruby in Waveland—wearing a wig, pushing a baby buggy. She followed her to the home of Mr. Enoch Byerly and ran straight to Penelope Cleghorn Lucas with the story.

Less than an hour later, Harvey Cleghorn had stormed the Byerly house. He purportedly confronted his estranged wife and was stabbed in the back by the man helping her flee.

Ruby disappeared again, this time with both her child and a man believed to be Felix Byerly.

The newspapers had a field day.

The headlines painted Ruby as a villainess, a faithless wife who'd abandoned her vows and her in-laws for some rich playboy next town over while the future of Cleghorn Farms hung in the balance.

On the porch of the Mottern house, Bernice sat in her rocking chair, still trying to make sense of it all nearly a month after Ruby had supposedly disappeared for a second time.

Jeanette Bretz, her youngest stepdaughter, waved from the road and joined her on the porch with a sigh.

"Fine day, isn't it?" Jeanette said, settling into the second rocker.

They chatted briefly about Jeanette's father—his health, his appetite—before the conversation drifted, inevitably, to Ruby Cleghorn.

"That girl's gone and lost her ever-loving mind," Jeanette said.

"You don't think it was actually her that did it, do you?" Bernice asked, lowering her voice. "Hiding out in Waveland of all places?"

Jeanette's brow twitched. Her tone soured—not in judgment, but in worry.

"I don't know. Part of me hopes it wasn't her, because if it was… that was dumb. Too dumb. Penelope Lucas lives just a few streets over from Byerly's house. You really think Ruby's that careless?"

"She wasn't always," Bernice murmured. "I swear, this all started after Justus killed old Elmira Lopp."

"That's only if you believe he did it," Jeanette said, eyes narrowing. "I heard it was Harvey. And Justus took the blame to protect him."

Bernice nodded slowly. She'd heard that version too. And frankly, it wouldn't surprise her. No one shed tears for Elmira—not even her family. Even so, decapitation was a bit gruesome.

They fell into silence. Both women were thinking of the ones left behind—Ruby's mother, stoic and uncharacteristically quiet, and Ray, who'd been fragile for years but had recently started to change. Jeanette had heard from her sister how proud she was of him. "Shaking the melancholy," she called it.

Jeanette stood a while later and walked down the path. Her eyes lingered on the spot where Enoch Byerly's car had once been discovered, abandoned near her father's house.

For a while, the police believed Ruby and her lover had taken refuge with her family. Everyone in the Mottern clan agreed to let the police search the property, even though it felt like a slap in the face.

Nick Mottern raised the most hell.

"If I was hiding my granddaughter and her killer boyfriend, why would I be dumb enough to leave their car abandoned right down the road?"

He had a point.

The name Byerly meant something else to Jeanette too. Mr. Byerly had once employed John Wesley Sutton, Ruby's father, back before he and her sister eloped. Odd coincidence, maybe. But life always had a way of tying things together.

A sick feeling twisted in her gut. If Ruby wasn't hiding, then someone dangerous was.

Jeanette broke into a run. She gathered up her skirt and hiked it as high as decency would allow. Panic gripped her chest.

She missed Ralph in moments like these. He would've known what to do. She only knew how to fret.

When she burst through her front door, she saw it. A hat—perched on the back of her favorite high-backed chair.

She nearly screamed. But then the man turned.

"Why Jeanette Bretz," he said, smiling. "I do believe I'm growing on you, sweet sister-in-law."

Jeanette's breath caught. Her stomach dropped.

John Wesley Sutton.

THE END

Made in the USA
Coppell, TX
26 July 2025

52365145R00225